BURN AWAY

Books by BV Lawson

Scott Drayco Series

Played to Death
Requiem for Innocence
Dies Irae
Elegy in Scarlet
The Suicide Sonata

Beverly Laborde & Adam Dutton Series

Steal Away
Hide Away
Burn Away

Burn Away

An Adam Dutton & Beverly Laborde Mystery

BV Lawson

Crimetime Press

Published in the United States of America.

For information, contact:

Crimetime Press
6312 Seven Corners Center, Box 257
Falls Church, VA 22044

Trade Paperback ISBN 978-1-951752-04-0
Hardcover ISBN 978-1-951752-05-7
eBook ISBN 978-1-951752-03-3

1

The firefighters had most of the blaze under control as Detective Adam Dutton stood surveying the still-smoking ruins of the building, once a thriving antiques shop called Vintage Vibes. He'd opted not to wear a mask but was beginning to regret that decision.

He turned to the fire chief, Bent Vinson. "You found the body near the front register?"

"So it appears."

"I'm surprised you could ID the register out of this mess."

"We got here in time to save some of the structure, but most of the interior is gutted. The cash register is surprisingly still intact. A little melted, but intact. You'll find the body right there beside it."

"Safe to go in yet?"

"We cleared out a path for the EMTs when they get here. So, yeah. But you know the drill."

Thankfully for Adam, the heat from the embers would keep out the bone-chilling cold. Vermont winters weren't for sissies. The best news was, it wasn't totally dark yet, although the firefighters had rigged some makeshift lights on stands. Just in case.

Adam pulled up the collar of his coat to use as a mask and walked along the "path" Vinson indicated. He coughed a few times, knowing the acrid smoky smell would cling to his hair and clothing long after he'd left the scene.

The body lay surrounded by a pool of firefighting foam. Adam stooped and used his gloved hand to gently pry up the victim's shoulder—no foam underneath. He turned his attention to the victim's head, and that was even more interesting. There was a gaping fifty-millimeter hole in the skull. From when he fell, perhaps? Hard to tell from the blackened ruins, but Adam didn't see anything nearby that would have caused such a wound.

He stood up straight and almost jumped when a female voice behind him said, "Looks like we've got an extra-crispy one."

Adam acknowledged fellow detective, Eliot Jinks, who was holding onto her hat to keep it from blowing off. "Yep. And one with a hole in his head."

"Extra-crispy and holey. Sounds a little unholy, if you ask me. As in, maybe this wasn't an accident."

Adam waved to department's forensics expert, Joe Brimm, who'd trailed behind Jinks. "He's all yours, Joe. The usual. But make sure you pay attention to his skull. Oh, and the lack of foam solution under the body."

Brimm's eyes widened. "Interesting. He was dead before the firefighters arrived, then?"

"I'm hoping you can tell me."

Brimm gave Adam a grim smile and put down the silver case he was holding as it blended in with the silver ashes and smoky foam. He quickly pulled out a camera and went to work.

Adam and Jinks left him to his task and headed toward Vinson, who was talking to some of his men. Adam asked, "Your fellows got any signs this was arson?"

"Don't know for sure yet. But there are a coupla things of interest. For instance, a witness from a house one street over heard a low 'whomp' noise."

"Is this witness the one who called it in?"

Vinson nodded. "Adding to the possible arson theory, the fire did spread unusually fast. Plus, there was some localized warping to the underside of a metal file cabinet. And one of my guys thinks he noticed unnatural floor burn patterns. Kind of a trailer shape."

"Accelerant?"

"Possibly."

Adam clapped him on the shoulder. "Thanks for getting here so fast, Bent. Kept it from spreading to other nearby businesses."

The other man tipped back his helmet. "We got lucky this time. But I'll take it."

Jinks poked Adam in the ribs and pointed to their left. "Sergeant Moody's kept the crowd at bay. The antiques store's assistant director and his wife are over there."

Adam followed her to the group of onlookers and addressed his question to Moody, "Which one is the assistant?"

Moody narrowed his eyes at Adam and grunted out, "The one wearing the green-and-red plaid coat. Lucas Barratt."

Moody might as well have said, "I'm not your goddamn flunky, Dutton." But his rigid stance and his eyes that held a fire of their own made it quite clear. Adam wasn't in a mood for another pissing contest with Moody, so he just headed toward Barratt along with Jinks.

He stopped in front of the thirty-something man sporting coal-black hair and a small goatee. "Are you Lucas Barratt?"

The man nodded, making a few of the ice crystals on his beard flake off in a mini-snowfall.

Adam pulled out his badge. "Detective Adam Dutton. You're the assistant manager of the Vintage Vibes store?"

Barratt stared at Adam with wide eyes. "I don't know what happened. It was all so fast."

"Then you were here at the start of the fire?"

"No, I mean, it burned down so fast. Only learned about it when I got a call from a friend. He has one of those police radios."

Adam frowned at that. He wasn't a fan of people listening to emergency communications and living out some sort of spectator-adrenaline-fantasy. "So the owner—"

He looked at Jinks, who helpfully added, "Jared Lake."

"Jared Lake, yes. Can we talk to him?"

"I don't know. Tried calling him. But I get no answer."

Adam and Jinks exchanged glances. After many years working together, they were on the same wavelength most of the time.

Jinks asked, "Mr. Barratt, could Jared Lake have been in the building during the fire?"

"He's usually so prompt, leaving right at the dot of five. Never once recall him putting in overtime. Can't imagine why he'd have been in there." Barratt shivered.

Jinks replied, "We just found a body inside. But we'll have to wait for the Medical Examiner to get a positive ID."

Barratt grabbed onto the auburn-haired woman at his side whose eyes were as wide as his. "Jeanne, it can't be him, it just can't."

Realizing this must be the wife Sergeant Moody alluded to, Adam said to her. "You're Mrs. Barratt?"

"Yes, and I do hope you're wrong about Jared. Maybe that body in there is a burglar. Maybe he set off the fire by accident. Or on purpose."

"That's one possibility. Can either of you think of any reason someone might want to set fire to Vintage Vibes?"

"Absolutely not." Barratt grabbed his wife's hand. "It's unthinkable. You really think it's arson?"

"It'll take some time to investigate. These things always do. But our fire chief is pretty good."

Noting the growing darkness, the cold, and the increasingly pale faces of the couple, he said to Barratt and his wife, "Why don't you go home. There's not much you can do at this point. And the investigators won't be releasing the scene anytime soon. Get some rest."

Adam added, "We'll check with you again soon." To see how they were doing, sure. But he had a lot of additional questions and no time to deal with the duo right then.

Jinks was scanning the crowd, occasionally taking photos of the scene, including the people standing around. She had a talent for doing it without people realizing she was doing it. She said to Adam, "That man over there is acting odd."

"Which one?"

She turned to point, then dropped her arm. "He's gone. Good thing I've got him in little bits and bytes." Flipping through the photo stream on her cellphone, she stopped at one in particular. "That's the guy."

Adam studied the man's face. "Don't recognize him. Do you?"

"Nope. But he didn't look shocked. Or afraid. Or worried, or whatever you might expect from a normal person. Maybe he's a 'fire tourist.'"

"Fire tourist?"

"You haven't heard of them? They go around to all the fires like a scavenger hunt. Guess it's how they get their jollies."

Adam thought of the police radio Barratt's friend had used. Yep, he really hated those civilian radios. As if law enforcement types didn't have their hands full enough as it was. Fire tourists. Bah.

"Print out that photo when we get back to the station, Jinks. Maybe someone there will know the guy."

Jinks saluted, and Adam glared at her. "Not you, too?"

"Me, too, what?"

Adam lowered his voice. "Moody. He's been giving me shade all evening."

"Guess he's pissed at having to do crowd control instead of being the 'big-shot' detective. As in, the *mayor's cousin*," Jinks made air quotes with her fingers, "shouldn't be just a lowly sergeant."

"Probably. But he's trouble with a capital T. As in threat."

Jinks added, "Make that turd, and you've nailed it."

The flashing red lights at the scene got even redder with the arrival of an ambulance as it screamed into view. Adam walked over to greet the crew and pointed out the body, giving them instructions on taking it to the M.E. When he rejoined Jinks, she said, "This is the second suspicious fire in the past week. There was the other one over in Woodstock."

"I heard about that. Another antiques store, wasn't it? Main Street Antiques?"

"Think so." She rolled her eyes. "You know me and antiques. Can't stand all those fusty doo-dads. Gimme IKEA any day."

Adam smiled briefly. "Two antiques stores in a row. Gotta worry a little bit about Harlan."

"Dear Harlan and his Tossed Treasures store will be there long after the rest of us. They're timeless. Maybe two antiques store fires are just coincidence."

"Still . . . you thinking what I'm thinking?"

Jinks frowned. "Hope not. Thought we were done with the Forsythes and that whole Northeastern Antiquities League crime-gang shit."

"Gotta wonder who's left of that 'gang,' since Reginald Forsythe the Third is dead. And Reggie junior is essentially brain dead in a nursing facility."

She sighed. "Ivon Kozak and Darnell Warner . . . sorry, *Redbeard*, are very much alive. And in Red's case, a bail skipper. And AWOL."

Adam frowned. "This would be taking their tactics in a whole new direction."

Jinks gave Adam some side-eye. "Now that you mention the Forsythes, where's Beverly Laborde? Gotta wonder why she hasn't turned up since she seems to magically appear at crime scenes. Especially if it might be related to a Forsythe."

"Hopefully, she's at the Apple Valley Resort enjoying some Christmas-time spa pampering."

"You mean hard cider?"

"Maybe some of their mistletoe or cranberry treatments."

Jinks stamped her boots in the thin layer of snow. "I could use some pampering right about now."

"Cranberry oil massage?"

"Hell, no. An imported beer, some of Felicia's homemade soft pretzels, and some basketball on TV. Without the kids pestering me about who did what to whom."

Adam chuckled. "Maybe I'll write you up a prescription."

"You're not a doctor."

"I'm an enforcer of the law. I'll make it an edict, then."

"And hell will freeze over before those kids pay any attention to it whatsoever." Jinks rubbed her gloved hands together. "Speaking of freezing over. Standing still is turning me into a Jinks-sickle."

"You take the remaining crowd on the right, I'll take the left, and we'll meet in the middle. That'll give Vinson's crew time to do their job."

As they started in on their questioning, Adam wondered what Beverly really *was* doing tonight. Hopefully, she was warm. And safe. And not getting into any more trouble.

But his discussion with Jinks about the Forsythes and the NAL had sent a little tingling burst up his spine. If his sixth sense was worth anything, he had a bad feeling about this arson business being more than it seemed. And he wouldn't be at all surprised if a con woman like Beverly Laborde somehow managed to figure into the middle of it all.

2

Beverly grabbed the spa menu card and ran her finger down the list. Merry Mistletoe Lip Special? Cranberry Pedicure? Buttered Rum Massage? Hard to tell it was Christmas time, ho ho ho. *Sarcasm this late in the day, Beverly?*

She tossed the card on the marble-topped table, a little annoyed at her snarky attitude. After all, what was wrong with the resort's efforts to add a little holiday cheer for their customers? Just because Beverly didn't like the holidays, it didn't mean everyone else had to suffer.

She stood in the middle of the cavernous lobby next to the monster granite fireplace, wondering what to do for dinner. Room service? Take out? Try that new Indian place in town?

It seemed she couldn't make any decisions these days, not even able to pick a place to eat. What was wrong with her? It wasn't like her to be morose and tentative. Unfinished business had a way of doing that to her, though, didn't it? Always had. Well, the morose part. The tentative part was new.

Standing up straight, she marched into the café. There. She *could* make a snap decision. Once inside the café, however, she lost a little of her new spine, looking at the gleaming white tables without much enthusiasm. That is until she spied a friendly face and headed over.

"Nyssa, I'm so glad to see you."

The other woman pushed a strand of her dark, curly hair behind her ear and studied Beverly's face. "Is something wrong?"

Beverly looked around and, not spying any other diners at the moment, flopped down at a table. "Nothing serious. But I could use someone to talk to. I'm so bored with sitting in my room and flipping through the TV channels."

Nyssa smiled, grabbed a couple of cups of coffee and some lemon poppy seed muffins, and joined Beverly. "Having a job helps keep you grounded."

Beverly had noticed Nyssa seemed much happier than the first time she'd met her—when her controlling and manipulative husband was a suspect in the murder of their former neighbor. "You like working here?"

"I love it. And thanks to you for recommending it for me."

"Since Gloria will only work weekends soon, seemed like the perfect solution."

Nyssa took a bite of the muffin. "Gloria's getting her life in order, going to college and all. I'm a bit jealous. Did you know she's even gotten close to Ramsay Ryall?"

"Ramsay?" Knowing it was his brother who Nyssa's husband had been accused of killing, Beverly was beyond surprised. "How do you feel about that, I mean, the Ramsay part?"

"I'm fine with it." At Beverly's skeptical look, Nyssa added, "Really."

"I guess they do both work here. If Ramsay's still a guide for outdoor sports, that is."

Nyssa nodded. "He is. I think he'd rather be doing what he and his brother used to do, building custom snowmobiles. But he's having some financial problems, so . . . "

"Ah. I think we all know what that's like."

"And how."

As they both spied a woman walking past the café door wearing a fur coat and expensive Gucci boots, Beverly said, "Most of us, that is."

Beverly leaned on the table. "Wasn't Ramsay Ryall dating someone up in Bangor?"

"He was. It didn't work out. Guess that's why he took a shine to Gloria, though I hope it's not just that rebound thing."

A sudden shrill laugh in the lobby caught their attention. A group of three women wearing matching red cashmere sweaters peered into the café, saw them, and turned around. Beverly had a twinge of guilt it might be her "down-with-the-holiday" vibes scaring off potential customers.

Nyssa sighed. "Vernon didn't want me working here."

The muscles in Beverly's neck tensed at the mention of the man's name. "Why would your husband care if you get a job?"

"Mr. Philandering Professor cares about his image. And his wife working as a clerk in a café? Oh, the horror."

"Nyssa, I know I shouldn't pry. But this whole open marriage thing . . . are you sure it's a good idea?" Beverly held the cup of steaming liquid up to her face to feel its warmth on her skin, though she felt pretty steamed already at her companion's situation.

"It's a horrible idea. I went along with it since trying to stop Vernon from doing anything is like trying to stop a tsunami. But he's targeting his students more and more for his conquests. And I'm a little worried he's not just sticking to the 'legal' eighteen-year-olds."

"How young?"

"I think there was one seventeen-going-on-eighteen. And I heard a rumor another was sixteen. She was a prodigy and likely naive. And vulnerable."

"You should report him to the police. In fact, I should tell Adam—"

"Please don't." Nyssa's eyes pleaded with Beverly even more than her words. "Not even to Detective Dutton."

"Why not?"

Nyssa looked down at her hands holding her mug, but Beverly hadn't missed the glint of tears in her eyes. "I know I should report him. But I don't have evidence. And if I do file for divorce, I need it to be as amicable as possible. I'm afraid of what he'd do to me otherwise."

Beverly considered that for a moment. "You're in an ugly bind, Nyssa, and I do understand that. Truly."

Nyssa's laugh was hollow. "Not that it isn't already bad. He wouldn't buy me a car to drive to work. I had to find someone willing to sell me a used clunker with my first paychecks from the café. And then there's Muttley."

"Your dog?"

"Vernon will say it's *his* dog and try to hold on to him out of spite. Even though Muttley clearly favors me."

Beverly made a mental note to consult Adam anyway, despite Nyssa's reservations. Maybe there was something he could do without getting Nyssa in trouble with her shitty husband. How could it get much worse? And Beverly wasn't about to let the man get away with what was technically statutory rape. Even if it was consensual between him and his underage students.

Her anger turned to concern when her cellphone rang, and she saw it was from Agnes Flamm. Agnes didn't usually call her at this time of day. "What's up, Agnes? I hope Blaine isn't giving you any trouble."

"Oh my, no. That young Blaine has proved to be a model employee. Despite his unsavory background. No, dear, I just wanted to let you know there's been a fire."

"A fire? Where?" Beverly uttered a silent prayer to whatever gods might be listening that it wasn't another bombing at Adam's house.

"An antiques store. Vintage Vibes. But that's not all. I heard a rumor the police found a body inside."

"A body?"

"I know the owner, Jared Lake. And I'm worried it might be him."

"Oh, Agnes, I hope not."

"And this is the second antiques store fire recently."

"The second?" That was news to Beverly. A serial arsonist targeting antiques stores, perhaps? That made her start to fret about Harlan Wilford and his Tossed Treasures shop. "Agnes, I must go see Harlan to make sure he's okay."

Agnes chuckled. "Don't think you need to worry about that. Harlan's with me in my wine shop right now, safe and sound."

"With you?"

"He's helping get the store ready for our first live performance. Did you know he's done some audio work in the past?"

"To be honest, I don't know much about his past."

"Neither did I. But he's such a multi-talented man."

A tone of something more than admiration crept through the cellphone connection. Maybe that time Beverly thought she'd seen the two of them flirting wasn't just her imagination. She should be happy about that, shouldn't she? Then why did it make her heart sink a little bit?

"Agnes, just tell him to be careful."

"Of course, dear." Agnes paused, then added, "Have you seen Adam recently? I'm sure he'd have more details about the fires. And other things."

"Not in several days. I hate to bother him since he's so busy." Agnes wasn't very subtle with her matchmaking. Not that Beverly hadn't wanted to see Adam. But ... there was always that "but."

"I'm sure he'd make time for you, dear."

Beverly forced a laugh. "Maybe soon."

After hanging up with Agnes and finishing her snack with Nyssa, Beverly headed to her room. Perhaps there'd be some interesting home-renovation show on. She slid onto the four-poster bed and flipped on the TV to surf through the channels, finding several. But they bored her, too. Who was she kidding? She'd rather watch the true-crime shows.

That was the problem with her, wasn't it? She wasn't at all "normal" in any sense of the word. No house, no home base, no husband, let alone a boyfriend, even a shady "employment" history—if being a con woman could count as employment.

Why did she feel so at loose ends? Maybe it was because her five-year vendetta against the NAL to avenge her grandmother's death wasn't finished. Ivon Kozak, the mysterious figure her friend, Mr. X, had mentioned, was still out there. And Redbeard, equally enigmatic and dangerous, was on the lam.

Nothing in her life had any sort of closure. Even her criminal louse-of-an-uncle, Reggie Forsythe, was in limbo— caught between life and death on a ventilator in a nursing facility. Beverly should feel sorry for him. But after what he'd done to so many people, including her and Adam, he didn't deserve much pity.

She stared at the cinnamon-scented pinecones the staff had put on the nightstand as a holiday touch. They were giving her a headache.

She got up to get some Zinfandel from the room's mini-bar when a knock on the door stopped her in mid-stride. She opened it to find a red-hatted bellhop standing there holding a letter in his hand.

"Special delivery for you, Miss Laborde."

"For me? From whom?"

"I don't know, Miss. Came via a courier."

She gave him a tip, sent him on his way, and studied the envelope. No return address, no postmark. Just her name in letters that looked like they were cranked out by an ordinary computer printer.

She pulled out the note inside, which was also computer-printed in several different colors and fonts, and studied the words. "A friendly word of advice. Don't pursue the NAL any further, or you might end up like your uncle."

Beverly stared at it in disbelief and then sank down on the bed, still clutching the card in her hand. Who would have sent it, and why? The enigmatic NAL kingpin, Ivon Kozak, the hired-goon, Redbeard, or someone else entirely? Just when she thought she might start having a more normal life.

Should she tell Adam about it? She got up to place the note in the drawer of the nightstand. Adam had an arson case and who knew what else to deal with. No, she wouldn't tell him about it just yet.

But that cranberry soak suddenly seemed a lot more appealing. With a double shot of vodka for starters. It's not as if she'd be getting much sleep tonight.

3

Saturday, December 12

Adam strode into the Ironwood Junction PD and headed straight for the reception desk. Arline Newton looked up when he handed over a bag. "What's this?"

As he headed toward his office, he said over his shoulder, "Crossroads Café had fresh eggnog donuts."

She called out after him, "Aww, you remembered. If you're trying to get on my good side, case closed."

He chuckled as he breezed through the hallway. Arline was a "nogaholic" if there ever was one, although Adam couldn't understand what she saw in that stuff. Sweet eggy cream. Ugh. Of course, he was fairly sure she preferred it with some rum, Kahlua, and bourbon.

Maybe he was fixating a little too much on the bourbon himself, because he collided with a dark blur that darted out in front of him. Great. Sergeant Mike Moody.

Moody growled at him. "Watch where you're going, Dutton. Or am I supposed to scrape and bow before the Great Detective as he prances into a room?"

"Knock it off, Moody. Go get some coffee or something."

Moody glared at Adam one more time, then scurried off toward the break room. Adam had intended to head there first thing and grab some of the station's extra-dark brew, but he didn't want to chance another showdown with Moody. Damn the man.

He was in such a bad mood after his encounter with the moody Moody, he almost ran into Sergeant Bill Naigle. "I'm two for two in the klutz department today, Bill. Sorry about that."

"My fault. Saw you with Moody and had to make sure he hadn't ripped off any of your skin with those bared teeth of his."

"It's getting worse every day."

"What kind of bee's up his ass? He owe you money or something?"

"Why would you say that?"

Naigle scowled. "Moody is always hitting me and everybody else up for money for this or that. When we eat out, he never pays his share of the bill. Says he forgot his wallet, or he had some medical thing and will settle after payday. But he never reimburses anyone."

"Ugh. I didn't know."

"It's getting bad enough people are starting to run the other way when they see him coming. Even Joe Brimm's been thinking about ways he can get back at him for it."

Adam's eyes widened. "Mr. Mild Mannered nerdy forensics guy?"

"Joe said he knew several ways to slowly poison Moody, and no one would ever know."

"Jeez, remind me not to get on Joe's bad side."

"Or Sergeant Gray's."

"What, did Moody stiff Charlene, too? The most notoriously cheerful officer in the known universe?"

"Yep. Borrowed a couple hundred and never repaid her. Think she went to the library to get a book of wizard spells."

Adam shook his head, and Naigle clapped him on the shoulder. "And you watch out for Moody, too, Adam. Everyone's been talking about how he's got it in for you. You know we've got your back, right?"

"Yeah, Bill. And thanks."

Adam had just sunk down in the chair at his desk when the in-house phone chirped. Cherry Steele, Chief Quinn's administrative assistant, was unreasonably calm as she said, "Good morning, Adam. The chief wants you in his office in five."

"Thanks, Cherry."

He sighed, but before he could muse any further on the less-than-stellar start to the day, Jinks popped by with a cup of java he recognized as being from Miralee's Market. Even better than the Crossroads coffee. "Here you go, stud. Figured you could use it."

Adam hopped up and immediately took a swig of the dark, smoky brew. "Thanks, Jinks. Would be better with Kahlua—or maybe bourbon—but other than that, it's perfect."

"You must have got the same invitation to the lion's den I did. We should walk down to the chief's office together. United front and all." She scanned his face. "Late night orgy? Or did you have some hemlock pancakes for breakfast?"

"Sergeant Moody."

"Ah." Jinks nodded in sympathy. "Then, I really *should* have put some Kahlua in there."

Chief Quinn waited as the two detectives poured into his office and sat in their usual chairs in front of his desk. And as usual, Adam had to squirm around in the chair to get comfortable. Maybe it was those casters that never worked right. Or the vinyl the color of dried blood that made him slip around.

Quinn gazed at their coffee cups with a wistful expression.

"God, I could use one of those right now."

"Still going decaf, sir?" Adam remembered the month after the chief's doctor had told him to cut it out. The staff now referred to it as the "Dark Ages."

"Have you ever tasted that stuff? Swill doesn't begin to describe it. If everyone had to drink decaf, coffee would disappear off the planet."

Jinks added helpfully, "There's carob or grain-based drinks. Ayurvedic roasts, rooibos."

The chief raised an eyebrow and didn't say anything.

Jinks smiled. "Hot chocolate, then."

"My doc says even that has too much caffeine. I still have some every now and then. But if you tell him I said so, I'll say it's all lies."

Quinn thumped a stack of papers on his desk. "Fire Chief Vinson and I are putting out a joint statement about the fire at Vintage Vibes. With a note about the tip line, if anyone has more information."

Jinks asked, "Did Vinson find any link between the fires here and the one in Woodstock? Arson at both?"

The chief shook his head. "Not yet. Could be coincidence the two happen to be antiques stores."

Adam piped up. "Props to the Medical Examiner, by the way. She stayed up late working on a prelim ID of the body and discovered our victim had two titanium dental implants. As did Jared Lake."

"How did you know that?"

"I made a call to his sister this morning to double-check."

Quinn frowned. "Did the prelim autopsy also verify your hunch, Adam?"

"The guy was dead before the fire. Head bashed in, no smoke in the lung tissue."

Quinn replied, "All things considered, certainly seems like

a match. And murder. Has Lake's sister been able to reach him?"

"Not since the fire."

"There's also that, too. Poor Mr. Lake."

Adam nodded. "The little research I did on Lake makes it seem like he's clean. No rap sheet, complaints, not even traffic fines."

Jinks said, "Could be a simple burglary. Lake surprised the perp, got conked, and our burglar set the fire to destroy any evidence."

Quinn leaned forward in his chair. "Bent Vinson seems to think the fire was set in a methodical manner with an accelerant."

Adam replied, "And therefore premeditation."

"Exactly."

Adam sighed. "I hate to bring this up so soon into the investigation, but my 'little research' last night found that Lake was a member of the Northeastern Antiquities League. Not terribly surprising. But it does raise more questions about any ties to the Forsythes, Ivon Kozak, Redbeard, and company."

Quinn got up briefly to pour himself a cup of an amber liquid from an aluminum dispenser. "Herbal tea," he said with a grimace. "Was Lake an active NAL member?"

"Not lately. But had been so earlier in his career. About ten years ago."

Quinn tasted the tea and shuddered. "Sounds like you have a long list of work to do. And Jinks, help as you can when you're not working that pharmacy robbery case. Farm some of that grunt work over to Bill Naigle."

Even as his words of dismissal made Adam and Jinks stand up, Quinn added, "Adam, could you stay for a minute?"

Jinks gave a sympathetic look before she left.

Quinn didn't waste any time with the reason for his

request. "I'm getting more irritated—make that furious—each day with Mayor Lehmann for trying to push Moody on me as a detective. And push you out in the process."

"Your golfing games with the mayor must get a little awkward, sir."

"Good thing I've run out of excuses because the mayor has stopped asking. No more golf games."

Adam felt a moment of sympathy for the chief. Quinn was in a bind and in the middle, even more than Adam.

Quinn tried another taste of the tea and scowled. "Damn the man. If I make Moody a detective, I'll have to find the extra money to pay for that position. Money I'd love to have, but just not for Moody. And where's this magical money going to come from? Otherwise, I'd have to demote you or Jinks, something I'm fighting."

Adam nodded but kept silent.

"I'm still hoping Lehmann will be ousted in the next election. But the polls show he's in the lead. Hell, maybe that egotist will finally run for governor like he's been threatening to do for so long."

"But he'll have even more power, won't he, sir?"

"Yes, but with a whole state to worry about, he won't have time to concern himself with one town and one PD. Except his cousin. Hell, maybe he'll even give Moody a state job. Far from here."

The chief paused to choke down some more of the tea and then looked at Adam over the rim of his cup. "Seen Zelda lately?"

Adam sighed inwardly, keeping his face blank. He'd been trying *not* to think of the odd relationship he had with his ex-wife, who was now warming the mayor's bed. And he definitely wasn't going to tell the chief about Zelda's offer to have an affair with him while her husband was out of town.

He replied simply, "Not lately, no."

"Good. Try to keep it that way."

The chief waved him off, and Adam hurried back to his office where Jinks was waiting, with her brown-booted feet up on his desk. "Not too bad, I hope?"

Adam patted his body. "Everything's still intact. And as for that 'lot of work to do' the chief mentioned, I'm thinking we should talk to Jared Lake's sister first. Then Lucas Barratt, the victim's assistant."

"Sounds like a plan."

Adam tossed his now-empty coffee cup into the trash. "How are Felicia and the kids?"

Jinks crossed her arms over her chest. "That whole Christmas commercialism thing really gets to me."

"They gave you two a long toy list this year, I take it?"

"What's a WiFi coding robot, anyway? I mean, whatever happened to basketballs and Barbie dolls? But if by long, you mean a list that stretches from here to the North Pole and back, then yep." She hopped up. "Decided on your Christmas plans? My offer still stands for you to join us for dinner."

"Thanks, but I'll have to check with Harlan."

"He's welcome, too. You could also invite Beverly."

Adam shook his head. He had no idea where that relationship stood. What would she say if he asked? Would she even hang around in town long enough to observe the holidays?

If there was one, and only one, thing he'd learned about Beverly Laborde, it was you could hardly learn anything about her at all. Not until she chose to let you into her world. What would he find there, if he did? Maybe he'd like it, maybe he wouldn't, or maybe it would still be too hazy to see anything.

Enough of that. Adam heaved a big sigh. It was time for one of his least-favorite parts of being a cop, talking to a family member of someone who was in all likelihood just murdered.

But there was no way around it. And with any luck, the victim's sister would be a strong first link in the chain to finding the killer. One link, one lead at a time.

He didn't want to think about the broken chains, the unsolved cases. He'd only had one before, and he'd told himself afterward that he'd be damned if he ever had another one. He looked over at Jinks, who was giving him a curious look but just said, "So, let's get this shit-show on the road."

4

Beverly was right to think she wouldn't get much sleep because she hadn't. And even when she did fall asleep for a few hours, the threatening note she'd received played a starring role in her nightmares. Maybe this was a sign she should just let it go, this vendetta of hers against a gang of crooks who'd helped destroy her grandmother?

But she was in far too deep to turn back now. And the sender of that note didn't know her very well, or he'd have realized it was more like a red flag to a bull than making her want to wave a white flag.

Deciding a complete change of scenery was in order to help her mood, she headed to Willem's Wine & Cheese to seek out her friend, Agnes Flamm. The store had only been open a couple of weeks, but the stream of customers was already cheering Beverly up a little bit.

She stood admiring the low walnut wooden platform at the end of a side room that was soon to be a café addition to the shop. "This is really nice, Agnes. It'll make a terrific space for music acts. Or poetry or book readings."

"That's what I'm hoping." The older woman stepped back as a teenaged boy with tousled blond hair and striking pale eyes carried a box of wine glasses into the room.

He asked, "Where would like these, Miss Flamm?"

"Oh, just right over there, Blaine. And thanks."

Beverly watched as he gingerly placed them on the edge of the bar and headed into the main shop area. She waited until Blaine was out of earshot to say, "He seems to be a big help."

"More than you know. He still has some abandonment issues. And is like a skittish feral cat at times. But he's getting better each day."

"Staying out of trouble?"

"Far as I know. With Adam as his police guardian and mentor, I'm hoping Blaine will turn out well. No thanks to his alcoholic father."

Beverly walked over to inspect the wine glasses. "It's incredibly sad his own father can't appreciate his son. Realize what he has."

Agnes patted her on the arm. "I know, dear."

She glanced at Beverly's face, but Beverly wasn't about to show any signs of the sadness that filled her at the talk of Blaine's father. The father and son still had each other, even after the death of Blaine's mother. So why couldn't the man realize that? It was more than Beverly had.

She pulled one of the glasses out the box and looked through it before setting it down on the bar. "Business doing well since you opened? The non-café side, I mean."

"We're doing quite well. Better than expected. Guess people in Vermont like wine and cheese. Who knew?" Agnes smiled and pointed to a side room. "The café side, well, I guess we'll have to hope it's not a bust when this part opens next. Christmas sales and parties should help."

"With your considerably culinary talents behind it, it couldn't help but be an overwhelming success."

"If your optimism is an omen, so be it."

Beverly ran her finger along a box labeled as containing wooden stirrers. "Heard from a friend that the body they found in the fire was Jared Lake, the owner of Vintage Vibes antiques.

I'm sorry, Agnes."

Agnes leaned against the bar, one hand gripping the edge. "I'd feared that would be the case. Poor Jared. A nice man, he was. I do wonder what happened."

"My friend seems to think it was arson. But Jared was already dead from an assault."

"Would that friend be Adam Dutton, perchance?"

Beverly shook her head. "I'm sure Adam is far too busy to talk to me right now."

Even if he wasn't, she didn't want to get in his way. Again. No, her "friend" was someone else Agnes had met briefly, Mr. Xenakis, or "Mr. X." A man still a little mysterious to Beverly. A man who knew everything about the NAL and maybe a bit about everyone else.

She said, "Two arsons in two antiques stores, two weeks apart, is beyond coincidental. Maybe I'm paranoid, but I'm still worried about Harlan's store."

Agnes nodded. "I understand your concern. I even told Harlan he should install sprinklers. And hire some security."

"What did he say?"

"You know Harlan. 'I'll be fine.'"

"Sure, he'll be fine. Like he almost got put away for murder after someone broke into his store and planted evidence." Beverly paused in mid-tirade. "Mr. X can help out. And Harlan's assistant is handy, too. I'm sure Prospero can think up something."

Agnes walked over to one of the brand new dining tables. She picked up a battery-operated flameless candle, the same type Beverly spied on all the tables, and said, "Harlan is such a love. He brought these over to add a little Christmas touch."

There went that smile again, every time Agnes mentioned Harlan. Beverly asked, "Do you think you'll have this room completed by the time your first holiday music act is booked?"

"It'll be down to the wire. Have to admit it's keeping me up at night since it's taking longer than I'd hoped."

"Who's the first act, by the way?"

"I tried to get Adam to play his guitar, but he said he was too out of practice."

"Couldn't tell it from the way he played a Spanish dance for me." Beverly chewed on her lip, knowing how that would sound. But when Agnes seemed to ignore it, she relaxed.

"Actually, our first act is none other than my little helper, Blaine."

"Blaine? He's a musician?"

"He has a hidden talent. Plays the guitar and sings and writes his own songs, although he's never shown anyone those songs before. He's a little shy. I had to get Adam's help to talk him into it."

"Adam seems to be getting closer to Blaine, too."

"Enough to keep an eye on him. And hopefully, steer him toward a different life from his ne'er-do-well friends."

"That's quite nice of Adam."

"You sound surprised."

Beverly shrugged off a reply. No more talk of Adam. "Will you be open on Christmas?"

"Christmas Eve. And on New Year's Eve, too."

"What about finding staff to work?"

"I plan on working, myself. And since Harlan's shop will be closed both days, he's volunteered to help out here."

"I'd be happy to pitch in." Not that Beverly had anything else to do or anywhere else to go. Might be nice to work on the holidays. Keep her mind off of family gatherings.

A young brunette woman sporting a new bob and stylish tortoiseshell glasses popped her head into the café. "Agnes, there's a delivery for you to sign. I think it's some barware."

When she popped back out, Beverly said, "Sharon Bogren

seems to be enjoying her new job here. Guess it beats being secretary at the Salt Rock Lodge."

"So she says. And I'm glad to have her."

Agnes hurried off to take the delivery, and Beverly went in search of Sharon, who was counting out a shipment of white cheddar cheese wedges. "I was just telling Agnes how happy you seem to be working here."

Sharon beamed. "And I have you to thank for that. I owe you big time."

At least Beverly was good at getting *other* people jobs. "How's Braddon?"

"He finally made Rapier Marshal. But that's not the best news. He's going to open an Olympics training facility for fencing. I'm so excited for him."

"With his background, makes a lot of sense. I wish him the best of luck."

"I'll tell him. And you and Detective Dutton must come visit when it's finished."

Beverly started to head out, but first, she had to duck into the café area where she'd left her purse. In her haste to grab it, it fell off the table, and some of the contents spilled out onto the floor. Including her gun. She really should have taken Mr. X's advice and got a shoulder holster.

Blaine, who was nearby after carrying in another box of wine glasses, bent over to help. He stopped when he saw the gun. "You carry this all the time?"

"Self-defense only."

"Can I see it?"

Beverly paused. But since he was fifteen and almost old enough to operate a gun in Vermont without a guardian's permission, she pulled it out and let him handle it. "It's not a good idea to use a gun except for self-defense, though."

His eyes were wide with admiration. "I'd love to try it out."

"Why don't we go to a range someday. So you can learn all the proper safety rules."

"Thanks. That would be dope." He hesitated, then added. "Maybe someday I'll be a cop, too. Like Detective Dutton."

"I'm sure Detective Dutton would be happy to talk to you about that any time." Beverly wasn't sure what she'd imagined him wanting to do with his life after the rough beginnings. But this had come out of left field.

Perhaps she could keep the whole gun business just a secret between her and Blaine? Adam had expressed reservations about her carrying a gun. And he might not approve of her going with Blaine to the shooting range, either.

But she was her own person with her own life and could do whatever the hell she pleased with that life, right? With or without Detective Adam Dutton's approval. She thought of her threatening note again. The secrets she was keeping from Adam were starting to pile up, weren't they? Far more than he knew.

Beverly sighed as beginning of another headache came on. After all those years of lying and cons, pretending to be someone else—all in the name of being an avenging angel— maybe that's why she couldn't completely rely on anyone. And maybe that's why she'd been feeling so out of sorts lately.

But after thinking about it, she'd decided one thing for sure. All of her recent musings about getting a job or settling down had suddenly disappeared into a fog of existential smoke. That threatening note meant she already had a job, one that wasn't finished.

There was no higher calling than making sure the people involved in bilking her grandmother and other elderly antiques store owners—and now murdering another owner, Jared Lake—were finally taken out, one by one.

An all-too-familiar sensation settled in the pit of her stomach. Like she'd swallowed a cocktail of stress pills and molten steel liqueur, followed by a chaser of adrenaline. Once again, it was showtime.

5

Adam and Jinks pulled up in front of an immaculate Victorian that was almost too immaculate, more like something fake from a Hollywood set. It was dotted with windows everywhere there could be windows and matching glass doors. The yellow color of the house with the dusting of snow on top made it resemble a frosted lemon cake. One of Adam's father's favorites.

Adam followed Jinks as they trudged up the varicolored quartzite walkway to the door, but they didn't have to knock when the door opened first. The woman who greeted them said, "I saw you coming. You have news about Jared, don't you?"

She showed them into the front room, filled with surprisingly modern furniture for a Victorian. Even the woman herself was dressed in a copper-colored pantsuit, with her white hair cut into a short, spiky style. No antiques-lover, this. She offered them coffee or tea, which they politely declined. Adam was already buzzed from the Miralee's Market espresso, and Jinks needed her hands free to take notes.

The victim's sister sat down across from Adam. "You must be the nice detective I spoke with on the phone this morning."

"Adam Dutton, yes. And you're Arabelle Lake—"

"Call me Belle. Please. The other sounds like a fairy. You know, Tinkerbell."

Jinks looked up from her notepad. "Or a fancy ballet move."

Belle smiled at Jinks. "I've thought of that, too."

Adam asked, "I'm sorry to have to discuss this with you, Belle. We won't have a positive ID on the body for a while, but—"

"It's him. I know it."

"How's that?"

"The dental implants I told you about, for one. The same type you said you found on the victim. And he hasn't answered my calls. That's not like him. Plus," she hesitated. "I know it sounds silly . . . but I have a feeling. I just know."

Adam nodded. "Does he have any other family?"

"Only me and his nephew—my son, Peter, who lives in California. Peter's father is deceased, a heart attack. Jared never married, never had kids."

"I see." Adam looked over at Jinks, who gave him a brief glance up from her note-taking. So, Belle was his only heir, then? He set that thought aside for now.

"Tell me more about Jared."

Belle clasped her hands together. "He was a good soul, my brother. But a lousy businessman."

"Oh?"

"He was always having problems with the shop. Even afraid he'd have to declare bankruptcy." She rushed to add, "I know what you're thinking. Insurance fraud. But he'd had an infusion of cash recently."

"From what source?"

"I assumed he'd got a loan. Finally."

"You say, 'finally.' He'd been trying to get a loan for a while?"

"Yes, though most banks considered him a poor risk. Can't blame them."

Adam frowned. "Insurance fraud isn't necessarily the first motive I'd name in this case. But we have to keep an open mind."

"I just know poor Jared wouldn't do such a thing, no matter how desperate. He's a good Catholic. Always worried about going to hell." She paused before adding, "Makes it ironic he burned in an earthly fire." Her voice trailed off, and then she uttered a half-laugh, half-cry.

Adam asked, "Do you need a glass of water?" He added, "In fact, why don't you go ahead and get something to drink. And I'll take a cup of that tea you were offering, after all."

When she returned, he gratefully accepted the cup of tea, and she sat down with a glass of something yellowish—lemonade?—to match the house.

He gave her a minute, then proceeded. "Did Jared have any enemies? Or had he received any threats you're aware of?"

"Enemies? Threats? Why would you ask that?"

Adam balanced the too-hot cup of tea on his lap. "That preliminary autopsy also discovered a skull wound we think occurred before the blaze. He was likely killed prior to the fire being set."

Belle put a hand to her throat. "Murdered?"

"It would seem so."

"I can't believe it. I . . . not Jared." She dropped her hand to her lap and shook her head. "Hadn't seen him in several weeks. My fault. Been so busy with my Christmas charity group. However . . . "

"Yes?"

"The last time I saw him, I got odd vibes."

"Odd in what way?"

"Maybe as if he was hiding something? Or, in retrospect, afraid of something. Strange behavior for a guy who's ordinarily fairly dull." She smiled briefly. "His idea of a big night out was watching hockey on TV with his dog and some pork rinds and warm beer. The dog is with Jared's neighbor since I have an allergy."

Adam couldn't help aiming a quick look at Jinks. Hadn't she said not long ago that her idea of a fun evening was an imported beer, some of Felicia's homemade soft pretzels, and some basketball?

He said to Belle, "But Jared didn't say anything unusual at his most recent meeting with you?"

"Not then, no."

Adam picked up the tea again. It was chamomile, not one of his favorites, but he wanted to be polite. "Your brother was involved with the Northeast Antiquities League. Did he talk about that organization much? Had you ever met anyone from the group?"

"I did hear him mention it once—that he was fed up with them. Though he didn't mention why, and I didn't press him on it. His business was the most important thing in his life. Not some fusty old-boys club with secret handshakes and keggers."

Belle sighed. "I admit I'm worried his creditors will come after me now. Or Peter. Though any money left will go to pay lawyers and claims."

"His estate won't be considerable, I take it?"

"I don't think so. Not that any of those sharks out there know that."

"Belle, I urge you to be wary of people claiming to be creditors. You shouldn't be on the hook for them personally, just your brother's estate. There are far too many scammers out there."

"As I say, might not be much left to scam. I think he did take out a business insurance policy within the last year or two. Maybe that will help."

"Did he also have a life insurance policy?"

"Come to think of it, I think he also bought one of those policies in the past year."

Adam gulped down a little more of the tea. "Were you and Peter the beneficiaries?"

"Suppose I'll have to talk to the lawyer about that. Jared didn't like to discuss financial things. But every now and then, he'd let a little detail drop." She shook her head. "That business policy makes it sound more like insurance fraud, doesn't it?"

Adam smiled at her. "I think that's all we need right now, Belle. And we do want to thank you for talking with us. Especially during such a difficult time." He put the chamomile down on an end table with relief. "And thanks for the tea."

When Adam and Jinks were back in the car, Jinks rolled her eyes, "Secret handshakes and keggers? Little does she know, right?"

"If by handshakes, you mean bribery, theft, and harassment, and by keggers you mean murder, well then, yeah. That about describes the NAL."

Jinks snorted. "She seems harmless. But a nice, fat insurance policy can turn sweet little old ladies into money-grabbing killers."

"Old, Jinks? I think she's maybe sixty."

"And you're forty-two. Half-old."

"Thanks, oh so much."

Adam shook his head, but he had to agree with Jinks on one thing, namely, the insurance money. That made two potential policies Belle might benefit from—the business policy and the life insurance one. From the looks of Belle's immaculate house and what appeared to be expensive furniture, one could argue Belle didn't need the money. But perhaps she just had expensive tastes she needed to pay for?

She hadn't seemed all that surprised that her brother was dead, let alone murdered. But people in shock often acted in odd ways. The beginning of an investigation was always one part intrigue but one equal part frustration.

Jinks cranked up the heater to the "blast furnace" setting. "So our victim seemed afraid of something or someone. And recently took out an insurance policy. Maybe Belle's brother wasn't so dull, after all."

"Could be a lot of things. Loan sharks, blackmail—"

"Or our favorite crime syndicate, ye olde Northeastern Antiquities League."

"I wish they *were* all 'olde,' aka retired, jailed, or deceased."

Jinks offered Adam some mints. "To cleanse the palate from the chamomile."

"How did you know it was chamomile?"

"From the look on your face."

He grabbed a couple of the mints, and she said, "If Beverly Laborde has her way, all of the NAL goons will soon be just a bad memory."

"I'd rather she didn't."

"Can't really blame her, can you? Have to admit, I admire her spunk. I'd probably have done the same thing."

"But you're a trained cop. She's—"

"A con woman extraordinaire."

Adam frowned. "Reformed."

Jinks lifted an eyebrow. "Um-hmm."

Adam reached over to grab the container of mints and downed most of the rest of them. "Let's go earn that ten dollars an hour of ours."

"My mother wanted me to be a supermodel. Said I'd be set for life."

Adam tried to picture Jinks in a frou-frou number with ruffles and sequins and a perennial pout. "You wouldn't have lasted a day."

She feigned a hurt look. "Not glamorous enough?"

"Don't think they'd have kept you on after you'd strangled the clueless designer and coldcocked the sexist photographer."

She grinned. "You owe me some mints."

6

Jinks and Adam stood in the center of the large two-story room with a net-enclosed area at one end and several little stalls along the outer walls. In the middle lay two large synthetic-grass areas with holes and flags poking out each hole.

Jinks said, "I cannot believe people pay money to do this. Little ball into little hole. Over and over and over."

"Indoor golfing facilities are all the rage, I hear. Especially in New England. Snow golf hasn't caught on yet."

"I'd be doing some raging right now if Felicia was into this."

"And little Jacob wouldn't find it fun?"

"I'm hoping he likes cheaper fun. I think this is beyond my pay grade."

They'd tracked Justin Garone here, the owner of the other antiques store recently hit by arson. When Adam asked a staff member which of the dozen or so men inside was Garone, she pointed out a middle-aged man on the farthest green. He wore knickerbockers with argyle socks—did people really still do that sort of thing?

Adam winced when Jinks elbowed him in the ribs and said, "Dude looks like he stepped out of a nineteenth-century painting."

As they got closer to the man, Jinks stopped in mid-stride. "Isn't that the same guy we saw at the scene of the fire at Vintage Vibes? The one I said must be a 'fire tourist?'"

"Let's find out." They trekked over to him, swerving to avoid an errant ball and another golfer cursing at them, "Get out of the way."

When they finally reached their target, Adam asked, "Justin Garone?"

"That's me. Who wants to know?"

Adam explained, "I'm Detective Dutton, and this is Detective Jinks. We're from the Ironwood Junction Police. Mind if we speak with you for a moment?"

Garone frowned and held up a hand. "Can't it wait? I'm only half-way through the hour I've already paid for."

"Sorry, sir, but we really need to speak with you."

The other man heaved an annoyed sigh. He bent over his ball, took a few wiggling steps, and then took his swing. The ball missed the hole by about a foot. Garone grumbled, "I usually make those."

"Is there someplace else we can go, sir?" Adam looked around the facility.

Garone hesitated, then pointed out a little room in the back. The putting-stance posters on the wall and stacks of instructional books and magazines made it clear this was a "coaching" room. Adam just hoped no one had coached Garone on his answers in advance.

"Mr. Garone, I know when the arson hit your Main Street Antiques store, you dealt extensively with the Woodstock police. But we need to chat with you now about another fire, this one at Vintage Vibes."

"Such a terrible tragedy. Yes, yes, of course. Anything I can do to help, Detective Dutton." He looked over at Jinks. "And Detective Jinks, was it?"

Adam said, "For starters, we saw you at the scene of the Vintage Vibes arson yesterday evening."

Garone nodded. "I have a police scanner. A small hobby of mine. When I heard there was a fire and then learned the address, I knew it was Jared Lake. And since I'd dealt with an arson recently, I feared the worst. Naturally, I had to go by and see if there was anything I could do."

"You knew Jared Lake quite well, then?"

"Not really. We were friendly rivals and colleagues. Even went golfing together once." Garone swallowed hard. "The ambulance that was there. Must have been someone inside that building. Was it . . . ?"

"Jared Lake? We believe so, yes."

"I was afraid of that. I'd hoped maybe it was someone else. But who else would it be?"

"Did you know of anyone who might wish Lake harm?"

"Harm? You mean, this wasn't an accident?"

"It might not be."

"I see. As far as I know, Jared was well-liked, a friendly guy. I knew he had financial troubles. An eye for antiques but not the stomach for business. Although stomach isn't the right anatomical term. You have to be hard-nosed and hard-assed most of the time."

"Did Jared offer up any details about those financial troubles of his?"

"Only hints. Everybody knew he was on the brink of bankruptcy."

Adam noticed Garone was standing in front of a poster of golfer Gary Player and could almost be a dead ringer for the Hall of Famer. "Jared had an infusion of cash recently. Did he mention that to you?"

"What? Heavens, no. How interesting. Maybe he won the lottery? Or perhaps he finally convinced a banker to take a chance on a loan. Most banks around here knew better."

Jinks asked, "Were you also a member of the Northeastern Antiquities League?"

Garone blinked slowly. "The NAL?"

"Yes, sir."

"I got into the business later in life after a stint in the military. Didn't really have much of an interest in the NAL. Oh, I knew I should make contacts and all, but I was sick and tired of bureaucracies and organizations. That's why owning my own business felt so freeing."

Jinks pressed him, "Did Jared ever talk to you about the NAL?"

"He tried to get me to join, oddly enough, when I first opened my shop. But after all that nasty business with Reggie Forsythe, murdering his father and all, glad I didn't get involved."

Adam almost told him he didn't know the half of it, but instead said, "Mr. Garone, I checked with the Woodstock PD, and they said you were going to receive a substantial insurance settlement."

"Thanks to my wife. She kept nagging me about getting some good policies in case something bad happened."

"Lucky for you, she did."

"It'll be enough for us to retire and move to Florida. Where I can play golf year-round instead of resorting to an indoor putting green."

"Except for when the hurricanes come through."

Garone chuckled. "I'll take that over our three-foot blizzards any day, Detective Dutton."

They thanked him for his time and stayed around to watch Garone and the other duffers from a second-story viewing platform. Garone returned to the same hole, did his little putting wiggle, and this time, he sank the shot.

Jinks watched Garone take a little victory dance. "You buying that about the police radio?"

"More people have 'em than you think."

"Could check on sales around these parts. See if he bought one recently."

"More paperwork. Hooray. But it's a good idea."

Jinks said, "Arsonists are often spied at the scene of the crime, watching their handiwork with pride."

"True, but he's also a victim, himself. Allegedly."

"If it's insurance fraud, then maybe not a victim."

"An insurance-fraud ring instead of an arson ring? With both Garone and Jared Lake involved? It'll be an interesting angle to follow up."

"I'm already in fraud mode after my internet-fraud case earlier this month. Just call me the fraud goddess."

Adam watched another golfer miss a six-inch putt for the third time. How much money did they charge an hour for this? He glanced over at a sign with prices and shook his head. Well, it was a cheaper hobby than owning a plane, a boat, or a horse. He'd just stick with his hand-me-down guitar.

They returned to the police station where Jinks got right down to business with some of that paperwork. Adam settled at his own desk to listen to new phone messages. The fire chief, a colleague at the Burlington PD, and Joe Brimm. One was from Beverly asking him to give her a call.

He rubbed his eyes and looked at his own stack of paperwork. He picked up the top folder, stared at it for a minute, and then put it back down. Phone calls first. He grabbed his cell and scrolled through the contacts. When his thumb landed on one labeled BLB, he stopped. Why had Beverly called? If it were urgent, she'd have called his cell, wouldn't she? One way to find out.

7

Beverly watched as the cobalt-blue Subaru pulled into the circular driveway and parked under an oak tree. Her pulse quickened as the handsome dark-haired man climbed out of the car and headed her way.

As he got closer, she said, "I see you got a new car."

"Couldn't save the old one. Guess being dipped upside down in a pond and then hit with a pipe bomb was too much for my old faithful steed. Imagine that."

"How's the house?"

"I've made some repairs after the bombing. Still have more to do. The eaves, gutters, some brickwork patching."

"Sounds hopeful." She moved toward the largest tombstone in a row of large headstones. "I know how busy you are. But thanks for coming."

He joined her in staring down at the inscription on the red granite marker which read, *Reginald Forsythe, II.* "I don't mind meeting you here, but have to admit I was surprised to get your call."

"Had a sudden urge to see this. Not really sure why. Yet, I couldn't bring myself to visit here alone. Imagine *that.*" She gave him a brief smile.

"Bad memories?"

She shook her head. "My grandfather was a rotten man in

many ways. But I also remember what Imelda Forsythe told me. That he had a tender side when he didn't know you were looking. And that if Grammie hadn't divorced him, things might have been different. Imelda said she wasn't sure he ever got over that."

"That doesn't excuse what he did. Not just the shady business dealings, but keeping his son away from your grandmother and raising him to be a monster."

"Wonder what my grandfather would think of that monster, his son, being in a nursing home, kept alive by tubes and machines?"

Adam frowned. "He brought it on himself. And both father and son were always at each other's throats, remember?"

Beverly nodded and stayed silent for a moment, listening to the wind whistle through the leaves, knocking several to the ground in a flutter of dying life. "Probably should have brought some flowers."

"Like black dahlias?"

That prompted a slightly bigger smile from Beverly. "He was pretty much my only family left. Along with my uncle-the-monster."

Beverly thrust her freezing hands in her pockets and looked at Adam. "What about you? I know Harlan's been like a father to you after your parents passed. But any grandparents? Uncles? Cousins?"

"I'm like you in that regard. Only an aunt and uncle who live in Alaska. Needless to say, I don't see them much."

"But you could. See them, that is. If you wanted to."

He stooped down to run his finger along the stone's lettering. "Guess Forsythe's ex-wife paid for this." He straightened up as he added, "I hate graveyards."

"You do? Whatever for?"

"None of that ghost stuff. Though when I was a kid, a

friend and I got lost in one overnight—that was one creepy experience. But that's not the reason." Adam pointed at two graves side-by-side in the far corner of the lot. "I visit my parents' graves on their birthdays each year."

"I haven't done that in a long, long time. Guess I move around too much." Beverly started to say something flippant but changed her mind as she looked into those lovely mocha eyes of his filled with the glint of a shared loss. "I don't like graveyards, either. And I was so young when my parents were killed. I barely remember them."

"What about your grandmother?"

"She wanted to be cremated. Hated the thought of being a bag of bones rotting underground. I scattered her ashes on Spruce Peak near Stowe. Up where we used to go picnicking all the time."

"I like that. Think I'll get cremated too."

"And where would you want your ashes spread, then?"

"Not sure it would matter. But maybe over the White and Connecticut Rivers where my father used to take me fishing."

"Ashes to ashes, dust to dust." Beverly tried for a teensy bit of humor, "And Adams to atoms."

"Seems fitting. Maybe even more environmentally friendly."

"And practical, I won't have any family to visit my grave."

Adam shook his head. "Maybe not family. But sometimes friends are even better than family. And you have more of those than you think."

Maybe he was right about that. She'd certainly developed more friends here in Ironwood Junction in the past few months than she'd formed in the past ten years. But she didn't want to delve too deeply into her future, something she still wasn't able to comprehend much beyond any given week.

Not wanting to get more maudlin than they already were,

Beverly walked along the adjacent markers, reading the inscriptions. "All of these here say Forsythe. Must have been a big family at one time. Wonder who these people were? I mean, they're all likely family of mine of one kind or another, right?"

"Maybe you should do one of those ancestry things."

She folded her arms across her chest in mock indignation. "So you law enforcement types can use my DNA without permission? Not a chance."

He grinned. "Now, you're the one getting paranoid."

He bent over to pick up something shiny in the snow, making his coat and shirt inch up and expose part of a jagged red scar on his side. That must be left over from his torture at the hands of the madman who kidnapped and branded him.

Beverly shivered, but when her eyes moved over the rest of his body, she suddenly felt much warmer and hoped he wasn't catching her frank appraisal. *Damn the man.* Forty-two going on twenty-two. How did he manage to keep in shape?

Adam hadn't seemed to notice her stare as he examined the object in his hand, a silver metal flask, that he stuffed into a pocket. He squinted at the headstone again, then turned to her with a serious expression. "About that 'monster' in the nursing home and all those tubes and machines . . . "

"Please don't tell me he had a miraculous recovery and then escaped like Redbeard."

"Not exactly. The doctors say there *has* been some new brain activity on the monitor."

"But he shot himself in the head. We saw him do it. And we visited him in the hospital just a couple weeks ago." Beverly frowned and stamped her foot. "I have to go see him—I need to see for myself he's still there."

"That's not a good idea."

"Why not?"

"For one thing, he's been moved to a nursing facility. And

I just don't think it's in your best interests."

She frowned at his words. "Shouldn't I be the judge of that?"

"Beverly, you've been obsessed with that man for years. You've already given up too much of your life trying to get revenge on him. And all the other NAL members you blame for hastening your grandmother's death."

When she opened her mouth to disagree, Adam said, "He can't hurt you now. You need to move on."

"Oh, really?" Beverly fished an envelope out of her purse and handed it over to him. "Good thing you've got gloves on."

He studied the marking on the envelope and teased out the paper inside. When he read it, his gaze darkened. "When did you get this?"

"A bellhop delivered it to me at the resort. Said it had arrived by courier. I debated whether to give it to you. Might just be a prank."

Adam turned the envelope over in his hand. "It looks similar to one I received. After my house almost got blown up."

"You didn't tell me about that note."

"You had a lot on your mind right then. I didn't want you to worry."

Adam studied Beverly's note further. "A computer-printed piece of regular paper with big fonts and crazy colors— although the red ink cartridge is low, more pink than red."

"Why that weird thing with the fonts?"

"It's like someone's trying to copy those threatening notes of yore when people cut text out of newspapers. No return address, just your name, also printed out."

Adam carefully folded the note back inside the envelope. "Might be traceable. All color printers have hidden microdots in them these days to foil counterfeiting. Well, at least laser printers. Not so much with inkjets. And my note was printed on an inkjet."

Beverly sighed. "There, you see? I can't leave the NAL and those crooks behind me. I'm not about to let someone just threaten me like that."

"That's what I'm afraid of. You getting yourself into danger again."

"It's my life to do with as I wish. And apparently, my quest isn't done yet." She stood with her hands on her hips. "You need to go and arrest Ivon Kozak right away for the two arsons and Jared Lake's deaths. Because he must be behind it all."

Adam stared at her. "How did you hear about all of that?"

"Mr. X."

"Of course."

"You don't seem to be keeping me in the loop these days, so what am I supposed to do?"

"Beverly, I don't want to see you getting hurt. Again." He sighed. "Look, if Kozak's guilty, we'll go after him."

"Of course, he's guilty."

"These things take time. We have to pursue all leads and follow procedures. We don't like arresting the wrong guy, and the courts really don't take too kindly to that."

"But Adam—"

"Look. There are other possible motives. Insurance fraud, theft, money laundering, or using the arsons to cover up the real reason for Jared Lake's murder. It could be a hundred different motives."

"But Jared Lake was a member of the NAL, Adam."

He frowned. "Mr. X tell you that, too?"

"Among other things."

"Looks like it's time I paid that man another visit. He does have a history with all of this, especially the Forsythes. Although my detective radar just can't seem to trust him completely."

"Well, you can trust him. *I* do."

"He certainly has been helpful thus far. Still—"

Beverly reached over to grab the threatening note, but he held it out of reach. "Ah, ah," he said. "I'll want Joe Brimm to take a look at this. See if matches up to my note."

She reluctantly relented. "You won't lose it, right?"

"I wouldn't be a very good detective, otherwise."

He was half-smiling, but she could tell from his defensive posture she'd offended him. She would say she was only joking, but she wasn't so sure that was true, was it? Maybe those trust issues of hers were getting out of hand.

But even though she'd told herself she didn't need Detective Adam Dutton's approval about anything, she also didn't want to hurt him. So she lightened the mood. "Now that you mention it, I sure could use some of Mr. X's yak-milk hot chocolate right now."

He pointed to his car. "It's not hot chocolate, but I've got a thermos of tea in there. And an extra cup."

They decided sitting inside the SUV was smarter than staying outside in the blustery winds, and Adam was soon pouring Beverly some of the tea. She took a taste and coughed. "This is unusual."

"It's an herbal tea the chief is using to wean himself off caffeine. He said he made too much and gave me this thermos." Adam chuckled. "Quite frankly, I think he just wanted to get rid of it."

Beverly choked down some more of the tea. It was warm, so it had that going for it, if not much else.

Before returning to her own car, she took one more last look at her grandfather's tombstone from a distance. What secrets, good and evil, had he taken with him to his grave? If things had been different and she'd gotten a chance to know him, would she have even liked the man?

Missed chances, missed experiences, missed life. Hardly anyone missed her grandfather. Would anyone miss her when she was gone? How many times had she asked herself that question in the middle of the night when she awoke with the aches, the longings, the raging fires of anger that kept her from sleeping?

At the thought of sleep, she yawned, prompting Adam to say, "Looks like we've kept you up past your bedtime. Maybe you should get some rest. You've gone through hell and back the past couple of months."

She surprised herself by agreeing. "Sleep sounds lovely. As Scarlett said in *Gone With the Wind*, tomorrow is another day."

Which was appropriate—Scarlett had battled hardship and ultimately won, hadn't she? With any luck, Beverly would end up showing Scarlett a thing or two about perseverance.

She yawned again. Perseverance later. A little shut-eye first.

8

Sunday, December 13

After spending the rest of his evening yesterday making mostly fruitless calls and handling more of the dreaded paperwork he hated so much, Adam *should* be in a bad mood this morning. He really should. But he couldn't help but smile as he looked over at his yawning companion in the passenger's seat. "Are you sure you don't need more coffee, Beverly?"

"Think I drank a gallon of the stuff already at the resort. The hazelnut was on sale."

"Had the usual Miralee's Market brew this morning, myself." Adam added, "Was it poor sleep that did you in?"

"You mean, was I up all night worrying about that threatening note?"

"Among other things. The trip to your grandfather's gravesite, too."

She sighed. "Maybe not all night."

Adam thought about turning the car around right then and there and making a U-turn for Miralee's and coffee with extra shots for Beverly but decided against it. "Sorry about your rental car."

"The agency told me the funny noise I was hearing might be something in the suspension. Not that it matters to me since it's on their dime. If they can't fix it, I'll just get another one."

"Adam's Taxi Service is happy to be of help."

She grinned. "Thanks. I told Harlan I was going to drop by the shop this morning, and I didn't want to let him down. Besides, he's another one of those worries that kept me up last night."

"Thinking his store might be next in line for an architectural french fry?"

"Oh, that turn of phrase."

As they parked beside the building with the lettering, "Tossed Treasures" on the sign, Adam was glad for the excuse to check up on Harlan. Maybe the other two fires weren't the work of a serial arsonist with a grudge against antiques stores, but he couldn't be sure of anything yet. Those fruitless calls and hated paperwork of Adam's certainly hadn't helped.

Once inside the store, Beverly led the way to the familiar office where the usual aroma greeted them from the vintage machine labeled, "Eat Butter Kist Popcorn." Harlan greeted Beverly with a hug as Adam spied an item on Harlan's desk and picked it up.

He studied the ugly clown clock. "You're keeping this in a place of honor, I see."

"I may regret that soon."

Adam asked, "Why?"

"That 1927-D Saint-Gaudens Double Eagle coin you found inside was appraised at a little over a million and a half."

"Then, this clock should definitely be front and center."

"You'd think so." Harlan rubbed his white beard. "But Ramsay Ryall has taken a cue from his late brother, you see. Suing me to get some of the cash from the coin sale. Makes me wonder if it'll be more trouble than it was worth."

Beverly's jaw dropped open. "What? Adam said Ramsay told him he didn't want any of his father's 'cursed' blood money. What changed?"

"Don't know, Beverly, I just don't know. But the smell of money can change people's minds real quick."

Beverly crossed her arms over her chest and huffed. "I run into Ramsay all the time at the resort since he's working there. I'll give him a piece of my mind."

"That's sweet of you, but we'd best let the lawyers take care of this." Harlan peered at Adam, "I've hired Duane Sher. You were right about him being top notch when he defended me about that bogus murder charge. Figured he could handle this, too."

Adam nodded. "One of the best legal eagles I know."

"Hope so. Legal stuff has never been my strong suit. Prospero takes care of most of the administrative things."

Adam placed the clock back on the desk as Harlan added, "When it rains, it pours, I guess."

"What do you mean, Harlan? More bad news?"

The older man opened his desk drawer and pulled out an envelope he handed over. "Got this delivered earlier this morning. Prospero said a courier dropped it off."

With a sinking feeling in his stomach, Adam examined the envelope. The note inside was almost identical to the ones he and Beverly had received—computer-generated, crazy colored fonts, and all. Only this one read, "Stay away from the NAL, or you might end up like Jared Lake."

Beverly peered over Adam's shoulder to read it, and she and Adam exchanged worried looks. Adam said, "Harlan, I—"

Harlan put up his hand and called out his office door, "Prospero, you got a minute?"

The young man poked his head into the room, and Adam thought he saw a new strand or two of gray hair among the black. Maybe Harlan's assistant was worried about the shop, too.

Harlan asked him, "Tell 'em what you told me. About security."

Prospero's face brightened. "I've been bugging Harlan here to add more security for months, Mr. Adam. Think I've finally won him over. A new alarm system and some video cameras should do the trick."

Beverly piped up, "I'm sure Mr. X can help. You should see all the security at his place."

Harlan furrowed his brow. "I know you like that man, Beverly. But I still can't help worry a bit you're trusting another crook."

"I trust him as much as I trust you, Harlan. He's out of that whole NAL scene for good."

Adam wanted to add a "Hear, hear" to Harlan's concerns about Mr. X but figured Beverly would punch him if he tried. He just said, "I can increase my patrols of the area. Maybe have some uniforms do it, too."

Prospero beamed. "That'll make my mother feel better. Made the mistake of telling her about the arsons. She hasn't stopped worrying since."

Adam asked, "Speaking of those fires, Prospero. Did either you or Harlan here know Jared Lake well?"

Harlan spoke first. "Bumped into him all the time. Good man. Terrible shame him dying that way."

Adam glanced at Prospero, who shrugged. "I didn't know Mr. Lake. But I do know his assistant, Lucas Barratt. We have a lot in common."

"You do?"

"We're both immigrants. Me from Guatemala, Lucas from El Salvador. We even both dated Lucas's wife, Jeanne, but Lucas won that battle. We stayed friends, though. They're obviously made for each other and quite happy. So I'm happy."

Adam asked, "Had you seen either Jared Lake or Lucas Barratt recently? That goes for you too, Harlan."

Prospero replied, "I popped into their store last week. Lucas had called me saying they'd got in some jade figurines, and they don't sell those. Harlan agreed we'd take the figurines and give them some porcelain plates in return."

Harlan verified that, adding, "Haven't seen either one myself. Last time I did, they seemed fine."

Prospero shrugged. "Mostly fine."

Adam studied him. "Mostly?"

"Mr. Lake seemed aloof. Kinda angry, almost. Not at me. But something. Or someone, I guess."

"Did your friend Lucas know the reason for this?"

"Just said his boss had been jumpy lately. But Mr. Lake didn't want to talk about it."

The bell at the front door rang, and a group of five customers wandered in all at the same time. Prospero scurried back into the store, and Adam decided he and Beverly should take that opportunity to leave, too.

Before they did, Adam told Harlan, "Let Prospero rig up those security devices. But call me if you see anything suspicious, night or day. No matter how trivial."

"Sure thing, Adam."

"Oh, and I'd like to keep this threatening note you received."

"Take, keep, destroy, whatever you wish. Likely just a prank, don't you know."

For once, even jolly old Harlan didn't look convinced by his usual optimism. Beverly scanned Adam's face with worried eyes as the duo headed to Adam's car. "A threatening note to you, I sort of understand. You're a cop. And mine makes sense, too. But Harlan?"

"Don't know what to make of it yet, Beverly. It's an escalation I didn't expect." Adam opened the door for her and added, "The surviving arson victim and also the dead victim's sister didn't mention a similar note. Though the sister said her brother might have been jumpy, even frightened, when she saw him last, several weeks ago."

"Wasn't 'jumpy' the same word Prospero used about him?"

"Yeah." Adam slid into the driver's seat and pulled out his cellphone. After dialing a familiar number, a voice boomed on the other end. "Adam, this had better be good. I'm in the middle of some exciting, death-defying paperwork."

"You need help fighting off those paper cuts, Cray?"

"Nah, I'll just wave my bottle of peroxide at 'em. Wouldn't dare attack me after that."

"Look, Cray, I—"

"Need something. You hardly ever call me unless you do."

"Because you're the best, Cray."

"Oooh, Detective Dutton, aren't you the flatterer. I'll bet you say that to all the private eyes."

"Look, Cray. Didn't you work with a local Salvadorian client not too long ago?"

"Diego Lopez. The philandering wife case."

"Thought I recalled that. Nice to know I'm not having senior moments yet."

"You sure about that? You are getting a bit long in the tooth."

Adam grinned, knowing that Cray was a good ten years older. "I want you to look into a man named Lucas Barratt. Worked at the Vintage Vibes antique store."

"That the one just burned down?"

"The same."

"Must be a suspect then. Okay, but I hope you pay me faster than last time. I got tabs at the Ironwood Pub & Brewery that need paying."

"I pay you out of my own pocket, Cray."

"You rich detective-types. Rolling in dough."

"If you mean phyllo, yes."

Adam practically heard Cray's mouth watering through the phone. "You throw in some of that double-nut apple strudel of yours, and you got yourself a deal."

"Fine, then. I promise."

When Adam hung up with Cray, Beverly poked him in the arm. "You promised me something, too."

"Yes, well, the something I promised you is a little riskier. Still not sure it's a good idea."

"A promise is a promise, Adam. It's still relatively early in the day. You'll have time to do all your other detectivey things later."

Adam pulled out of the parking lot and pointed the car toward the western edge of town. He had a good idea Chief Quinn wouldn't agree to this little excursion. But Beverly was right—he'd made her a promise, even if it was under the influence of nostalgia last evening before he and Beverly left the cemetery.

Adam sniffed the air and said, "I don't smell much in the way of perfume. Did you bring any with you?"

She replied with an indignant frown, "That's a rather chauvinistic thing to say."

He grinned. "Eau de smoke tends to linger with you long afterward. After this, you'll probably wish you'd drowned yourself in it."

9

From the way Adam was gritting his teeth, Beverly could tell the closer she and Adam got to the scene of the Vintage Vibes fire, the antsier he got. She didn't want to put him in a difficult position. But damn it—she needed to see the scene of the crime. In the past, before she'd started in on one of her cons, she'd always liked to know exactly what she was dealing with. This wasn't all that different, was it? And he'd promised.

A few blocks from the site, Adam got a phone call from Jinks. When he hung up, he told Beverly, "An insurance rep from the victim's policy is already at the scene. I called the office to clear it first. Quinn said the fire investigation team had gathered most of the evidence they could, so it should be fine. As long as I supervise."

"Then, our timing is perfect."

"It would appear so. But a word of warning, Beverly. There might still be hot pockets of flames. And even though the scene's been mostly released, I'd like to avoid any further contamination. Just in case."

When they arrived, a blonde woman with what looked like an expensive Canada goose-down coat, with matching feathery hairstyle, was taking photos with a professional DSLR camera. She introduced herself as Jenny-Lee Salant. Beverly wrinkled her nose as the other woman stood next to Adam and smiled up at him while batting her eyelashes.

Salant nodded toward burned-out husk. "I've taken hundreds of photos and made measurements. I'm also going to get a report from the fire chief. When it's ready."

"Sounds like more work than a typical insurance claim."

"My office is concerned this is a fraud case since the policy was new. I haven't spoken with the victim's heir, the sister, directly yet. Or even the victim's staff, particularly his assistant, Lucas Barratt. But I will. Soon."

She moved to stand so close to Adam, they were almost conjoined twins. "You'll let us know if they find anything that's linked to fraud, I hope?"

"Of course."

Salant said, "This is so reminiscent of the Garone arson. You've probably heard of it, the Main Street Antiques fire up in Woodstock."

"You're involved with that one, too?"

"Indeed, we are. On the surface, I haven't found any fraud. Yet. But there's a reason they call me 'Bulldog Salant.'"

Beverly almost gagged at that one but smiled sweetly at the other woman. "I find it hard to believe Jared Lake would commit insurance fraud and then kill himself before he could get any money."

Salant frowned. "Maybe he didn't plan on that happening. Or got careless. Or it was his sister who set the fire and made a mistake. Who knows?"

Adam partially agreed with her, saying, "There *might* have been an accidental component."

Beverly almost smacked him. Was he trying to flirt with a woman who actually wore three-inch heeled boots to an arson scene? She'd thought better of him than that.

Salant said, "I'm kind of sorry to see a couple of items burned in the fire that were listed on his insurance inventory sheet. Like a rare French antique art nouveau bakelite cicada brooch pin, circa 1900s. And this whimsical little 1890s beetle bug playing a mandolin."

At Adam's raised eyebrow, she added, "My brother's an entomologist."

Adam smiled. "Jewelry bugs are the best kind."

"That's what I tell him. He can have the others."

"Good thing your brother doesn't study bakelite beetles. Bakelite plastics don't burn, but if cracked, that plastic can release toxic formaldehyde and asbestos."

Salant replied, "Then I take back my admiration for that little mandolin-playing figure. It can stay lost."

Tired of having to focus on the plastic-woman, Beverly turned her attention to the blackened frame before her with its charred wood and twisted metal frame. The bleak starkness of the scene was bad enough. But it also gave her a twinge in the gut as she thought of the unfortunate Jared Lake.

When she saw the glint of sunlight on something half-buried under some rocks several feet away from the building, she headed over. Very gently, she pulled it out from under the pile. It looked like almost like an ashtray with an octopus attached—and was it wearing goggles? It was a curious, but rather ugly little thing.

Salant startled her when she said over Beverly's shoulder, "What's that?"

Beverly showed it to her, but Salant wrinkled her nose. "Not worth much. It's even dented."

Guess that meant Beverly could pocket the item, then. A reminder of the man, his store, his life, and something else she couldn't quite identify. She wasn't sure why she wanted to keep it, but she did.

When Salant seemed satisfied she'd taken all the photos she needed, she gave Beverly a curt nod. But she made sure to grab Adam's hand and hold on to it in a way that didn't seem entirely professional. Salant said, "Hope to hear from you soon, Adam. Call any time." And there went the batted eyelashes again.

When she'd finally left, Beverly huffed. "She seemed quite taken with you."

He shrugged. "Insurance reps do whatever they can to get cops to give them ammunition. So their company doesn't have to pay out. Don't read anything special into it."

"I wasn't. Just seemed unprofessional."

Adam gave her a sharp look and said, "Getting close to noon. Weekends are BOGO day at the Crossroads Café. Hungry?"

Her stomach rumbled, and she was surprised to realize she was ravenous. Maybe not surprising since she'd skipped breakfast. They headed straight for the café, and as they walked in, she was relieved to see they'd beaten the lunch crowd.

They placed their orders and ate in companionable silence for a bit until Adam asked, "Thought any further about buying a place or getting a job around these parts?"

"You may recall what I told you when we discussed this before. No résumé and no references. Ten years without a 'real' job. Who'd want me?"

"Both Harlan and Agnes, for starters. I'm sure they'd welcome the help and would pay you well for it."

"I wouldn't want to impose. And I'm not all that keen on being dependent on someone else for money."

She did a quick mental calculation of the funds still sitting in her Seychelles bank account. Her wheeling-and-dealing had made it possible for her to live a nomadic existence with enough money for room and board. But if she didn't keep up that con-woman life, those funds wouldn't last forever.

Adam replied, "There's the whole private eye thing we talked about, too. Since you love disguises and acting so much."

"Me and Cray. I can see it up on the nameplate. Laborde and Querry Investigations."

"You'd get top billing?"

"Naturally."

Adam chuckled. "I do believe you could tame that hulking bear-of-a-shamus into submission."

She took a bite of her chicken wrap. The chipotle-mayo sauce was tangy, spicy, and a little bit . . . smoky. "Going back to the arsons, we need to focus on Ivon Kozak."

"We?"

"The police, of course," she half-lied.

"The only information I even have about the guy and his shady NAL connections come from Mr. X."

"Then I think we need to visit Mr. X again and find out more. After all, when I called the car rental agency, they said my SUV wasn't quite ready for pickup."

Adam mused, "I still don't know what to think about Xenakis."

"Oh, he's harmless enough. Now, anyway."

Adam just shook his head

Beverly wasn't about to tell Adam of the conversations she'd had with Mr. X concerning some of the less-than-legal behavior he'd engaged in while under the employ of her grandfather—before Xenakis got out in disgust. Or about the time she'd seen him K.O. a thug with what he called shuto, or a knifehand strike, that he said, "can be deadly . . . when you want it to be."

She'd be the first to admit she knew very little about the man's past. But then, most people knew very little about hers.

Maybe that's why she liked him so much. They were two islands adrift in a sea of sharks just wanting to be left alone.

After they'd finished their quick bite and returned to the car, Beverly decided she didn't like the troubled look on Adam's face. So she reached over to dial up a local rock station and cranked up the volume. Jinks had once told Beverly that Adam hated the electric-guitar screeching of heavy metal. Beverly said, "You like Metallica, right?"

In reply, he glared at her, and she just laughed.

10

Adam looked out over the fields as they drove up the winding driveway past the many security devices he'd noticed on his first visit to Mr. X's place months earlier. Beverly had a valid point when she'd said Mr. X could give Harlan some security tips.

The two yaks didn't seem to care much about all those devices, standing in their fenced-in area and appearing to be much more interested in Adam and Beverly. Unlike Adam's last visit, the shaggy Yin and Yang sported red and green blankets.

After a recent round of light snow and melting cycles, the moat around the mini-castle was a little higher than usual. As Adam and Beverly navigated the walkway above it, he glanced over at her to make sure she was okay. "You don't seem too bothered by this."

"My fear of drowning mostly applies to deep or running water. This isn't so bad."

Xenakis greeted them warmly and immediately ushered them into his lair, offering up some of his customary yak-milk hot chocolate. Adam said, "No, thanks, I think I'm already over-caffeinated."

Beverly replied, "I'm not, and he's driving. Give me the alcoholic version this time."

Mr. X disappeared long enough to fetch Beverly's drink. When he handed it over, he said, "In Mongolia, they make an alcoholic beverage out of fermented yak's milk itself. One of these days, I should make you some Tibetan butter tea."

Adam's stomach churned at the sound of that, but he asked, "What's in it?"

"A salty mixture of black tea and Tibetan butter made from yak milk. Yak butter is really more of a cheese broth rather than butter. It has a smell and taste similar to blue cheese or Roquefort."

Cheese Adam could handle. Might be good in an omelet. He asked, "What's with the red and green blankets and halters on Yin and Yang?"

"I thought it looked rather festive."

Adam suppressed a grin at that. Christmas yaks. Why not? When Mr. X returned with Beverly's drink, Adam got down to business. "You probably know why we're here."

"The arsons. Naturally."

"And any new information you might have about Ivon Kozak and his connections to the missing Redbeard, aka Darnell Warner."

"Where do you want to start? It's a rather lengthy subject."

"A source of mine said Ivon Kozak's a nasty piece of work who has his tentacles into everything. And you told me, yourself, that with Forsythe out of action, Kozak pretty much has a corner on the dirty dealings market."

Mr. X nodded. "All quite true."

"Is it possible Kozak or Redbeard were behind the recent arsons and the death of Jared Lake? I only ask due to your connections to the NAL, and Lake allegedly being a member."

"He was. Not one of the more high profile figures. A little on the slippery side, but mostly kept his head down to avoid becoming a target of Forsythe's wrath."

"What would he have done to worry about that?"

"Reggie Forsythe was narcissistic that way. If you didn't sing his praises or crossed him in any way, you paid for it. One way or another."

"If Jared Lake was such a little figure in the NAL, I don't see why he'd be a target."

"For murder, you mean?"

"You heard about that, I see."

"Via my own sources. I like to keep an ear out even though I'm no longer part of that group. I never know when I might be a target, myself."

Adam let that go, for now. "Speaking hypothetically, if Kozak took over Forsythe's role as the NAL kingpin, what sort of breach would Jared Lake have committed that could lead to his murder?"

"The number one motive for Forsythe's wrath—and now Kozak's—is always betrayal."

"We haven't found any dirt on Jared Lake that would indicate such. Although he did receive a large infusion of cash recently."

Mr. X considered that for a moment. "Possibly, by honest means. More likely, not so honest."

"Are we talking theft, blackmail, fraud, what here?"

"Unknown. Perhaps even a double-cross. Either way, it seems poor Mr. Lake's ambitions ultimately exceeded his grasp."

Beverly stopped sipping her chocolate long enough to ask, "Did you know the owner of the other store that burned down? Justin Garone?"

"Garone I don't know much about, other than he's a neophyte in the business. And because I don't know much, that must mean he's pretty clean. As far as the NAL goes."

Beverly wrapped her hands around her cup. "Wonder if Sergeant Moody plays into all of this? Adam's friend, Cray, found a link between him and Ivon Kozak. And he has that background in military explosives. Couldn't he be involved in this?"

Xenakis smiled at her. "I've always thought you make a good detective, Beverly. You really should hang out your shingle."

She gave Adam a sideways glance, and he smirked. Great minds and all.

Mr. X added, "I'm intrigued by Moody, not having heard of him and his connections to the NAL crime syndicate before. I must put out some feelers."

"About those feelers, Xenakis." Adam leaned forward so he could look at the other man more directly. "Care to be more forthcoming about those?"

Mr. X shook his head. "Sorry. As I told Beverly, my origins are . . . original. And secret. As are my sources. We'll leave it at that."

Beverly asked, "How big is Kozak's influence now that my uncle is in the nursing home?"

"Kozak took a back seat to the Forsythes while they were still in power. But he's been emboldened after their demise. He may seem like a little weasel, but you should never underestimate him. In Greek culture, a weasel near one's house is a sign of bad luck, even evil. Fitting, that."

"We'll keep that in mind." Adam leaned forward a little more. He was getting too comfortable on that plush sofa. "And it's possible Redbeard has changed his allegiance from Forsythe to Kozak?"

"That is quite likely. Perhaps I can help a bit more with that angle. I've heard of a possible Redbeard sighting in Stowe via my connections."

"How recently?"

"A few days ago."

Adam nodded his thanks. "I'll put out a BOLO on the guy."

"That would be wise."

Beverly drained the last of her mug and set it down on the table beside her. She had a little chocolate mustache that made Adam want to whip out his cellphone camera.

She said to their host, "Adam found out there's been activity on my uncle's brain monitor."

Mr. X tented his fingers together. "That is most interesting. I had not been made aware of this."

That came as a surprise to Adam since the man seemed to know everything about the whole Forsythe clan. "It's just a minor change, but it was enough to shock the nurses."

"I see. I hope for his sake, he doesn't come around. It would have been better for everyone if his clumsy attempt at a cowardly suicide had been successful."

Adam suddenly became aware of music playing in the background, something exotic-sounding. He followed it to some speakers mounted on the walls. "Is that music from Indonesia?"

"Gamelan. You have a good ear, Detective Dutton. Are you a musician?"

"He plays the guitar," Beverly replied and then asked, "But why gamelan instead of opera?"

Xenakis wrinkled his nose. "This is much better."

Adam thanked him for his time and urged him to call Adam directly if he had more information. He didn't want Beverly going behind his back again for one of her crazy schemes. Not to mention he was getting mighty tired of being kept out of that loop between her and Xenakis.

As Adam and Beverly retraced their steps over the moat, he asked her, "What's with that whole opera comment?"

"Mr. X was once married to an opera singer. For all of one month."

"Ah, I see. Bad 'ex' memories." Adam felt more sympathetic toward the guy. He had a few of his own bad memories from Zelda.

Beverly smiled. "Since he has a background in Asia, I'd say it's more bad karma."

"I could use some good karma right now. Like having a witness who saw one or both of the recent fires. Or maybe the culprit walking into the PD and turning himself in. That would be *great* karma."

She stopped to take a photo of Yin and Yang. "Patience, grasshopper."

Adam grunted. He was ready to get out of the exotic realm and back to the ordinary world of investigation. But he stopped to stare at the curious yaks. What were they thinking? If they were capable of thinking.

"I don't think we should put all of our investigative theories in one basket. Jared Lake's arson might have nothing to do with Kozak or Redbeard. I know you're obsessed with them, but—"

"Have you forgotten about my threatening note, Adam? It warned me specifically to stay away from that line of investigation. And Harlan's note even mentioned Jared Lake by name."

He wasn't ready to concede the point. "They might also be more general threats, a misdirection. Jared's death could be courtesy of a bad business deal. Or since we're on the subject, a bad 'ex.' Again, this could go a hundred different ways."

"How does Jinks feel?"

"She's a good cop. Keeping her mind open, like a good cop should."

"Then why did you even come here to ask Mr. X about the whole NAL thing?"

"That's part of keeping an open mind." He grinned at her and pointed at her mouth. "You still have a little chocolate there."

She wiped her mouth with the sleeve of her coat and glared at him. "How long were you going to let me go on without mentioning that?"

"It was rather fetching. Might even make a good disguise someday."

She folded her arms across her chest. "Now you're just making fun of me."

"Not in the slightest. Although maybe if you added some lederhosen and a little felt cap with a feather . . . "

With a loud *harrumph*, she stormed over to Adam's car and called out over her shoulder. "Next time, I'm calling a cab."

"All the way out here? That would cost more than a day's rental fee." Adam started after her but stopped for a moment to look back at the yaks. He nodded over at the mini-castle and said to them, "Keep an eye on that one."

In reply, one of them actually snorted.

Beverly popped out of the rental car office and poked her head through the window of Adam's SUV. "My other car isn't ready, so they're giving me a different SUV loaner. Much more deluxe." She pointed to a Mercedes in one corner of the lot.

Adam said, "So that's what it feels like to be wealthy."

She grinned. "Think I'll drive it to Boston and waltz into a Saks store. Might as well look the part."

"Good. You do that. It'll keep you out of trouble."

Her grin faded. "Me? Trouble?" Okay, so maybe she deserved that. A little. But he didn't have to keep harping on it.

Beverly watched him drive off and then pointed her new rental car not toward Boston, but toward the Apple Valley Resort. She needed to check on a few supplies, anyway. And grab the special effects-kit from her room to add to the trunk of the new rental. Despite half-promising Adam not to "get into trouble" or practice her con-woman expertise, she didn't like not being prepared. Scout motto and all.

Before Beverly headed to her room, she ducked into the resort's café and was pleased to see Gloria working there again. The other woman gave her a quick hug, and Beverly asked, "How's the prep work for business school going?"

"Got my schedule lined up. One dull professor, a couple of great ones, and too much research. In short, I think I'm going to love it."

"Good to hear. You'll be elbowing all those Wall Street types before you know it."

"Wall Street? More like Main Street. I want to open my own business. Not sure what yet. If you have any ideas, I'm open to suggestions."

Beverly smiled. "I'll have to get back to you."

"Maybe not an antiques store, right? I mean, they tend to burn down, or so I hear."

"Only two so far." Beverly paused and added, "Gloria, are you still dating Ramsay Ryall?"

The other woman's cheeks flushed a crimson pink, and she winked. "We've been having some fun, sure. I hadn't dated much since Adam put my abusive ex behind bars. So this is kind of new to me again."

Beverly blurted out, "Did you hear about Ramsay's lawsuit against Harlan Wilford?"

Gloria frowned. "Lawsuit? No, he didn't breathe a word about any such thing. Whatever for?"

"It's that valuable coin Harlan found in an old clock from Ramsay's father's estate."

"Ramsay told me he didn't want any of the estate. That it was tainted. I thought he was secretly glad his father left everything to Harlan."

"Apparently, Ramsay thinks that coin belongs to him and not Harlan."

Gloria grimaced. "I'm not a law expert, but it doesn't seem like he'd have a viable claim, would he?"

She excused herself long enough to deliver some food to customers at a table and then started to head back to Beverly. But when a few more customers poured into the café, Beverly waved to her and headed to her room, leaving Gloria to her work.

Beverly sank onto the four-poster bed, looking from the mini-bar to the Jacuzzi. She envied all the tourists and ordinary guests who were here to relax and get away from it all. The temptation to slip into the inviting Jacuzzi in the corner was almost too great to pass up. But there was something else she needed to do more.

§ § §

Beverly stowed her effects-kit in her rental car. She used the GPS to punch in the address of her target and headed out past the west end of town. When she arrived at her destination, she had to admit the location was spectacular—and possibly wasted on the poor patients in the nursing facility in front of her. One in particular. Her uncle.

He'd been moved since she and Adam paid him a visit not all that long ago. From the ICU at Dartmouth-Hitchcock hospital to this place where the frailest of the frail and oldest of the old were left to rot. If her time came, and this was what awaited her, she'd just grab some tequila and pills and head to Mexico for one last binge on a tropical beach.

She parked in a far corner of the lot to give herself a little distance and privacy to dip into her kit. She opted for the same disguise she'd used at the Southeastern Vermont Regional Hospital to gain access to her grandfather's autopsy records two months ago.

She adjusted the short, layered wig of ash-brown-and-silver to go with her navy dress and flats. Then she added the stethoscope, white lab coat, and fake "Dr. Liz Smith" ID tag.

Once inside the lobby, she pretended to be talking on her cellphone and sat on one of the visitor chairs. What she needed was for the front desk receptionist to step away for just a couple of minutes so she could find out which room her uncle was in. But when nothing happened, Beverly got restless. Time to make something happen.

Beverly stood up and walked around, continuing the conversation with her non-existent caller as she wandered around the corner and out of sight of the receptionist. Then she saw a half-empty cart of cleaning supplies standing in the hallway unattended, not far from a public restroom. Bingo. She nudged the cart a little bit down the hall and then pushed it over, making its contents spill onto the floor with a loud clanging that reverberated through the live space.

Beverly ducked into the bathroom and peeked out the door as she waited. She was rewarded with a glimpse of the receptionist rushing to see what all the commotion was about, which was enough for Beverly to make her move. The patient roster was on a clipboard on the desk, and she flipped through it quickly. There it was. Forsythe. Room 158.

She slipped down the opposite hallway from the cart mess, with a twinge of guilt at the trouble she'd caused someone. But it was for a good cause.

She tried to look confident as she navigated the meandering halls that jutted out this way and that until finally found Room 158. She was in luck—it was empty of staff. She approached the one bed in the room and gingerly tiptoed to the railing.

The man's face was the color of eggshells, and he was just about as weak-looking. Not at all like the mocking criminal who'd haunted her nightmares ever since he attempted to kill both her and Adam.

But Adam had mentioned there was activity on the brain monitor, right? She stared at the lines on the machine he was hooked up to but wasn't exactly sure what she was seeing. How to tell what was normal and what was closer to a coma pattern? Some fake doctor she was.

She moved even closer to the bed, staring at the controls and gauges and buttons on the monitor, trying to make sense of it all. Shouldn't those lines be straighter if he was essentially brain dead?

Then she heard a faint sound, sort of like a cat wheezing. As she looked down at Forsythe, her heart stopped for a moment when she saw his lips moving. Was he having his own nightmare? Was that even possible in a coma?

When Forsythe's eyelids suddenly flipped open, she almost screamed. The clouded gray eyes had a flicker of light in them as he seemed to focus on where she was standing. He licked his lips as he tried to form words. She couldn't hear what he was saying, so she bent over to get closer.

He croaked out the words, "Dutton . . . will pay . . . and so will you."

Beverly stood rooted to the ground with her mouth hanging open. She waited to see what else he might say, but he closed his eyes again as movement on the brain monitor caught her eye. The line seemed to be flatter, and Forsythe's breathing turned deeper.

Had she just imagined the whole thing? If so, she needed her own head examined. But if not, then her worse fears had just sprung to life along with Forsythe. The man was still dangerous and quite capable of scheming and directing his remaining minions, including Redbeard and Kozak.

She backed out of the room and spied a nurse's station down the hall. When a nurse looked up as she approached, Beverly asked, "I just popped into Mr. Forsythe's room, and there seemed to be unusual brain activity." Beverly spied a row of monitors at the nurse's station, one for each patient in that wing. "Did you notice anything?"

The two nurses on duty looked at each other and then at the monitor for Forsythe's room. Beverly had a feeling from the guilty way they were acting, they'd not been paying attention to their duties but more to the little TV they had under the counter.

One of the nurses spoke up, "We didn't see anything. But you know how these things are."

Beverly didn't, but also didn't want to appear un-doctor-like, so she just hurried off down the hall. Well, then. This put her in a bit of a dilemma, didn't it? She'd promised Adam she wouldn't go see Forsythe or get into trouble, and here she was doing that very thing.

What to do? Perhaps Forsythe wasn't really recovering, and it was just a temporary drug-induced babbling of a madman on his last legs. So, nothing to worry about, right?

Maybe, but that thought wasn't making her feel any better or any safer. And what about Adam? The figment-of-her-imagination in that hospital bed had also threatened him.

If she were even half as evil as her uncle, she'd have taken the opportunity to smother the man with a pillow and put the universe out of its misery. But no. Maybe she took a few ethical detours now and then, but she'd never wanted to hurt anyone. Not the way he'd hurt her and so many others.

Beverly made her way back to her car and shed the disguise, returning it to her kit in the trunk. She couldn't tell Adam about her visit to see her uncle, she knew that.

For one thing, there were no witnesses, not even the nurses. For another, she didn't want to face Adam's anger about going around him again and with disguises, no less. He'd be even less likely to tell her anything about this case after that.

And then there was the fact she was tired of making empty promises. Mr. X was right—she was who she was, and if Adam couldn't accept that, so be it.

She'd just have to find another way to tackle Forsythe and Kozak. On her own.

12

Monday, December 14

Jinks strolled into Adam's office and tossed an envelope onto his desk. "Thought you might like a little laugh with your caff. Sure woke *me* up this morning when I found it in my mailbox first thing."

Adam recognized it right away and grabbed a pair of nitrile gloves to tease the note out of the envelope. "Looks identical to the ones sent to me, Beverly, and Harlan. Joe Brimm is going to have kittens over this."

"Mine is a little more friendly than yours. I mean, 'Keep your nose out of NAL affairs' seems tame by comparison. I feel slighted."

Adam stared at the note. "Doesn't make much sense to send these to the rest of you. Makes me think they aren't related to the arsons but directly to me."

"How's that?"

"Someone trying to take revenge on me for something I've done. Maybe Forsythe and company. Or someone entirely different. But it pisses me off they didn't come after me instead of threatening my friends."

"Maybe it's just the last gasp of a dying crime syndicate."

"Perhaps. Hope you're right."

Jinks pointed at the note. "I'm not worried about myself. I'm more worried about Felicia and the kids. Especially after what happened to you and the pipe bomb at your house. I mean, what if a package arrives and Felicia is home with the kids? Or even worse, the kids are by themselves?"

"I know it's Christmas time, but have packages delivered to a drop box somewhere and don't let the kids stay by themselves for now. Don't worry them, but drill it in that they are not to accept any mail or packages."

"That'll be hard for those Christmas-crazed kiddles."

"You can put a stop on your mail for now and pick it up at the post office every few days."

"And have it blow up the post office? They don't deserve that, either."

"Maybe we'll get a little Christmas miracle and solve this whole mess before too long."

"Mess is right." Jinks peered over at a half-eaten cheese Danish on Adam's desk. "You gonna eat that?"

Before he could reply, she'd grabbed it and stuffed her face. She said, with her mouth full, "Stress eating."

Adam just shook his head. It was a mystery how a woman so thin, she almost disappeared when she turned sideways, could eat the way she did and not weigh four hundred pounds. "How about we deal with that stress by doing a little legwork. I'd like to talk to Jared Lake's assistant, Lucas Barratt."

Jinks played chauffeur in Adam's car as they headed over so Adam could call Prospero. Since Harlan's assistant was friends with Barratt, Adam hoped he would smooth the way for their visit. Even so, Barratt didn't seem all that happy to see them when they arrived.

He led them into his house but didn't offer them a seat as he said, "I can't talk long. My shift starts in forty-five minutes."

Adam took note of his uniform, with the matching brown pants and shirt and the cap he clutched in one hand. Definitely not antiques-related.

Barratt saw Adam's appraisal and explained, "I'm working at a fast-food restaurant to bring in more money until I find something better. You don't know how demeaning it is to work at a taco hut as if that's the only kind of food I know about. Tacos aren't even Salvadoran, they're Mexican."

"Maybe you could strike out on your own. A new antiques business."

"Actually, I'm a good cook. If anything, I dreamed of opening my own restaurant one day. And now I'm stuck making crappy tacos." He winced. "Don't tell my employer I said they're crappy."

Adam said, "Barratt doesn't sound like a Salvadoran name."

"My mother was Maria Martinez. My father's family was originally from Britain, but generations ago moved to San Salvador and settled down to work in the coffee industry."

"Ah. When did you emigrate to the U.S.?"

"Eight years ago. I'm worried I might get deported. I mean, if I'm accused of being involved in the arson somehow. Time's running out on my green card, anyway."

"We don't like to arrest innocent people, Mr. Barratt."

"Since there are so many Salvadorian gangs, I know I'll be tarred with that same brush. Hell. And I'm even afraid of guns."

Adam glanced around the room, and his eye landed on an unusual item sitting on top of an end table. He walked over and picked up a figurine, a curious little black ceramic beetle playing a mandolin. "This is interesting. Unusual."

Barratt shifted his stance and fiddled with the cap in his hand. "I guess so."

"Funny—the insurance adjuster I bumped into after the fire mentioned something exactly like this on the property manifest. Bakelite."

"That is funny. I mean, odd and all."

Adam stared at the man for a moment. "Wonder how it got here?"

"I don't know. I mean, that is, I guess ... " Barratt swallowed hard. "Guess I might have taken a couple of items from the shop without Jared's knowledge."

Before Adam could respond, Barratt rushed to add, "I needed money to help my wife pay for some medical bills after the birth of our son, Lyle. He was premature. Had a lot of health problems."

Barratt sank against the nearby wall and cleared his throat. "And then we had to pay for his burial."

Jinks walked over to put a hand on his arm. "Our condolences for your loss, Mr. Barratt. I can't imagine how hard that would be."

Children were one of Jinks's weaknesses, one reason she really hated taking on cases involving kids. Adam himself hated to grill the guy under the circumstances, but he had a job to do. "I can understand the reason for the theft, but that doesn't make it right."

Barratt nodded. "I'll pay Jared Lake's sister back. I swear."

"Maybe we can work something out. Right now, I'm more interested in the arson. Do you know if Lake had received any threatening notes? Or been acting odd, even felt threatened?"

"Maybe. Though he didn't mention it to me. I know they say don't speak ill of the dead, but he wasn't the friendliest soul. Didn't talk about himself much. And he'd been drinking more."

"You mean after work?"

"But I also caught him drinking at work, too. Had this little antique solid-silver hip flask he hid in his desk drawer."

Adam exchanged a quick look with Jinks. Maybe it just had to do with Jared Lake's financial problems. But then again . . . "Mr. Barratt, did Lake mention getting a big cash infusion recently?"

Barratt's eyes widened. "Cash infusion? I didn't see any signs. The place was held together by paper clips and duct tape. There were mice in the walls. And some of the ceilings leaked."

Adam took a shot in the dark. "Did you ever hear Lake mention the names Forsythe or Kozak?"

The other man avoided Adam's gaze. "Kozak, I'm not sure. But Forsythe . . . that was the antiques dealer who killed his father, wasn't it? And then shot himself?"

"That's the one."

"Yeah, Jared mentioned him. But he was just shocked. Couldn't believe it."

"Mr. Barratt, how did you hear about the fire the evening Vintage Vibes burned down? You and your wife were already there when Detective Jinks and I arrived."

"A friend of ours just happened to be passing by the store and called 9-1-1 and then us. We got there as fast as we could, but . . . " He passed a hand over his eyes.

Adam looked at Jinks, who patted Barratt's arm again and said, "Thank you for your time, Mr. Barratt. And our sincerest condolences for your loss." She didn't say whether it was for the man's son or his boss, but maybe both.

Back outside and out of earshot of Barratt, Jinks said, "Barratt could have been behind the murder and fire when Jared found out about the thefts. Maybe threatened to turn him in and get him deported."

"I thought of that. FYI, I looked up Barratt's wife. She's a U.S. citizen. But it might not matter, he could still get kicked out. Pretty good motive."

"Yeah, but to lose a kid like that. I sure hope it's not him. You gonna report that theft?"

"Where's the proof? Most of it burned up in the fire."

As they returned to the police station and walked into the lobby, they spied a man that made Adam want to run the other way. Not out of fear but just to avoid another confrontation.

But Mayor Titus Lehmann had spotted them, too, and immediately focused his ire on Adam. "Hope you're looking for another job, Dutton. Things will be changing around here soon. For the better."

Jinks asked in a tone of voice dripping with saccharine, "How's your dear wife, Zelda, Mayor?"

Lehmann glared at her and didn't answer. Instead, he turned to Adam and poked him in the chest. "You'd better watch it, Dutton. Because I'm watching you. You so much as squint at my wife or piss in the wrong place, and I'll have your badge."

Adam kept his face blank and replied in his best could-care-less attitude, "Last I checked, a mayor doesn't have that authority, sir. And I suspect you have more important things to do for this great town than vendettas against people you don't like. I have a feeling that's what the voters want."

Adam nodded at Jinks to indicate they should head toward the back of the station as he aimed one last parting shot at Lehmann, "And have a nice day. Sir."

Jinks grabbed a couple of donuts on the way to her office, and Adam almost joined her, even though he hated the things. A little sugar high might be what he needed to offset the bitter taste in his mouth.

Why couldn't Zelda have married someone else? If money and power were what she was after, Adam's ex would have been better off aiming higher—all the way to the state house.

Or maybe a U.S. Senator. But then again, with Lehmann's political aspirations, that might really happen.

It wasn't as if Adam couldn't take the heat, he was used to that. But he didn't like the scumbag mayor coming down hard on the chief or Jinks because of the man's dislike for his wife's ex-husband.

Adam stopped at the door of the break room, glanced around, and lunged inside long enough to grab a chocolate donut. And he hated chocolate donuts. It was going to be a long, trying day.

13

Beverly stood inside the front door, taking a look around. So this was the famous Miralee's Market, more of a re-purposed house than a tacky convenience store. The former house's front quarters were now home to a snack bar and a couple of ice-cream tables in one corner. Its usual red-and-white decor had been easily "Christmas-fied" with the addition of green garlands dripping with glass and wooden ornaments in purple, blue, and white.

She eyed a case of maple fudge and briefly toyed with the idea of buying some for Adam. After all, she was here because of him, wasn't she? He's the one who'd said their coffee and breakfast sandwiches were the best around. And to be honest, she was getting a little tired of the Apple Valley Resort fare.

She almost bumped into an attractive woman with shiny blond hair that contrasted against her equally shining brown eyes. The woman corralled a couple of small children closer to her to keep them from wandering too close to the candy aisle. Beverly studied the woman a little more closely and realized she'd seen her before—from the photo on Jinks's desk at the police station.

She ordered Adam's fudge and then approached the woman. "Are you Felicia Ramírez?"

The woman tilted her head. "I am, but I don't recognize you, I'm afraid."

"We haven't met, but I've worked with Detective Eliot Jinks and Adam Dutton." She held out her hand. "Beverly Laborde."

The other woman's eyes widened. "Oh, I've heard of you."

Beverly smiled. "And I'm probably better off not knowing what was said."

Felicia shook her hand and laughed. "It's all good, I promise."

The older of the two children, a young boy, backed into a display of apple crisps, which threatened to set it toppling. Beverly vaulted over the other child, a little girl, and managed to prop up the display to keep it from tumbling onto the floor.

When Felicia started to scold the boy, Beverly said, "It's my fault. I got in his way."

The boy looked up at her, and they exchanged a little conspiratorial wink.

Beverly said, "So this is Jacob, and that adorable little girl must be Krystianna."

"These are our rugrats." Spying a small area with toys, Felicia told the two kids, "You can each pick out a small toy. But don't knock into anything else."

The kids raced over to the shelf, and Felicia added to Beverly. "It's that 'bouncy' time of year, you know—they go from being energetic whirlwinds to energetic dynamos. Toys, candy, parties, presents. I worry we spoil them too much."

Thinking back to Beverly's own humble background, with Grammie always having to scrape by due to the demands of her antiques store, Beverly was pretty sure what Felicia and Jinks were doing wasn't spoiling. She said, "They're lovely children. Quite striking."

"Since I'm half white and half Hispanic, and their father was Greek, it's about what you'd expect."

Beverly frowned. "Is their father . . . "

"Dead? No, he ran off with another man. So when Eliot and I got together, it seemed to balance out somehow. We were all living a lie of sorts."

She paused to check on the kids and then laughed. "And since Eliot is half-Asian, half-black, our family is like a mini-United Nations. Our bucket list includes trips for the family to Asia, Spain, Greece, and god knows where else. It would be great for the kids to see the world. When we can scare up the money."

"Detective work doesn't pay as well as it should, I know. Jinks and Adam deserve a lot more for what they do."

"And how. I think combat pay should be figured in there." Felicia again eyed the kids who were excitedly picking up one toy after another and just shook her head.

"I'm glad Adam has a wonderful partner like Jinks."

"The reverse is equally true. I was worried Jinks would get stuck with some low-brow-ridge type who'd give her all kinds of grief. But Adam's quite the opposite."

Beverly almost laughed at that. Right before she'd met Adam that first time, she'd also half-expected he'd be a low-bridge ridge type, hadn't she?

Felicia added, "On second thought, scrap the combat pay. I think they should get the kind of money CEOs make. They certainly deserve it more. Putting their lives on the line every day." She lowered her voice. "And after what happened to Adam. You know about that, right? The kidnapping and torture?"

Beverly nodded. "After that, they couldn't possibly afford to pay him what he's worth."

When the clerk called out "Number forty-five," Felicia walked over to the counter to grab a tray of three hot chocolates. She said to Beverly, "Are you going to be around at Christmas?"

She replied slowly, "I'm not sure."

"If you do find yourself in town, you're welcome to join me and Eliot and the family for Christmas dinner. Eliot is trying to get Adam to come, too."

Beverly was surprised at how touched she was at the offer but just said, "That's sweet of you. I'll let you know one way or the other."

How could she say otherwise when she wasn't sure where she'd be or what she'd be doing? And presents? Should she buy presents? Cards? What did normal people do for Christmas these days?

A slide show of all her recent Christmases she'd spend on the run passed through her brain. Alone in hotels with room service watching *It's a Wonderful Life* on TV. If she even had room service. In some cases, she was lucky if the place had a working TV, let alone any food.

Well, she wasn't about to stand around feeling sorry for herself and being reactive instead of proactive. That wasn't her style. It was time to start being a little more like Beverly, the con woman again. It was what she knew best, and Mr. X was right—she was damned good at it.

Where to next? Adam and Jinks had wondered if the Vintage Vibes fire was tied to another recent one in Woodstock. Perhaps she should have a chat with the owner of that store? Adam was busy doing his own thing so he wouldn't really mind if she helped out a teensy bit. Just one antiques aficionado chatting up another, nothing wrong with that.

Her mind made up, she headed to her car and to her handy effects-kit. The only question left was, who was Beverly going to be this time?

14

Beverly was surprised when she was able to find a phone contact for Justin Garone that worked and even more surprised when he agreed to meet her. Granted, she'd said it was on the pretext of some "business" she had to discuss with him, but still . . . In fact, for a man who'd just lost everything related to his business in an arson, he sounded quite chipper.

She donned her "flabby-but-curvy sweater" under her coat and added a short black wig with bangs and then some tinted glasses. They'd agreed to meet at a sporting goods store since Garone was going to be there looking at some golf clubs. Beverly wasn't into golf, herself, but she lied that she was starting ski lessons soon and wanted to look at gear.

The business was appropriately named "Golf & Ski," almost as if it were tailor-made for her little deception. The building itself wasn't much to look at, certainly not like the many other quaint stores so endemic to Vermont. The place looked more like a pawn shop, complete with neon lettering, bars on the windows, and garish fluorescent signs painted in the front windows.

The interior wasn't a lot cheerier, but she was relieved to see it was a bona fide store and not a front for some other sleazy business. She didn't know much about this Justin

Garone, and he could have picked up on her bluff despite her best efforts to sell the con.

He'd described himself well, though, and she immediately spotted the balding man with the wood-print glass frames and orange bow tie. She sidled up to him and said, "You must be Justin Garone. I'm Lizabeth Furmanski." She looked at a putter the man held in his hands. "Looks like you've found a winner."

Garone swung the putter a few inches. "Seems like a better choice than my current one."

Beverly noticed the price tag. Nine hundred fifty dollars. Then she saw the gold plating. Well, then, the man's business must have been quite successful before the fire. Or else, he was getting a hefty insurance check.

She saw a rack of skis in the back of the store and said, "Do you mind if we move over there? I can talk business while I'm scouting the snow gear."

He dutifully followed her over to the skis—a little too closely for her liking. In fact, he stood so close to her when she finally arrived at the ski display, she could feel his breath on her face. She sighed a little inwardly. It's not that she didn't know the drill. She'd used her feminine charms on many a susceptible man in the past. It bored her silly, but she could always use it to her advantage.

Maybe that's one reason she was drawn to Adam when she first met him. He hadn't been influenced by those charms at all. Hell, he'd been ready to arrest her if he had to. You had to love that in a man.

Beverly batted her eyelashes at Garone. Take that, Jenny-Lee Salant. "About that business talk. I understand you just lost your antiques store in an unfortunate fire."

He heaved a dramatic sigh. Maybe a little too dramatic. "*Most* unfortunate, yes."

Still not much emotion from a man who'd just lost everything. She said, "I'm working toward opening up my own antiques shop. Nothing fancy, mind you, just a little leg up into the business." She shifted her feet to put her right leg, in all its leather-leggings glory, closer to the man.

He licked his lips. "Oh, I see. It's not an easy business. You have to be passionate about it."

"I think I'm a very passionate person." She smiled up at him.

"Yes, well, I'm, uh, I'm not sure how I can help."

"I was wondering if you had any items left over from the fire you might be willing to sell to me on the cheap. I've heard that's a good way to get started with stocking a new store. Closeouts, buyouts, damaged lots."

"I'm afraid there wasn't much left. Only a few items weren't burned completely."

"Those are the ones I'm interested in."

Garone shook his head. "Hardly worth much."

"Doesn't matter. A dollar here, a dollar there, it all adds up in the end."

He thought about it for a moment. "We might be able to arrange something. I'd have to look through things and see what's what."

"I would be so grateful." Beverly smiled again and added, "I've got a couple of bankrupt businesses I'm eyeing for the store. And then I suppose I'll have to worry about all the legalities and licenses and such." She said off-handedly, "And I guess I should join the National Antiquities League."

He stared at her. "The NAL? I'm not sure that's necessary."

"Isn't it? I'd heard you couldn't get anywhere in this business without their seal of approval. And dues, of course."

"I wouldn't know. I never joined."

She hid her disappointment. He didn't have anything to do with the NAL? "I spoke to Jared Lake about it not too long ago. He was most encouraging."

Garone's face darkened. "Jared Lake is dead, Miss Furmanski."

She feigned surprise. "Oh, my lord. I had no idea. Was it a heart attack? He seemed so healthy when I spoke with him."

"His business burned, too. But he was unlucky enough to be caught inside and perished with it."

Beverly put a hand over her chest. "That poor man. Did you know him well?"

"We weren't close, no. Just in passing."

Beverly stifled a sigh over the double disappointment of dead ends but trying to salvage her time and efforts, she pressed on. "I heard he was friends with Reggie Forsythe. That's two tragedies in a row. Maybe the antiques business is cursed."

"Well, now, Miss Furmanski. I wouldn't go that far. Just a string of bad luck lately. Running a business is hard work." He put a hand on her shoulder and added, "As I said, you have to be passionate. About work and life."

She wanted to shrug off that hand and slug that leering kisser of his. But she exercised what she thought was rather remarkable restraint. "Oh, I understand all that, of course. I was just wondering. I mean, Reggie Forsythe. Were all the rumors true?"

"Rumors?"

"That he murdered his own father. And was a shady antiques dealer." Beverly lowered her voice, "And that he was involved in bribing a state representative to make it possible to shut down Forsythe's competitors."

The muscles around Garone's mouth tightened. "Forsythe doesn't represent all antiques store owners. There are bad eggs everywhere."

"I've also heard rumors about Ivon Kozak. Made me have second thoughts about antiques. That I should look into something else." She picked up one of the skis and ran her hands along the edge. "Like sporting goods."

"Kozak is a tough wheeler and dealer. I'd stay far, far clear of him."

"Did he threaten you or something?"

Garone's lips tightened even further. "He can be very . . . persuasive."

Beverly pretended to cower as she held the ski closer to her. "That does sound threatening. Did you report him to the police?"

Garone's laugh was hollow. "They couldn't help. Kozak is untouchable."

"Untouchable how? Is he just like Forsythe? Has he killed anyone?"

Garone added in a rush, "On second thought, I'm not sure the few items left from my store are worth your time."

"But I—"

"It was nice meeting you, Miss Furmanski. Good luck with your business plan." The man clutched the putter in his hand and backed away toward the front of the store.

She could hear him as he muttered half under his breath, "You're going to need it."

Beverly returned the ski to the display and plodded out the store and toward her car, a little dejected. So much for her detective skills. Adam, or even Creighton Querry, would have done much better. Still, she'd learned one thing—Garone was afraid of Ivon Kozak. But was it because he'd really been threatened? Or just by the man's vicious reputation? Garone *had* mentioned Kozak could be very persuasive, hadn't he?

On the way out, she purchased a pocket knife she'd spied when she first arrived. Scout's motto again—be prepared and all. She looked around to see if Garone was anywhere in sight and thought she caught a glimpse of him pulling away in his own Mercedes. The man was definitely not hurting financially.

Round one of her sleuthing into Kozak's domain hadn't gone the way she'd planned. But she wasn't licked yet. She just had to decide her next move and try to stay off Adam's radar in the process.

15

Adam was more tired than he had any right to be. Sure, the interview of Lucas Barratt earlier in the day hadn't been as helpful as they'd hoped. And Adam and Jinks had then spent the better part of the afternoon making phone calls and checking databases—the usual thankless police-related tasks most people didn't know about. Not exactly hard manual labor. So why the fatigue?

Adam decided to leave a little early and head for one of his favorite places after a frustrating day. He was pleased to see Frank Ethridge already suited up, boxing gloves in hand when Adam strolled into Jim's Gym.

They sparred for an hour, with Adam getting in a few more licks than he did ordinarily. Frank even made the comment, "You seem to be in a fighting mood today. Somebody steal your lunch at work?"

He grinned, but Adam didn't grin back. "Just the usual, Frank."

"You know what they say. A man may work from sun to sun, but a policeman's job is never done."

"I thought that saying was about housewives."

"Whatever. Works either way."

They both turned at the sound of a deep cough as a man the size of a grizzly walked toward them. As Adam waved at him, Frank looked at the bear-man and said, "You're not fighting *him*, are you? I'm certainly not that stupid."

Finally, something that made Adam grin, and he took off the gloves to climb out of the platform and speak to Creighton Querry. Cray said, "You got a quieter place to yak, Dutton? It's so loud in here, I may go deaf."

"Why don't you meet me in my portable office."

"Portable office?"

Adam led the way out the door to his new Subaru. Cray looked at him askance. "Adam, it's twenty-five degrees out here."

"This car has heated bun warmers."

In reply, the other man grunted in disgust, then turned up the collar of his coat and stuffed his gloved hands in his pockets. They climbed in and Adam cranked up the heat. "Is that better, you wuss?"

"It'll do."

"Cray, glad you stopped by. I've been meaning to call you."

"If it's about that poker money, I'm good for it."

"We haven't played poker in over a year."

"Guess it's Stan I owe the money to. Good. I can blow him off more easily."

Adam turned the heat down a little since he was beginning to feel like a turkey basting. "I wanted to see if you've received any anonymous threatening notes lately."

"Notes? You mean letters or email?"

"Letters. I got one after the bombing at my house a month ago. Then Beverly Laborde, Harlan Wilford, and Jinks got notes more recently. Printed out via computer but made to look like the old-fashioned notes people used to make by cutting letters out of the newspaper."

"That doesn't compute, pardon the pun. Sending one to you, I can understand. You're a cop. Maybe even to me, but the others?"

"Got the lab working on the letters to see if they can turn up any evidence to link it to the sender. I suspect it's a personal vendetta, but I can't be sure."

"Someone targeting people close to you?"

"Possibly."

"And you thought this jerk might have sent one to me, too? Oh, I'm touched, Adam. Truly."

Adam snickered. "Just let me know, 'kay?"

"People close to you—and one of the targets is Beverly Laborde. That's interesting, wouldn't you say?" Cray grinned at Adam, who ignored him.

Cray just ignored Adam's ignoring and pressed him further, "How's Beverly doing? Staying out of trouble?"

"She promised to be careful. That's about as good as I can expect."

"Right." Cray glanced over at Adam but apparently decided to let it drop. "Like you asked, I checked into the background of Jared Lake's assistant from El Salvador, Lucas Barratt. Couldn't dig up any dirt. The guy's been keeping his nose real clean, far as I can tell. No ties to gangs I could find. No sexual romps or angry boyfriends."

"I suppose that's something. But he's still not cleared yet. He stole some items from his boss's shop."

Cray whistled. "Good motive. But I didn't get hints from my black-market contacts of anyone matching his description fencing stuff."

"He said it was to pay for his son's health care."

"If true, who could blame him?"

"Anything else?"

Cray nodded. "You're going to love this one. Lucas Barratt's wife, Jeanne, used to work for none other than Arlen Strudwick. And it was around the time he was pushing through the legislation that closed so many rival antiques stores of the Forsythes. Including Beverly's grandmother's shop."

"Seriously?"

"Thanks to Forsythe's little blackmail scheme against Strudwick, that makes Jeanne Barratt a link between the Gestapo tactics of the Forsythes and the murder of Jared Lake. Coinky-dink?"

"Maybe." Adam's reply didn't sound all that convincing even to his ears.

Cray continued, "Found something else out about Jared Lake, the victim. Friend of mine said Lake owed people money."

Adam digested that bit of news. "Lake's sister told us he'd fallen on hard times and might have to declare bankruptcy soon. But he'd got a sudden infusion of cash. She didn't know from where."

"Well, that friend of mine I mentioned is Leroy Schick."

"The bookie and loan shark?"

"He prefers to be called a 'wealth consultant.'"

That made Adam snort. "So maybe Jared Lake was in hock due to gambling debts, not just bad business practices. Interesting. But what about that sudden infusion of cash?"

"One of his gambles finally paid off, literally? If so, it's good he's dead. Because some of the people Lake owed money to might have planted him six feet under, themselves—if they'd got wind of the guy getting money and not paying 'em back."

"Maybe one of them did. Except they didn't so much plant him as barbecue him."

Cray took his gloved hands out of his pockets and thrust them in front of the heat coming out of the vents. "How are things with Sergeant Moody?"

"Moody? Why do you ask?"

"I saw him and Mayor Lehmann together in the back of the Dragon's Teeth Bar."

"That dive? Doesn't seem like the sort of place Lehmann would even know about."

"They were acting like they didn't want to be seen together in public. And they're cousins, so why would that matter? Naturally, I did some more deep digging on Moody. I mean, especially after what my friend Joey McCulloch told us a couple weeks ago."

"Seems like I recall you saying that after Moody framed his former colleague, Joey, for some planted evidence, Moody told Joey he should just walk away. That he was friends with a guy who could make Joey regret it if he didn't. Namely, Ivon Kozak."

"Gives you all kind of feels, doesn't it?"

"Feels I can do without, thank you very much." Adam rubbed his forehead. "Did you uncover anything else in your deep digging?"

"Not a lot you don't already know about Moody. Former military weapons expert. Left under a dark cloud at his previous police gig. Eats puppies for breakfast."

"What?"

"Had to make sure you were still awake. Did find out one other thing. Moody is also a gambler. Likes to renege on his bets."

"Thanks, Cray."

"No offense, but I think I need to blow this office of yours stat."

"So soon?" Adam said in mock surprise. "Why ever for?"

"All this heat is making you stink. Like a pair of gym socks left in the hamper too long, Adam. Hit the showers. Anybody's showers. Just quick, will ya?"

§ § §

Adam took Cray's advice and took a quick sponge bath in the men's bathroom at the gym before heading to his house. But he didn't go straight home, he made a stop by Miralee's Market to pick up a few dinner makings.

When he saw who was coming out of the store right as he was heading in, he regretted his decision to make the stop. First, he'd bumped into Mayor Lehmann at the station, and now . . .

Zelda Lehmann set her bag down and smiled at him. "I've wanted to give you a call, Adam."

"Really?"

"Really. Do you remember what we talked about at the courthouse that day?"

"It's a little fuzzy. Early senility and all."

She walked up to him and put a hand on his chest as she lowered her voice. "Titus is going to be out of town in a few days."

"That's swell. Good for him."

"Do you still have the key to my house?"

"Not on me. And if I did, I'd hand it right back."

Zelda's lips formed into a pout. "Why don't you at least come over for dinner? Maybe you can make me one of your signature gourmet dishes like you used to make. Perhaps the Coq Au Vin. You remember, don't you? You cooked it for me on my birthday. And you made it in your birthday suit."

"I don't think your husband would approve of me making you dinner and definitely not in my birthday suit."

"He doesn't have to know a thing. It's just old friends getting together."

Adam sighed. "We're not *just* old friends, you know that."

When another car pulled into the parking lot and headed for the closest space to them, Zelda backed off but added, "I'll be expecting your call."

As she headed toward her car, he scurried into the store. Was this another of those encounters he should mention to Chief Quinn? How many did this make now? And not one had been initiated by Adam, yet it was Adam the mayor blamed.

Oy, what a mess. If he took Zelda up on her offer, that would be like crossing a field full of land mines. If he ignored her, and she took offense, would she make up some sort of lie to tell her husband just to get Adam in trouble as revenge?

No matter what he did about his ex-wife, the chief wasn't going to be happy. And as for Adam . . . would he be happy?

Adam knew he should just ignore Zelda's invitations. But on the other hand, it had been a long time since he'd been intimate with anyone. In fact, the last time was a one-night stand on the day his divorce was made final. More of a pity fling than anything that mattered.

Just as he tried to push all thoughts of sex out of his head, the image of a raven-haired beauty popped in as if to say, "Aren't you forgetting someone?" No, he wasn't forgetting Beverly Laborde. Not that they'd ever been anything but professional. Except maybe in his dreams. That was another matter altogether.

Adam almost felt like heading to Jim's Gym for a few more rounds but decided against it. He grabbed some penne and fresh plum tomatoes. With a little wine and some herbs, he'd have a nice Pasta Pomodoro in no time.

16

Determined to follow up her less-than-successful chat with Justin Garone, Beverly pondered her next move. She was itching to try another disguise and tackle the big kahuna himself, Ivon Kozak, but perhaps taking a different course was more in order.

After calling up Agnes Flamm to see how she was doing, Beverly got the name of one of Agnes's acquaintances who owned an antiques store in the eastern edge of the county, named True Gems. And since Beverly had an "in" as a friend of Agnes, she wouldn't need a disguise.

The shop was in a standalone building with a stand of balsam fir trees behind. A picturesque spot, like on a Vermont tourist postcard. And customers didn't have to fight with any nearby businesses for parking, unlike Harlan's shop.

The store closed at five, and Beverly was about ten minutes shy of that. Hopefully, that would mean she had the place—and the owner—to herself.

Even though part of her was already convinced Ivon Kozak must have his hand in the arsons, if she was going to go at this like Adam would, she needed to rule out other motives, right? What if it were a different antiques thug dispatching rivals? It might take a while to get to all the store owners in the area, but one thing Beverly had plenty of was time.

Yet, when Beverly walked into True Gems and introduced herself to Annika Grimes, it was difficult imagining this cheerful woman with wavy gray hair and a ready smile as a serial arsonist. Annika's smiled threatened to go nuclear-bright when she learned who Beverly was. "You're Genevieve Glas's granddaughter? Oh, my dear, you're every bit as lovely as she was."

"That's quite a compliment. When I was a little girl, I remember thinking that Grammie was the most beautiful woman in the world."

"A wonderful soul, indeed. Did you go into antiques, too?"

"I dabble." That was mostly honest, if by dabble, you meant recovering stolen pieces from crooks by pretending to be a buyer and then exchanging the real antiques with fakes.

Annika smiled. "It's a fun business. If not a lucrative one."

Beverly looked around her store. Lots of carved wooden folk art and duck decoys in the front. And also some pine butter molds and oak Amish bread boxes. Not high-value items but treasures to some hunters, no doubt. "You heard about the arsons?"

Annika rubbed her arm. "It's the talk of the town. Among antiques folks hereabouts, anyway."

"Aren't you afraid it might be someone targeting businesses like yours?"

"Not sure why anybody would be interested in my store. Makes no sense whatsoever."

Beverly eyed a display of celluloid dolls and picked up a windup doll wearing a sombrero. A curious little thing. "Are you a member of the NAL?"

"Used to be. Got out years ago when all the evil sorts starting elbowing their way in."

"Evil sorts?"

"The Forsythes, for sure." Annika didn't bat an eye as she said that. Maybe she didn't know about Beverly's familial connections? Beverly rather hoped not.

Beverly replied, "They were all in the papers. After the murder."

"Wasn't at all surprised. My mother always said I had the gift of seeing people's auras. And those two, Forsythe father and son, had some of the darkest auras I've ever seen."

Beverly replaced the celluloid doll on its stand. "Who were some of the other bad actors in the NAL? I'd like to stay far away from them." That was more of an out-and-out lie, and Beverly didn't feel too comfortable with it.

Annika thought for a moment. "There was one other I took an instant dislike to. An Ivon Kozak. He wasn't at the meetings much. Thank heavens I didn't have to be around his negative energy."

"I think I've heard some rumors about him."

"Just don't know what happened to the NAL. Used to be such camaraderie. This is going way back, mind you. But when the Forsythes and their minions entered the picture, it became more cut-throat. Those two tried to dominate the group and the antiques business like mob bosses. It was sickening. Kozak, well, he's cut from the same cloth."

"Surely, not murder?"

"Who knows? One of my friends, Martyn Agoston, who's still part of the NAL, told me he once bid on an antique car at auction, a 1937 Ford Club Cabriolet. And won. The fellow he outbid was Kozak. Three days after the sale was complete, that car mysteriously caught fire. A total loss."

"And your friend believes Kozak did it?"

"It was too coincidental. Next time Martyn saw Kozak, the guy was more smug than usual. Told my friend, 'you know the saying, you play with fire, you get burned.'"

Beverly made a note of that. Maybe she should tell Adam? He couldn't exactly get on her case about visiting a friend of her grandmother's and "accidentally" learning something of interest, could he? She sighed inwardly. It had been so much easier when she was on her own and didn't have to wonder about whether to share intel with someone else.

Annika pointed to the little celluloid doll Beverly had replaced on its stand. "You like unusual dolls? I've got a box of different types that just came into the store." She looked at the Seth Thomas clock on the wall, which now said five, and turned the sign on the front door to "Closed."

"Come with me." She gestured to Beverly to follow and led the way into a stock room in the rear of the building.

For a stock room, the shelves were unusually empty. Just a few boxes here and there and some office supplies. A big contrast to Harlan Wilford's filled-to-the-brim shelving at Tossed Treasures.

Annika grabbed a box from the floor and put in on a table, then dug into the contents. Beverly was getting a little impatient but tried not to show it as the older woman pulled out the items one by one.

"I know it's in here," Annika mumbled. "At least it's supposed to be."

Other than the sound of Annika's rummaging through the box and the slight humming from the heating vent, the place was quiet and still. Peaceful, even. Until the sound of glass shattering made Beverly's heart stop. An intruder?

Annika stared at her with eyes as wide as twin mini-moons. Beverly put her hand to her lips and tiptoed along the wooden floor to the door, trying not to make any sounds. She paused with her hand on the door knob, taking deep breaths to still her pulse. But those deep breaths made her explode into an uncontrollable coughing spell. And a whiff of something that shouldn't be in the air made her realize exactly why.

She lunged into the main room to see shards from the front door's glass pane mingling with pieces of a broken bottle. The bottle lay in the middle of a river of fire that was spreading rapidly from the door to the counter and getting dangerously close to their position. Clouds of thick, choking smoke began to billow throughout the space.

Still coughing, Beverly grabbed her sweater and pulled it up over her mouth and nose, making motions for Annika to do the same. Beverly ran toward the counter looking frantically for a fire extinguisher. When a flash of red paint caught her eye, she grabbed the canister and started spraying the foam onto the fire.

It hardly made a dent. Those wooden butter molds and bread boxes—and dear god, the flammable celluloid dolls—along the front of the store were making for a tasty pile of fuel for the hungry flames.

Beverly yelled out to Annika, "Is there another way out of the store?"

"Just the front door. A tiny window in the bathroom, but it's over there," Annika pointed to a small room at the far corner of the store. If they tried that, and the window failed, they would be totally trapped.

No, there wasn't time to futz around with dead ends. With a look of apology at Annika, Beverly took the fire extinguisher canister and hurled it through the plate-glass window, obliterating it and all traces of the True Gems lettering.

She grabbed Annika's arm and pulled her toward the opening in the broken window. Beverly kicked out some of the last jagged pieces of glass along the bottom of the window to make it safer for them to climb over. And then, she half-pushed Annika through the window and out into the cool air beyond.

Once she made sure she and Annika were far enough from the building to be safe, she piled into her rental car to move it to a safer distance while she called Adam on her cellphone.

Everything after that was a bit of a blur, but she was impressed by the speed at which Adam and the police, the firefighters, and the EMTs managed to get to their location. Beverly told the EMTs, "I'm fine. I don't need to go to the hospital. But please check on Annika."

She did allow the techs to give her some puffs of oxygen, which made her lungs feel much better. Adam and Jinks stepped off to one side as the firefighters trained their gear on the by-now raging fire that had engulfed True Gems. Beverly noted Adam kept looking at her with a worried expression, so she made an "A-okay" sign with her fingers.

As the EMTs piled Annika onto a gurney and loaded her into the ambulance, she said to Beverly, "I want to keep an eye on the store. Maybe there will be some items not burned. Don't want them looted until I'm able to salvage what I can."

Beverly patted her hand. "Things can be replaced, your health can't. Besides, the police and fire department will be investigating for quite some time. They'll keep an eye on it for you."

After the ambulance drove away, Beverly walked over to the two detectives as Jinks asked, "You sure you're okay, Beverly? You were almost roasted like a Thanksgiving turkey."

Beverly rubbed her elbow. "Minor scrapes and bruises. Some smoke inhalation. But not too bad."

"Quick thinking." Adam smiled at her. "Using the fire extinguisher the way you did."

"I'd hoped to put out the fire, Adam. I really wanted to save her store."

"You say you think it was a Molotov cocktail?"

"Pretty damn sure of it. It spread fast because of all the wood."

"The thick smoke you described could be a thickening agent added to a flammable liquid. That's only done if you want to create a lot of smoke. And I guess it worked."

Beverly frowned. "Did the fires at Justin Garone's and Jared Lake's businesses have that?"

Adam shook his head. "It's almost as if this arsonist wanted to make it hard for someone inside to see their way out."

Jinks added, "Well, this arsonist would also have noticed the parked cars outside."

"And known someone was inside," Adam said. "That means they might have intentionally targeted Annika. Or you, Beverly."

She tapped her foot on the cold asphalt. "The sender of that threatening note?"

"Crossed my mind."

The trio turned to watch as the firefighters finished spraying the front of the building, with the fire seemingly out. But clouds of smoke still filled the evening air, along with the pungent smell of charred wood and melted plastic cables. Fine pieces of ash flitted down like snow.

"That makes three antiques stores, now, Adam."

"Actually, that makes five."

Beverly stared at him in confusion. "Five?"

"There were two more businesses that burned in the past year. One up in Montpelier and the other in Burlington. They weren't on our radar due to the timing and the distances between them and our cases. But the pattern seems to fit."

Beverly wrinkled her brow. Now she was even more worried about Harlan's shop. "What's the connection between them? I mean, they're all antiques stores. But why these particular stores, not others?"

"That's one of the things we're trying to find out."

Adam and Jinks urged Beverly to return to the resort, take a nice long soak in the hot tub, and get some rest. She decided to follow their advice. They were going to be on the scene for some time, and there wasn't anything else Beverly could do right then.

But maybe not the hot tub. After feeling the scorching heat from those flames that were dangerously close as she and Annika escaped out the front window, she didn't think she wanted to be around anything hot again for quite some time. A cool shower followed by a mint julep with extra ice would be just about right.

Once showered, robed, and julep'd, Beverly stretched out on the bed, trying to recall every detail from the fire. Maybe she'd caught a glimpse of someone leaving the scene but had been too focused on Annika to make note of it at the time? But as hard as she concentrated, no such detail sprang into focus.

She rubbed the soft terry fabric of the robe, and for once, she was grateful for the strong cinnamon coming from the pine cones. Adam had been right—the acrid smoky smell still seemed to cling to her hair and nostrils despite the shower.

Had Annika really been personally targeted or had Beverly? If so, and it was the same culprit behind Jared Lake's arson, then the arsonist was going to be mighty disappointed his target wasn't a charred corpse this time.

She sighed and gulped some more of the julep. She was surrounded by luxury spa-pampering possibilities at the resort and didn't have time for any of it. And instead of wrapping presents and singing carols, she was chasing crooks and arsonists. She lifted her julep glass in a mock toast. "Merry Christmas, Beverly. Ho ho ho."

17

Tuesday, December 15

Jinks yawned as she grabbed a copy of the *Herald-Gazette* and *Junction Jive* newspapers from the stack on the counter. Adam asked, "Did we keep you up past your bedtime last night?"

"Sometimes I wish I was a kid again like Jacob and Krys. So I could hit the hay at eight."

"Kids don't have to deal with investigating crime scenes. Thankfully."

Jinks paid for the papers and her slice of breakfast pizza and two coffees and followed Adam out the door of Miralee's to their waiting car. She asked, "How's Beverly?"

"I checked in with her last night after she'd gone back to the resort. She sounded good. Made me think we should stop by the hospital to see how Annika Grimes is doing."

"You read my mind." Jinks started up with a tuneless humming, as was her habit.

"Mind if we take a little detour first?"

"Detour? For what?" Jinks stopped humming long enough to take a sip of coffee.

"I found out where Lucas Barratt's wife, Jeanne, works. You'll never guess."

"It's too early for guessing games, sport."

"Just so happens to be Lehmann's office. Turns out, she's an aide to the mayor."

Jinks almost spit out her coffee. "This should be good."

In fact, Jeanne Barratt was a "junior" aide to the mayor—which meant she had a smaller office down a smaller hall on the opposite side of the mayor's cavernous suite. Adam was almost sorry for that because he was almost itching for a good verbal brawl. He wasn't quite sure why.

Barratt's wife looked like an extra straight out of Hollywood casting. Sensible unobtrusive navy pants suit, flats, and straight, dark hair—parted in the middle, no less. It was as if even her hair was trying to be nonpartisan.

Jinks took the lead in the questions this time, something she and Adam had naturally fallen into when questioning a man versus a woman. Privately, Jinks thought it was funny she'd taken on the "womanly" role of female-on-female questioning. But in their experience, it seemed to help reassure interviewees. Jinks was always quick to note, "Nothing sexist to see here."

Jinks added a reassuring smile as she said, "We're very grateful you agreed to talk with us. Your husband was quite helpful when we spoke with him yesterday. We understand how upsetting this must be for you both."

Jeanne's office was even smaller inside than it looked from outside, which meant Jinks and Adam had to stay standing with Adam shoehorned into one corner. Shades of Creighton Querry's shoebox office, except the private eye's was by choice.

Jeanne kept apologizing for the lack of space, adding, "I probably should have arranged to meet you somewhere else."

Jinks said soothingly, "This is fine. Mrs. Barratt, we understand you're a U.S. citizen, unlike your husband?"

"I was born in Bangor, Maine. I moved here about five years ago. I met Lucas not long after, we hit it off immediately, and got married a year later."

"Prior to moving here, you were in Montpelier, isn't that right? As an intern?"

"Why, yes. I worked for Representative Arlen Strudwick."

"Were you aware of legislation he worked on around that time to change the state code involving antiques stores?"

"Sure. At the time, it didn't seem like a big deal."

"The fact is, by changing that piece of regulation, Strudwick made it possible for the Northeastern Antiquities League, particularly Reginald Forsythe, III, and his son, Reggie, to shut down competitor businesses. And then buy their antiques at rock-bottom prices."

Jeanne stared down at her perfectly manicured hands, which were spread out on the desk. "I got that job in college because I was a Poli Sci major. Guess I was naive and still thought legislators were demigods."

She shook her head. "When the news came out about Mr. Strudwick's murder and how Reggie Forsythe was behind it, I felt sick to my stomach. I mean, I really had no idea."

"You never witnessed Representative Strudwick talking about that legislation at the time?"

"I once overheard him taking a call from Reggie Forsythe, but Strudwick seemed angry I'd overheard him. I decided I'd better keep my nose where it belonged. That is if I wanted to have any sort of career. Maybe that makes me a coward, I don't know."

Adam chimed in, "I'm not sure there's much you could have done. Just overhearing one heated phone call."

She sighed. "I suppose so. Poor Mr. Strudwick. I feel so sorry for his family. I met them briefly once. He had those six children, one disabled. This will be their first Christmas without their father."

Jinks spoke up, "I'm sure they wouldn't mind hearing from you. If you feel comfortable, that is."

Jeanne brightened a bit. "I think I will. That's a great idea."

Adam asked, "When you came to work for Mayor Lehmann, did he say anything about the Forsythes? Especially relating to Strudwick?"

"Now that you mention it, he did ask if I'd known either of the Forsythes, father or son. I told him I hadn't had much to do with them. And I remember thinking that's what sealed the deal for my hiring. Weird, huh?"

Adam wasn't about to go into all the gory details about Lehmann's connections to Forsythe and other unethical types right then. Maybe Jeanne didn't know—or maybe she did and was just a good actress.

She wrinkled her brow. "I thought you were here to talk about the arson. About poor Jared Lake."

"That's the focus of our visit, yes."

"He wasn't an easy man to be around sometimes." She grabbed a pencil on the desk and rolled it around in her hand. "But he didn't deserve to die like that."

"Not easy to be around?"

She nodded and then looked Adam directly in the eyes. "Lucas is a suspect in Jared's death, isn't he?"

"We're still collecting leads and information. We don't have any official suspects yet."

"You won't have any shortage of those, I'd imagine."

"Why is that?"

She sucked in a breath. "I'm not sure how much Lucas told you. Jared liked young girls a little too much. Lucas had to stand between him and the teenagers who came into the store to keep Jared from hitting on them. But Jared was also a thief. He stole things from other people's stores and houses and then sold them in his own store."

"Your husband never reported the thefts?"

"Lucas needed that job. And frankly, we were both afraid Jared would blame Lucas. The Salvadorian immigrant and all. Lucas wanted to get a better job. He'd tried, but with the baby . . ."

Her eyes teared up, and she looked away. Jinks said, "Your husband told us about that. We're very sorry. And I can imagine a prospective employer wouldn't want to take on those medical bills."

With a bitter laugh, Jeanne said, "You don't know the half of it."

Adam did know. A police department staffer had gone through something like that, a nightmare of never-ending bills. "I don't suppose Lucas has any names of some of those people Jared Lake stole from? Or any young women who were the victims of his unwanted advances?"

Jinks started to pull out her little notebook but stopped when Jeanne replied, "I'm not sure. But I think it was of one of those 'don't ask, don't tell' kind of things. Sorry I can't help you there."

Jinks and Adam thanked her again for her time and retraced their steps down the maze of offices. Jinks stopped to get a drink from a water fountain, then said, "She seems innocent."

"Don't they all."

"We've got better suspects and motives. I'm putting my money on insurance fraud. Maybe the owners of the five buildings targeted for arson were 'fraud friends' trying to bilk the system. If our dead dude, Jared Lake, was involved, maybe he changed his mind at the last minute and paid with his life?"

"And Annika Grimes?"

"Doesn't *seem* like she'd want to go to the extreme of committing suicide as a fiery end to her part in such a scheme, I'll grant you."

Adam grunted. "Our perp could also be one of Jared Lake's victims, either the thefts or the girls. If he ever followed through on any of that."

They were almost out of the building when a voice boomed behind them. "Are you harassing my employees, now, Dutton? Isn't it enough you're already harassing me?"

They turned to find a red-faced Mayor Lehmann, shaking his fist at them. Adam grimaced. Wonder if the man realized how much that made him look like a tantrum-throwing toddler when he did that?

Adam counted to five and replied, "Certainly not, Mayor. We only want to solve the arsons and Jared Lake's murder. Since Jeanne Barratt's husband was employed by Lake, we just needed to talk to her to see if she might have helpful information."

Jinks gave the mayor an even more fake smile than she had last time. "And Ms. Barratt was quite helpful and cooperative. You should be pleased with how well she represents your office."

Adam owed Jinks big time for that. Especially how she'd emphasized the word "she." The way Lehmann's red face got even redder resembling a giant bald strawberry was just a bonus.

Lehmann's voice took on a whiny edge. "I should have the two of you thrown out."

"On what grounds, sir?" Adam asked innocently.

"Disturbing the peace. Harassing an elected official."

Adam looked around at the curious faces of a couple of people walking past them. "I doubt these fine constituents would agree with your assessment, sir."

Lehmann looked daggers at Adam before whirling around on his heel and stalking off. Adam noted that one of the "fine constituents" was even chuckling. Perhaps the mayor's poll ratings were a little off. Or some few Ironwood Junction residents weren't fooled by the man's fake charm.

Jinks clucked her tongue as they finally exited the building. "I think the mayor got up on the wrong side of the bed this morning."

Adam muttered, "Or maybe Zelda made him sleep on the couch."

Jinks raised an eyebrow but didn't say anything. She knew about Zelda's proposition to Adam, even though he hadn't told Chief Quinn. Well, the Lehmann duo were the least of Adam's worries. It was a much bigger problem that their serial arsonist might strike again if they couldn't nail his ass soon.

And what about Beverly? His heart had almost stopped when she called him last night from the scene of the fire and before he found out she was truly okay. Still, seeing her covered in soot, with her face and clothes blackened had scared him more than he cared to admit. He knew she could take care of herself—she'd proved that time and time again.

So why was this particular incident so worrying? Had she been the arsonist's target all along? Maybe Adam's note-giver was taking his personal vendetta against Adam one step further.

Jinks studied his face. "You look a little pissed. But I wouldn't worry about Lehmann. He's his own little mini-hot-air balloon." She shot Adam a wicked look. "Maybe Zelda just needs to buy him some Viagra."

18

As Beverly walked through the halls of the Southeastern Vermont Regional Hospital, she experienced something she hadn't felt before in such a place. A sudden sense of foreboding that made her a little cold and clammy. Must be the lack of sleep last night after the fire.

Then she remembered her visit to her uncle at the nursing facility. She was sure it wasn't just a dream, that it had really happened. That Forsythe had become conscious long enough to threaten both her and Adam. But it was silly to think the encounter was giving her a little touch of PTSD. After all, what harm could a man who was attached to machines do?

One thing was for sure—Beverly still didn't want to tell Adam about it.

She didn't have to pretend to be a doctor this time to find her target room on the second floor. But she was quite surprised to see Annika Grimes fully dressed and sitting on the bed.

Beverly smiled at her. "Looks like they're ready to send you home."

"So they say. Kept me overnight for observation. Just because I'm an older woman, I told them, doesn't mean I need 'observation.' But since insurance pays, I guess they think they can get some money out of me."

"I'm glad they kept you for a while. People can develop bronchitis and pneumonia from breathing smoke. You know what they say, better safe than—"

"Dead. Yes, I know. Just wish I had a change of clean clothes." She looked past Beverly and added, "Looks like we've got some company of the official kind."

Beverly turned around to see Adam and Jinks standing in the doorway. That was a bit of a shock. Beverly had expected them to want to talk to Annika later, but here? Adam didn't seem shocked to see Beverly, however, when he first caught sight of her. She was getting too predictable.

As the two detectives walked into the room, Adam said to Annika, "The doctor on duty told me they were discharging you. I'd say that's good news."

"For me, yes. For them and their bottom line, not so much," Annika grumbled.

Adam replied, "Think of it this way. Things could have turned out differently and been far worse. Jared Lake worse."

Jinks added helpfully, "A hospital room is better than a room in the morgue. Bigger, too."

Annika frowned. "I still don't see why someone would go around setting fire to antiques stores. Porn shops, maybe. Pawn shops, maybe. But antiques? Unless some soul has a grudge against porcelain dishes."

That elicited a smile from Adam. "Those evil instruments of the devil." He studied the woman as if assessing her medical state for himself. "Do you feel up to a few questions?"

"Can it wait 'til later? I want to go by the store. Or what's left of it."

Beverly piped up, "Are you sure you want to do that so soon?"

"Vermonters are made of sturdy stock, you know that."

Beverly patted her hand. "Then I'll drive you."

Adam looked at Jinks. "I should tag along just to keep an eye on things. You okay going solo and taking the car to the police station?"

With transportation arranged, Beverly drove Annika and Adam to the still-smoking shell of True Gems. Yellow caution tape, sawhorses, and orange cones circled the area, but Beverly was pleased to see no potential looters lurking nearby.

Since the firefighters had arrived quickly, there was more left of this building than Jared Lake's store. But Beverly had a good idea of how much it would cost to rebuild.

Annika choked up at the sight and put her hands over her face. After a few moments, she stood up straighter and wiped her eyes with a clean patch of her sooty knit top. "I'm so grateful you were with me, Beverly. You saved me from certain death."

Beverly wasn't so sure about that. Maybe if she hadn't been there, the store wouldn't have been targeted. She gave Adam a quick glance, but his expression wasn't giving away his thoughts.

Annika continued, "Looking at my life's work being reduced to this in mere minutes . . . "

"Were you insured?"

"Yes, but maybe not enough to rebuild."

"There are plenty of folks who would contribute items to help get you up and running. I know several people personally."

"Thank you, dear. I'm not sure what I'll do. Need to talk to my rep and see."

"I'll bring some people to salvage what's left. Once Adam's department clears the site, that is. We can put it in secure storage for you."

"*If* anything's left. Looters, you know."

Adam said, "We'll have patrols in this area keeping an eye on things."

When Annika decided she couldn't stand looking at the blackened store any longer, Beverly played chauffeur for her and Adam again and followed the older woman's directions toward her house. It looked to be a restored old farmhouse, with its red siding and stone trim, although the "farm" part was long gone, given over to newer houses instead of horses.

As Beverly and her companions piled inside, she noted the interior was furnished like True Gems had been. An Italian Majolica ceramic wall plate here, a Florentine box there. Even a celluloid doll that made Beverly wince for a brief moment. Maybe there was hope for a rebirth of that store, yet, if Annika wouldn't mind parting with some of those treasures.

Beverly also noticed Annika's hand was shaking, and she offered to make some coffee for her. The machine was a very modern coffee-pod gizmo, so it was a fairly easy task. Beverly soon had three cups of something called butter toffee roast she handed out.

Annika accepted the cup gratefully. "Adam here was telling me about Justin Garone. How he showed up at Jared Lake's arson after hearing it on one of those police scanner things. Can't imagine wanting to see anything like that again, myself. Guess it takes all kinds."

Beverly frowned. Garone hadn't told her about it, but she hadn't even thought to ask. She was some super detective, all right. "You were probably working at that time of day, anyway."

"Actually, I closed early and went shopping at the new Green Mountain Outlet Center in Brattleboro."

"By yourself?" Adam asked.

"You mean an alibi?"

When Adam looked a little uncomfortable, Annika smiled. "Don't think any of the store owners would recall me. Plus, I like to pay in cash. Hate using credit cards. Afraid I'll overspend and then there are those damned interest charges. A modern form of usury and a crime in my book. I'm not about to let those big corporate bastards use my money to finance their lavish lifestyles."

Adam shifted around in his puffy chair that was so big it almost swallowed him. "Mrs. Grimes, have you ever heard the name, Ivon Kozak?"

"You bet I have."

Adam shot Beverly a quick side glance. He asked, "In what capacity?"

"Through his reputation, for one. But Kozak, through an intermediary attorney, approached me about selling my business to him. I thought he was lowballing awful bad and didn't take his offer seriously. So I turned him down."

"And no one else offered to buy it before or since?"

"No, just Kozak. I'd planned on leaving the shop to my grandkids, so why on earth would I sell it?"

"Did you know either Justin Garone or Jared Lake well?" Adam must have given up on getting comfortable, choosing to sit on the edge of his chair.

"I met Garone a few times, and we hit it off since my late husband was also in the Army. Garone had such a nice wife, too, into meteorology. A big weather buff. Has one of those deluxe home weather stations."

Annika sipped more of coffee, and Beverly noted she was draining the cup pretty fast. Annika continued, "As for Jared Lake. He's younger, so I didn't associate much with him or his wife. Young people don't really like to hang out with older people. We're too stodgy. Little did he know I'm taking skateboarding lessons." She grinned.

Adam asked, "You were part of the NAL, like Jared?"

Beverly felt a little bad for not telling Adam about her previous conversation with Annika on the topic. But Annika didn't seem to mind talking about it again. "Until recently.

Attendance is way down. No doubt, due to all that bad press about the Forsythe and Strudwick murders. That's why I left. In fact, I'm helping to spearhead a new antiques organization separate from the NAL. We're going to call it the New England Antiquities Alliance, or NEAA, a rival group."

Beverly frowned. "Maybe that's why you were targeted?"

"Could be, now you mention it. Everyone's beginning to believe the NAL, or the top brass, was just one big crime syndicate."

Beverly noted Adam looking at her again. Crime syndicate was an appropriate term, for sure. Beverly was also pleased to see some of Annika's spunk beginning to return. Maybe she should look into getting some of that butter toffee roast if it had that effect.

Warming up to her coffee and the topic, Annika said, "After Kozak's attorney contacted me, I looked him up. He owns a chain of antiques stores in the northeast. All with similar names. And come to think of it, none of *those* stores have burned down, have they?"

Beverly said, "And Kozak's also a member of the NAL."

Annika nodded. "People in the organization don't know much about him, other than he's successful. He's rarely at meetings and keeps to himself. Oddly, I remember him as being quiet, polite, kind of unassuming."

"Maybe he was just keeping a low profile."

"At meetings, perhaps. But I learned he's been building his business forcefully." She peered at Adam. "You should talk to Kozak's cousin. He's about the man's same age, as I think they grew up together. Although they're not close these days."

She brightened, "I know what, I'll call her and tell her you're coming because you want to talk to her."

Adam made a motion to interrupt her, but before he could, Annika had already picked up her landline and dialed the number. "Norma, dear. I have a very nice police detective and also a lovely new friend of mine, Beverly, who want to come talk to you about your cousin Ivon. Is now a good time? It is? They'll be right over."

After Adam and Beverly made sure Annika was settled in and didn't need anything, Adam shook his head as he and Beverly walked to her car and climbed in. "Guess you and I are going for a ride."

Before Beverly started up the engine, she said, "By the way, I almost forgot to tell you something Annika told me. One of her friends bid on an antique car at auction and won after outbidding Kozak. Three days after the sale was complete, that car mysteriously caught fire. And the next time the friend saw Kozak, he said 'you know the saying—you play with fire, you get burned.'"

Adam frowned. "I'll have to get the name of that friend from her."

"She said it was Martyn Agoston."

While Beverly drove to the address Annika had given them, Adam took out his cellphone and mouthed "Justin Garone" to her as he punched in the number and waited for the reply. From Adam's end of the conversation, she could tell what they were talking about. When Adam hung up, she asked, "Kozak's attorney offered to buy Garone's business, too, didn't he?"

"Yep. But he didn't trust the attorney or Kozak. Got bad vibes when the attorney was insistent it was the best offer he'd get from anyone. And it might be his last chance."

"He took it as a threat?"

"Not at the time. Merely that the attorney meant it was his last chance to sell due to a depressed market. But after the fire, he's not so sure it wasn't a bona fide threat."

Adam dialed another number but hung up after a few seconds. "I was going to ask Belle Lake the same question. To see if she knows if her late brother had a buyout offer from Kozak. But no answer."

"Guess it's off to see the cousin, then. The wonderful cousin of Oz."

"Let's just hope Ivon Kozak isn't as great and powerful as the literary Oz was supposed to be. Drive on, Dorothy."

Beverly grinned. "Thanks for not calling me the Wicked Witch."

19

Adam would have thought by now, he'd be used to losing control of the narrative when Beverly was involved. He'd even taken her to the scene of Jared Lake's arson after his shared scorn with Jinks about "fire tourists." He found he wasn't entirely comfortable with Beverly tagging along this time, either.

But it was her car, and she'd insisted, arguing, "Annika Grimes gave Kozak's cousin both our names and said we'd drop by within the hour. It will look too suspicious to her if I don't show up. And she might be less likely to talk to you."

"Me, as in the cop?"

"Naturally."

Although Beverly was doing the driving, she battered him with a barrage of questions along the way. "But what about Harlan and Agnes and security? And also the other antiques store owners in the area? Are you warning them? Are they getting armed guards?"

"All store owners have been warned to keep a close eye out. As if the news alone wasn't enough to do it. But local police departments everywhere are stretched thin. There's simply no way we could protect all those businesses."

When she started to protest, he said, "However, if each store owner wishes to hire their own private security guards, it's not a bad idea. Maybe Harlan should too."

"You think Kozak's only been targeting store owners he'd tried to buy out that refused him? As a warning to others?"

Adam opened his mouth to reply, but she continued, "I mean, was he just expecting word to get around that not being bought out meant a 'curse' was in their future? Surely he'd know suspicion would fall on him?"

"Perhaps. *If* Kozak is behind all this. But it's also possible no one put two and two together. Though having five such arsons now, one death, and an attempted murder might change all that."

"Mr. X always says when people get desperate, they make mistakes. Like Reggie Forsythe. And maybe even Redbeard. By the way, why haven't you caught Redbeard yet, Adam? He can't have gone far, especially if Mr. X heard he was seen in Stowe."

"The Stowe PD are on the lookout. But there are plenty of rural areas and mountains where anyone could hide if they want to."

When they arrived at the address Annika had given them, Adam was surprised to see it wasn't just an ordinary house but part of a compound. There were several outbuildings, including what looked like a big red barn, the type that dotted so much of Vermont's countryside. From the smell of the place, with dried hay and pungent natural "fertilizer," it was evidently a working farm.

They climbed out of the car and headed toward the house, but a faint voice made Adam turn toward the barn where a woman was waving energetically to them. Norma Ellery greeted them like old friends when they got closer. "Hope you don't mind if we talk while I do some brushing. Abbey and Alibaba here were getting a little tattered. It's horsey-salon day."

Beverly seemed fascinated by the two chestnut Morgan horses but also was hesitant and awkward as if she didn't know where to stand. Norma seemed to sense it and asked, "You ever been around horses before, Beverly?"

"I've seen them in the fields. And on TV."

"What do you think?"

"Seeing one up close is amazing, like some sort of imaginary animal come to life."

Adam reached out to stroke Abbey's muzzle and cooed softly to her. The horse nudged him gently in the shoulder, and he smiled. "Such a lovely girl you are."

Norma said to him, "You've been around horses before, I can tell. And so can they. She's usually not that affectionate around strangers."

Adam hated to turn the talk to business. He'd much rather saddle up one of the horses and go for a canter. It had been how long now? Three years? "I guess Annika Grimes told you why we're here."

"You want to ask about my cousin. Long story, short, he's not welcome here. Horses can tell if people are good or bad, kind of like dogs. They know Adam here is good people, and you, my dear," she nodded at Beverly, "they're just as curious about you as you are about them. But when Ivon and I were young, my horses would kick and whinny and get agitated whenever he was around. It was funny back then. But the older I got, it wasn't funny anymore."

"And yet, he found a successful calling in the antique business?"

"Oh, he's quite good at it, but I hear rumors from folks he's Mr. Mild Mannered Everyman to their faces even as he's using cut-throat business tactics. You know, to drive out his competitors."

She stopped brushing for a moment, "Quite honestly, not sure I need to know all those sordid details. And I want to stay as far away from him as possible."

"Were you afraid of him?"

She hesitated. "When we were younger, he threatened me once. I thought he was just joking. But he has this way of seeming normal, and then it's like someone flips a switch, and he takes immediate offense. Kinda like that whole Jekyll and Hyde thing."

"Is he on any medications or take any drugs that would contribute to this behavior?"

"None I know about. His major vice was pulling the wings off of flies." When Beverly wrinkled her nose, Norma added, "Clichéd, yeah. He was one of *those* kids. Never had any friends, as I recall. Guess he gave off stay-away-from-me vibes."

Adam reached over to pat Alibaba's mane. Equal time and all. "I know it's been a while since you interacted with him, but did he mention anyone named Jared Lake or Justin Garone?"

"Sorry. Those names don't ring a bell."

"How about a Darnell Warner?"

Norma looked uncertain, so Adam described him, "The man is about my height but built like a linebacker. And he has a head full of red hair with a red beard and mustache to go along with it. Ivon might have called him Redbeard."

"Oh, yes, I saw them together once. He looked like a red Wookiee. Big and hairy. Although I would prefer the Wookiee."

"Was this meeting business or leisure?"

"I recall they were talking about something and seemed to be in earnest conversation until I showed up. They stopped right away at that point. That seemed odd. I mean, this being my cousin and all. I even laughed about it, and he just shrugged it off as 'business.'"

"When was this?"

"About three months ago. I wouldn't have ordinarily been near Ivon except I needed to give him something his mother, my aunt Rose, loaned me once. Didn't want him accusing me of making off with anything that rightfully belonged to him. She's passed on now, you see."

Adam frowned at that. Three months ago? That would have right before Redbeard was arrested and then released on bond and went AWOL. And around the time Reggie Forsythe shot himself and ended up in the nursing home. Thereby leaving a big gap at the top of the NAL mob hierarchy.

Beverly seemed to be reading his mind again as she asked, "Did your cousin talk much about the Forsythes?"

"Said once he hated Reggie Forsythe more than anyone else in the world. Hated how he had a privileged background. Since Ivon had to rise from dirt to get where he is and all. He hated that Forsythe threw his weight around. Wanted to be the antiques kingpin."

"Forsythe was Ivon's main rival, then?"

"I guess, in a way." Alibaba nickered, and Norma rubbed the side of his neck. "This here is my oldest 'child.' I've had him for fifteen years now." She pointed at his coloring and laughed. "His coat is on the reddish side, too. I'll have to start calling him Redcoat."

Adam thanked her again for her time and asked Beverly if she minded dropping him off at the station. She was quieter on the way back, so much so he was starting to worry.

But she finally broke the silence. "Ivon Kozak sounds a bit like a monster from his background. Equal to Reggie Forsythe in his own way."

"One was born rich, the other not, yet both obsessed with becoming top mob boss in their own little criminal domain."

"For what? Ego?"

"When I was first dragged into Forsythe's shady world, I thought it might be a front for money laundering. Nothing turned up along those lines for him, but maybe Kozak. The investigation is still too early yet. And don't forget, we have zero proof Kozak had anything to do with the arsons."

"But Adam, who else? The guy offers to buy up competitors, they refuse, and poof, their business burns to the ground?"

"It just seems a stretch for a man who's been waiting in the wings for years, so to speak, to suddenly resort to murder."

"People snap all the time."

"I know that. And maybe something or someone triggered this guy. But don't fixate on Kozak exclusively. We've got Redbeard and Sergeant Moody as suspects, as well as people involved with the other arson victims, and that's likely just the tip of the iceberg."

Beverly looked like she would have folded her arms across her chest if she weren't driving. Her eyes were certainly on fire as she said, "It has to be him, Adam. If there's one thing my con artist experience has taught me, it's how to read people."

"About that," Adam turned to look at her directly. "You're taking my advice to heart, right? To keep all that play-acting for a future private eye business?"

"What else?" She replied, a little too quickly for Adam's peace of mind.

They rode the rest of the way to the station without saying much, which felt like an uneasy truce of sorts, to Adam. He hated to keep bringing the subject up, and he certainly couldn't keep her from being curious. Wouldn't want to. She had as much of a stake in all this antiques crime business as anyone. But he couldn't pretend he felt toward her as he would with Jinks or any of the other cops. It was something . . . else. He didn't have to chew on that thought as they arrived at the station.

He slid out of the car and said in parting, "Why don't you check up on Agnes Flamm. See how that Christmas shindig of hers is coming along."

"A great idea." She smiled at him and waved as she drove off, but he had a funny feeling about the way she'd agreed so quickly. Again.

He looked toward a group of chattering crows in the bare maple trees nearby. Crows seemed to be following him these days. He muttered in their direction, "You said it."

The crows' calls continued to follow him all the way into the building as if trying to tell him something. He didn't believe in omens, but wasn't the term for a group of crows a "murder?"

20

Beverly didn't stop by to check on Agnes Flamm at her shop like she'd half-agreed to before dropping Adam off at the police station. No, she had something better in mind.

She checked the time. Close to five. Ivon Kozak's main antiques shop closed at five-thirty, so her timing was good. She chose her salt-and-pepper wig this time, with some horn-rimmed glasses and a little added cheek prosthetics. And the reporter's notebook, of course.

When she arrived at the site, she couldn't help but be impressed. Kozak's Antiques Mall was on a five-acre lot with an impressive building rising up in the center like an antiques cathedral.

The architecture was a take on Vermont country kitsch, but almost aggressively so. A slate roof topped off tall glass windows with painted lettering, and the wraparound vinyl porch was designed to imitate white wood. At the start of the long driveway, a sign taller than Beverly—surrounded by a circle of landscaped rocks, gravel, and winter plantings—pointed the way to the entrance.

When she walked into the store on the dot of five, one of the two employees in the place greeted her. "May I help you, Miss—"

Beverly stuck out her hand. "Lizbeth Furmanski. I'm looking for a Scandinavian folk art box. I do hope you have one."

The crew-cutted employee, whose name tag read "Colin Parton," shook his head. "Nothing like that, I'm afraid. Would you be interested in some early American keepsake boxes instead?"

Beverly feigned disappointment. "Oh, I don't know . . . well, I guess it wouldn't hurt to look."

Colin herded her toward a table with several of the boxes, and Beverly picked each one up in turn. "Hand-painted with these lovely flowers and birds of prey. This is nice."

And it was, too, top quality with inlay and some type of exotic wood—koa, maybe? Kozak must have quite an eye because Beverly hadn't seen such pieces this fine before in person. When she saw the price tag, she almost whistled. They were selling it for about ten percent under prices she'd seen elsewhere. How could Kozak afford to do that and stay in business?

She thanked Colin and said she wanted to look around some more. Mostly, she was waiting until the other customers in the store left. She browsed through some Lalique crystal and Tiffany sterling silver, truly admiring the items—a George III cut-glass bottle with sterling silver lid, a Persian teapot, and much more. Grammie had never been able to afford items as exquisite as these. And Harlan specialized in more folksy pieces and homewares.

Finally, she carried the hand-painted keepsake box up to the counter where the other staffer, Millie Lamper, stood waiting to ring her up. Both Millie and Colin weren't smiling much, and their hunched postures, listless movements, and monotone voices screamed unhappiness.

Beverly paid for the box and said, "How is Mr. Kozak? I'd hoped to get a chance to talk to the man himself. I mean, he's an expert on Burmese sapphire jewelry, isn't he?" Beverly had done a bit of homework and learned that much.

Colin replied, "Mr. Kozak isn't here right now. He should be back later. Or maybe tomorrow."

At the mention of his name, the duo seemed even less happy than before. Beverly decided to poke the hornet's nest a little. "It must be so much fun working here. Especially having the chance to work with such a legend in the antiques world."

Colin licked his lips, and Millie looked down at the cash register. Finally, Colin cleared his throat and said, "We certainly love our customers."

A good feint, there. Okay then, time for more poking. "You'd think antiques would be so boring. But I heard the horrible news about the other antiques owner, Reggie Forsythe. Must be quite the talk among antiques stores in the state, right?"

Millie picked at the sleeve of her leopard-print sweater before answering, "We never saw him. He was kind of a rival for Mr. Kozak. I guess we never really expected him to show his face here."

Colin blurted out, "We heard Mr. Kozak once say he was looking forward to the day when he'd see Forsythe six feet under."

He and Millie laughed nervously, and Beverly joined in. "You know how people love gallows humor."

Colin excused himself and hurried to the far corner of the store, pretending to be neatening up a display of demitasse cups, although Beverly could tell it was already neat enough. Millie looked at Beverly warily as if to say, "You want to buy something else or not?" so Beverly decided to leave.

She wasn't sure what more she could get out of the two reluctant employees, anyway. But their behavior was certainly interesting. Why all the nervousness and, dare she say, something akin to fear?

Beverly sighed as she stood next to her car. She hated to waste a good disguise. After a little quick research on her phone, she found out more about Ivon Kozak's wife. The woman owned a small tea shop across the border in New Hampshire just a few miles away.

§ § §

Beverly called ahead to see if Kozak's wife was there on the pretext Beverly was a reporter doing a human interest story and wanted to talk to her. She was in luck—Sheila Kozak was at work.

Beverly realized a little too late she'd used this reporter con too many times before, but it seemed to work with women. Appealing to their sense of vanity, perhaps? But that wasn't exactly fair since she'd known plenty of vain men in her day.

She made sure to grab her fake generic press pass ID she kept in her effects-kit and took a deep breath as she stared at the entrance to the café. It was named "Sheila's," no doubt after Kozak's wife. Yep, the vanity thing might be just the ticket.

When a waitress ushered Beverly into a small office, a woman with platinum hair and icy blue eyes greeted her. She left the office door open as the two women sat down. That might be trouble, but it couldn't be helped.

Beverly started her spiel right away. "I'm so grateful I found you in today, Mrs. Kozak."

"It's a pleasure. What did you say your article was about?"

"Successful women business owners in the region. I don't want to take up too much of your time since the article will cover several people. But I found your story utterly fascinating."

"Is it? Typical hard-working, ladder-climbing woman trying to make it in a man's world. And usually getting her fingers stepped on by male boots on the way up that ladder."

Beverly nodded sympathetically. "I understand your husband also runs his own successful business. Makes the two of you a power couple. I imagine how challenging it must be to have two such successful people in the same household. When do you have time for family life?"

"Our two kids are grown with families of their own and have moved away. So that's not a factor. Early on, it was difficult, for sure."

"Do you get to see them often?"

Sheila hesitated a split second, but enough for Beverly to sense there was an undercurrent of something strange there. "Not as often as I'd like," she forced a smile. "I've only seen our four-year-old grandson once. And Ivon hasn't met him yet at all."

"I'm sure your husband is as sad about that as you are."

Again, that small hesitation, only a little longer this time. Reading between the lines, Beverly was beginning to think there might be an estrangement, and that Kozak wasn't close with the kids. He hadn't bothered to see his new grandson in four years?

Changing tacks, Beverly said, "There must be so many challenges to owning your own business. The legalities and accounting. And insurance, too—look at the recent antiques store arsons. I'm guessing you and your husband must be afraid of that happening to you."

Sheila waved a hand in the air. "Ivon doesn't seem concerned at all. In fact, he said he had the kind of insurance that would ensure no one burns down his place."

"That's reassuring. I'd talked to another female business owner of an antiques store," Beverly made up a name on the spot, "Anna Gables. And she is most definitely concerned. But she said your husband had made an offer to buy her out."

Sheila narrowed her eyes. "I don't know anything about that. You'd have to ask my husband. We tend not to get involved in each other's business affairs." Then she asked, "What newspaper did you say you worked for again?"

Beverly made up another name, the *Entrepre-nous*. "We're a new startup focusing on female entrepreneurs."

She really was slipping. She'd used that line before on someone else and not all that long ago. Was she really getting that sloppy? She needed to come up with some more original ideas, stat. Either that, or she was going to have to go back to college to get an actual journalism degree.

Beverly added with a smile, "I'll be happy to send you a copy when it's published."

To put Sheila's mind at ease, Beverly asked some more typical questions, and Sheila did seem to relax. So much so that she was laughing at the end of the interview. Maybe Beverly hadn't blown it, after all.

As Beverly left the tea shop, her notebook full of useless information in hand, she bumped into a man carrying a shovel. She fell backward, just catching herself in time.

The man reached over to steady her. "I'm sorry, miss. Are you all right?'

"I'm fine, it's nothing."

He peered at her. "You were just talking to Mrs. Kozak, weren't you?"

"Yes, I was."

"I'm a handyman here. I was inside, picking up some materials, and overheard your conversation." He looked around and then lowered his voice. "If you want the real story of the Kozaks, you should talk to Lucas Barratt."

At the sound of a car driving up, the man clammed up, gave her a quick look, and disappeared around the building. Beverly stood looking after him. Lucas Barratt? What did he have to do with Kozak? And how was she going to let Adam know about this tip without mentioning how she came upon it?

Maybe Adam was right about her not sticking her nose into the investigation. Her attempts at sleuthing were only dredging up more questions than answers. Well, he wouldn't find out about this little outing, would he?

She sighed and slid into her car, whipped out her phone, and immediately went to register the *Entrepre-nous* domain name. Thankfully, it wasn't taken. She was definitely getting sloppy, when she used to make sure the details were all squared in advance.

Maybe Adam was right, and she was fixated on the wrong suspect. Kozak—and his wife—might just be red herrings like in mystery novels. But her comment to Adam hadn't just been an idle boast. Her con-woman past *had* honed her character-judging skills to a fine point. There was an old saying in the con trade, "It takes a scammer to truly know a fake."

21

"You really think he'll talk to us?" Jinks leaned on the car as she and Adam stood in the parking lot. "If he's there, that is. A lot of business owners sleep late. It's just the grunts who have to come in early."

"It's only a friendly courtesy call. He'd be a fool not to talk to us." Adam studied the imposing facility with the fancy entrance sign and the white porch that wrapped around the front and sides. Kozak wasn't doing badly to afford something as fancy as his "Antiques Mall." He was glad Beverly wasn't around to get involved with this guy.

Adam had spent the time at the station, after Beverly dropped him off the previous evening, digging into every database he could. It was almost as if Kozak took pains to keep his nose clean, as far as the records went. No rap sheet, no business complaints, not a single overdue library book, or even a parking ticket.

When they went inside, an employee named Colin Parton led them past an array of expensive-looking antiques, including a locked case filled with jewelry, toward an office in the rear.

Kozak might be an antiques tsar of sorts, but the office they entered was modern looking. Adam guessed the massive floor-to-ceiling bookcase along one wall and the equally large executive desk in front cost half a year of Adam's salary.

The man who introduced himself as Ivon Kozak was also a surprise. An altogether unimposing figure, no more than five-seven and about a hundred fifty pounds. His pale face and beak noise made him resemble a bird. Make that a raptor, because Adam caught a glimmer of something hawkish in the man's eyes. It was only there for a moment, but Adam knew he hadn't imagined it.

The man indicated a couple of leather seats for Adam and Jinks, much more plush than those in Chief Quinn's office. Adam smiled and thanked him for taking the time to "chat" with them.

Adam started with, "You may have heard about a string of arsons at antiques stores in the state recently."

"Oh, yes, yes, I'd heard all about that. Such a pity. And that unfortunate Jared Lake. What's the world coming to? All that nasty business with the Forsythes. Good riddance to them, I say."

If a voice could be described as unctuous, Kozak's filled the bill. Adam took a deep breath. "We're going around to the other antiques store owners just as a precaution to remind them to be on the lookout for anything odd or suspicious. I hope you haven't seen anything of that nature, yourself."

"I've instructed my staff to keep their eyes open. But so far, we've been lucky."

"Yes, you certainly have." Adam was still smiling, but his slight emphasis on "you" hadn't gone unnoticed by Kozak, who pursed his lips. Adam continued, "You have a nice place here. You're quite successful, it would seem."

"I've had my successes, yes. It's incredibly hard work. Had hardly a penny to my name when I started out."

"Rags to riches, quite a feat."

"A feat of perseverance. And learning not to take 'no' for an answer." Kozak uttered a half-laugh as if he'd said something incredibly humorous.

Adam did a little persevering, himself. "I understand you've been trying to expand your empire in the past year or so. Buying out other shops, like Justin Garone's Main Street Antiques. And Annika Grimes's True Gems." He still hadn't been able to get in touch with Belle Lake about her late brother's shop.

"We've been expanding, it's true. I'm not sure which stores we've approached. You see, my attorney handles those little details. I'd have to ask him." Kozak's eyes bored into Adam's. The warning was clear . . . said attorney was on standby to get involved in case of any accusations.

Adam asked, "Which attorney might that be, sir?"

"A very fine one, Detective Dutton. Mr. Douglas Marcell, Esquire."

Adam sat up just a little straighter at that. The same sleazy guy who'd bailed out Redbeard and also represented the sleazy Forsythes. "I believe I've heard of him." Jinks, who was taking her usual notes, cleared her throat, and Adam saw out of the corner of his eye the slight tensing of her jaw.

"I retained him years ago on the advice of other antiques shop owners. Such a fine man. Very effective at his craft."

"Yes, sir, I'm sure he is." Adam added nonchalantly, "I don't suppose you've seen a man around here by the name of Darnell Warner? You couldn't miss him. Tall, with thick red hair and matching beard."

"I'm sure I would have noticed such an odd individual, Detective. And his name is Darnell Warner, you say? You must think he's tied up in all of this. I'll definitely have to keep my eye out."

Kozak's lips turned up into a joking smile, exposing the man's perfectly matching teeth. He was playing with Adam and didn't seem to care if Adam knew it.

Kozak stood up and walked toward the door. "It's been such a delight to talk to you fine officers of the law. I do hope you don't mind if I get back to work? An empire doesn't get built with a lot of dilly-dallying."

"Of course, sir." Adam handed over his card. "If you wish to contact us."

Before they could leave, Kozak had one parting shot. "Oh, Detective Dutton . . . that whole business with the Forsythes. I believe I'd heard a name from some of my colleagues. A Beverly Laborde. I'm not quite clear what her involvement was with that whole affair, but I'm sure you know all about that. Perhaps she should be on your list of possible suspects."

Adam gritted his teeth, trying not to let Kozak's verbal stabbing get to him. He pasted on a smile and said, "You won't mind if we chat with your employees out there? To see if they've seen anything suspicious?"

Kozak nodded at them dismissively. "Be my guest. They're free to tell you whatever they feel like telling you. Although I believe one of them, Miss Lamper, is out on an errand."

That was a bit of odd phrasing, "tell you whatever they feel like telling you." But Adam let it go as he and Jinks made their way to the counter where Colin Parton was operating the register. Colin said he hadn't seen anything unusual, certainly nothing related to arson, but promised to call them if he did.

Adam also asked, "You must have been aware of the whole Reggie Forsythe saga. Was all over the news."

Colin scratched his head. "Funny you should mention it. You're the second person who's asked me that in two days."

"Who was the first?"

"A customer who came in yesterday. I believe she said her name was Elizabeth something. Furman, no. That wasn't it. Furmanski, Lizbeth Furmanski, yeah, that was it."

Adam felt his blood pressure rising. He thanked Colin and felt like steam must be pouring out of his ears as he stalked back to the car. Jinks, who'd been close behind, stared at him as they climbed in. "You look like you're ready to spit nails. No, make that nail guns."

"That name. Lizabeth Furmanski."

"What about it?"

"I'm pretty sure it was Beverly. She used a similar name on me before. I thought we'd come to an understanding about her not using her disguises and con-woman routine to interfere in investigations."

Adam wasn't sure who he was most upset with—Beverly or himself. Was she teasing him or defying him? And she must be getting careless to use the same name twice. Or did she somehow want him to know she'd done this?

His cellphone rang, and he noted the caller. Jinks peered over his shoulder and saw the name. Zelda. He let it go to voicemail, and Jinks shot him a sympathetic look. "And the woman troubles keep on coming. Zelda just won't leave you alone, will she?"

"I'm not sure why. She's got everything she wanted. Money, a taste of power, prestige."

"Funny. I didn't hear you say anything about love in that list of 'gots.'"

Adam stared at the car's ceiling, noting his blood pressure hadn't fallen much. "Can't help but wonder what she'll do if her husband, our 'esteemed' mayor, does run for the governorship."

"It'll get him out of our hair."

"We'll either be greatly relieved or greatly screwed. And that's just if he wins. If he doesn't, who knows what havoc he'll wreak out of spite."

"He hasn't declared his intention of running yet. Neither a borrower nor a lender be."

Adam squinted at her. "What?"

"Don't borrow trouble, ace."

He shook his head. "Kozak is trouble, for sure. I had my doubts about him being behind the arsons. But that smug bastard knows something."

"Knows Redbeard, too, if I'm any judge of smug bastards. And Kozak is high on the smarmy meter."

Adam tapped out a pattern on the steering wheel, not realizing until Jinks pointed it out that it was from the song "A Whole Lot of Trouble for You," making him shake his head.

She asked, "Where to next, Kemosabe?"

Adam grabbed his cellphone again and looked up Jenny-Lee Salant's number. "You up for a trip to the exciting world of insurance?"

§ § §

They navigated across town to Salant's office and caught her in before she headed out to an early lunch. They didn't bother going inside, chatting with her in front of the door. "Miss Salant—"

"Please. Jenny-Lee."

"Miss Jenny-Lee, we know that Jared Lake was insured through your company. But did you also cover Justin Garone's Main Street Antiques and Annika Grimes's True Gems stores?"

"As a matter of fact, we did." She stepped a little closer to Adam, making them only a few inches apart. He tried not to notice. she added, "That means I'm not going to be out of a job any time soon, thanks to the investigations involved."

"Have you uncovered any evidence of insurance fraud?"

"Not so far. Certainly nothing that would prove any of the three, let alone all three, were working together. Or Jared Lake's sister, since her brother died in the fire."

"What type of policies did they have?"

"Substantial policies, which was prudent on their part. Standard procedure. Except for Grimes. Hers wasn't nearly as big."

"I was hoping you could show us a copy of those policies."

"Unh-uh. Confidentiality and all. Of course, I'd be happy to obey a court order." Jenny-Lee smiled up at Adam. "Do *you* have any leads to help prove it's fraud? My company would be eternally grateful. And so would I."

"Nothing yet. But we'll certainly keep you posted. And hope you do the same."

"Of course, Adam. Anything to help you. I'd definitely not turn down the chance to see you again."

On their return trip to the station, Jinks couldn't stop ribbing Adam about Jenny-Lee's blatant flirting. "She only had eyes for you, tiger. I hardly even registered on her people-meter."

"I'll tell you what I told Beverly. Insurance reps do whatever they can to get cops to give them ammunition not to pay out. Don't put anything special into it."

"Right, partner." And then she added, "You told Beverly that? Why, was she upset this she-beast was flirting with you? A little green-eyed monster? Battle of the she-beast versus the green-eyed monster. I'd pay to go see that."

Adam snorted. "Just for that, I'm taking back the Christmas present I got for you."

22

Beverly sat on the sofa nearest the front window that had a nice view of the moat and the yaks. She'd skipped breakfast at the resort, so Mr. X had kindly offered her some "enhanced" yak hot chocolate with a little egg and bourbon added in.

Mr. X was not at all happy she tried to see Ivon Kozak, even though she'd missed him, and had also paid a visit to Kozak's wife. "He might get suspicious when he looks up the newspaper you mentioned and not be able to find anything."

She grinned. "When I returned to the resort last night, I used their computer to create a fake website for *Entrepre-nous*. Even social media accounts, back-dating them."

"Impressive and quick thinking. It doesn't alleviate all of my concerns."

"With all the fake interviews I've arranged lately, who knows? I might go 'straight' and start up my own magazine."

He smiled at that. "Your talents seem to run toward the less conventional type of work. I still think you should try your hand at becoming a private eye."

"You and Adam." Beverly stretched her legs out on the sofa. "Mrs. Kozak's handyman told me something interesting. He said if I wanted to know more about Ivon Kozak to talk to Lucas Barratt. Do you know who that is?"

"Jared Lake's assistant at his antiques business. That makes me curious." Xenakis stared off into space. "I thought I knew all the Kozak and Forsythe connections. But Barratt never crossed my radar as being connected, just a typical employee."

Mr. X leaned forward, an earnest expression on his usually blank face. "Why are you pursuing this, Beverly? Adam Dutton and his partner and colleagues seem quite competent to handle it."

"Because my uncle may be involved. And because Harlan and all the other antiques store owners might be targeted. And because after what happened at Annika Grime's place with the two of us almost roasted, it's even more personal than ever."

"I can't fault you for playing detective there, Beverly. You do good work, even if it's unorthodox."

"Speaking of 'orthodox,' have you ever thought about starting a store with your yak products? Milk, shawls, socks . . . .?"

"Like you, I'm not sure I'm cut out to be a conventional businessman. Unless you want to run the store for me?"

"Nice to know I have one thing to fall back on if I can't find a way to make a living."

Mr. X studied her face. "It seems something else is bothering you."

She sighed. "I went to see my uncle. In the nursing facility."

"Whatever for?"

"Adam said there was brain activity. I just had to see for myself."

"And what did you find?"

"He woke up. That is, I think he did. Only for a moment."

Xenakis frowned. "How could you tell?"

"His eyes fluttered open, and then he seemed to be muttering something. He looked directly at me and said, 'Dutton . . . will pay. And so will you.' I was so shocked, I thought I'd imagined it."

"Have you told Detective Dutton this?"

"He'd be furious. Maybe that makes me a coward. On the other hand, I don't have any witnesses, not even the nurses."

"It might mean nothing."

She chewed on her lip. "Part of me is wondering if it's like when people with dementia get suddenly coherent right before they die. A man's last gasp. And we'll read about his death in the papers tomorrow."

"How would that make you feel?"

"Now you're starting to sound like a shrink." She looked at her feet spread out on the couch. "Then again, I'm already on the couch. If shrinks still do that sort of thing."

"I was just wondering if his death would make you sad in some way."

"I'd have preferred he go to prison."

When Xenakis didn't reply right away, Beverly asked, "You do believe me, don't you? About the waking-up part?"

"I do. As you say, it might be temporary. Or it may mean we need to watch him more closely. To make certain he doesn't pull off a vanishing act like Redbeard."

She nodded, relieved. She also knew deep down she'd have to tell Adam . . . when the time was right. She reached over to grab her purse and pulled out the odd little ashtray with the octopus she'd rescued from the rubble at the Lucas Barratt arson site. "Do you know what this is?"

He walked over to take it from her and studied it. "Fairly lightweight. Cold cast resin, I believe, painted with a black-and-copper veneer to look older. Not a true antique, but I haven't seen anything quite like it. Where did you find this?"

"In what was left of Jared Lake's antiques store after the fire."

"Doesn't seem very valuable."

"That's what the insurance adjuster said." Beverly wrinkled her nose.

Mr. X handed the octopus-ashtray back to her. "You don't seem to have a favorable opinion of this adjuster."

An image of the woman flirting with Adam flashed in Beverly's mind, but she pushed it away. "Just not sure I trust her."

"Your instincts are usually quite good. Perhaps I should look into this woman."

"Maybe hold off for a bit. I'm trying not to irritate Adam too much these days. Any more than I already do. Change of subject, please?"

"Well, then, since you're thinking about opening up a private eye business," Mr. X raised an eyebrow in a half-mocking way. "Perhaps you should join me in a little excursion. Up for a bit of that investigating?"

She drained the last of the chocolate concoction, grateful for something active to do rather than dwelling in navel-gazing. "Lead the way."

§ § §

They took Beverly's car since Xenakis wasn't fond of driving. "What did you say this place was again?" She put the address into her GPS.

"An 'antiques' store of a different stripe. A museum of curiosities."

When they stopped at a sleazy building with orange paint and purple trim that looked like it was more of a second-rate pawn shop than a museum, she looked askance at Mr. X. "Should I have my gun handy? Of perhaps you carry your own?"

"I don't like guns on the whole. Too noisy and messy. I much prefer up-close action, hand-to-hand. So much more civilized . . . and accurate." He added, "I don't necessarily trust you alone with this man. Although I'm beginning to think you could take him. He's let himself go."

They climbed out, and Beverly was instantly fascinated when they entered the place. There were plaster-face casts and what looked like voodoo dolls everywhere. "What is all this?"

"Gorrie Sidman, the owner, collects these things in his spare time as a sort of hobby."

"Gorrie? His name is appropriate." She peered into the back of the room. "Where is he?"

"He's probably in his office."

The office was down a long flight of stairs in a dank basement that made Beverly want to put something over her nose. That space was even stranger than the first floor, with jars of various body parts in formaldehyde, some skulls, teeth, books with bindings made of human skin, and complete skeletons.

She said, "Shades of the Mutter Museum in Philly."

Sidman was as colorful and odd as his "museum." His gray beard was set off by a pink felt hat, a magenta tie, black suspenders, and an electric blue scarf. The scar on his cheek and his barrel chest told Beverly the man had seen his share of tough scrapes, but he welcomed Xenakis as someone who was almost cowed by the taller, much paler man.

His voice sounded rusty as if he didn't use it much. "Xenakis, long time no see. Last time was, what . . . when you had a mustache?"

"I'll have to check my photo album to see."

"Haha, still the same iceberg humor. So, what are you here for today?" He gave Beverly a long scrutiny. "And what's with the classy dame?"

"I'm here about Ivon Kozak. As for the 'dame,' she has an interest in the matter."

Sidman sat down on an oversized wooden crate that seemed to serve as his desk. "And here I was hoping you wanted to talk about something cheerier."

"Rumors have tied him to a series of arsons recently."

"And you think I might know something about that? Me with my honest little business?"

Mr. X just stared at him as Sidman thrust his hands in his pockets and shrugged. "Kozak tried to buy out a bunch of antiques stores. They refused. The stores burned to the ground."

"It doesn't seem likely Kozak would be willing to get his hands dirty."

"Oh, no, not that weasel. He's much more likely to have someone do it."

"Darnell Warner, for instance."

Sidman looked from Mr. X to Beverly. "Redbeard, eh? Yeah, that would fit."

"Is it possible Kozak or Redbeard had any bomb-making experience?"

"Sure, Redbeard was in the Army. He worked in an explosives unit."

Beverly blurted out. "Sergeant Moody was in the Army for a while, too. And was also attached to an explosives unit."

"Moody? You mean Mike Moody?" Sidman curled his lips. "I've heard of that guy. A bit of a gambler. As I recall, he was discharged dishonorably from the Army. Fighting and such. Got worse after he was kicked out. He was in debt, too."

Mr. X asked, "How badly?"

"Bad. In debt up to his eyeballs or maybe even higher. He turned to certain unsavory means to get money."

"Theft?"

"An old friend of yours, Reggie Forsythe. And maybe even Kozak. I heard tell he also has ties to Leroy Schick, a bookie and loan shark to the rich and famous. Only takes high rollers."

Mr. X nodded. "I'm familiar with Mr. Schick."

Beverly frowned. "High rollers? Where would a police officer get enough money to be a high roller? They aren't paid that much."

"Indeed." Mr. X added, "Perhaps he inherited it."

Sidman guffawed. "Good one, Xenakis. That's what they all say. Like, I 'inherited' some money from some horses. Or football players by beating the spread. Or mobsters."

"One more thing, Gorrie. Have you heard of any insurance-fraud schemes in play in the state?"

"The arsons, you mean? Nah, not a peep. Insurance fraud's a tough racket. Too many schmucks have tried that. The companies are spooked."

"You've been very helpful, as usual. I'll let you get on with your . . . whatever it is you do down here."

"Don't think you'd want to know." Sidman leered at Beverly. "You've got gorgeous hair. Wanna part with a little bit of it? I got some scissors right here."

Beverly stared at him. "I already donated at the office. Blood, too. And some of the extra fangs I didn't need anymore."

Sidman guffawed. "Now I see why you like this dame, Xenakis. She's like a female version of you."

Beverly and Mr. X made their way out of the basement into the colder, but much fresher air of the outdoors. Beverly shook her head. "Strange little gnome of a man."

"But always a fount of information."

"He gets all that from running a museum?"

"He has friends in many low places. Sub-swamp-level low."

Beverly tapped her foot on the ground. "I'm worried about Adam."

Mr. X seemed to know what she was thinking. "It certainly sounds like Sergeant Moody may be involved in all of this."

Beverly sighed. "And that makes him a danger to Adam. I'm not getting a lot of sleep lately."

"Worrying won't help. Only action."

"You're right." Beverly smiled at him. "So . . . where are we going next?"

23

Once back at the station, Jinks made a beeline for the breakroom hoping to get fresh coffee before the pot was left on too long and turned to sludge. Despite the fact Adam didn't really want any more coffee, he wished he'd gone with Jinks when he bumped into Sergeant Moody ... again. If Adam didn't know better, he'd think the guy was angling for a fight and made it a point to seek out Adam for these "chance" encounters.

Moody sneered at him, "I hear you're stumped by those arson cases, Dutton. Beyond your skills, I'd say."

Adam groaned inwardly. "Not now, Moody. I don't have time for games."

The other man stared at him for a moment and then gave him an odd look. "Heard you were looking into Ivon Kozak as a suspect."

Adam stood very still. He hadn't told anyone inside the department about Kozak except for Jinks and the chief. And he knew beyond a shadow of a doubt neither one of them would have leaked that bit of intel.

Adam didn't have time to reply before Moody quickly changed the subject, crowing, "I hear I'm a shoo-in for detective real soon. Better watch your back, Dutton."

He aimed a triumphant sneer at Adam and headed down the hall, crossing paths with Jinks, who was walking in Adam's direction. When she'd made sure Moody was out of earshot, she told Adam in a low voice, "On my way to the breakroom, I caught Moody in your office. He was rifling through papers on your desk. Tried to look into your computer, too."

"Did he see you?"

"I scared him by breezing in there. He had some lame excuse about you having a report ready for him. That he was just there to pick it up and save you some time." She rolled her eyes. "As if. I've got kids. My lie detector gets tons of practice."

Adam grumbled, "Glad I wasn't the one to catch Moody. I might be out of a job after I decked him."

The chief's administrative assistant, Cherry Steele, appeared around the corner just then. "There you are. Chief Quinn wants to see the two of you."

Adam said, "Did he say what it was about?"

"No, but he seems really wired. If I didn't know better, I'd think he'd snuck some caffeinated coffee."

Adam and Jinks made their way to the chief's office and "assumed the position," as Adam called it, he in the right-hand chair and Jinks in the left. He used to tease her about always choosing the one closest to the door and escape.

Quinn wasn't in the worst of moods, thankfully, but he wasn't exactly dancing a jig. Cherry was right about being wired—the chief kept cracking his knuckles and wiggling in his chair. "Just wanted to get an update on your progress with the arsons."

Adam said, "We're still looking into insurance fraud, but my money's on Kozak or Redbeard. Finding the tie is going to be hard unless we locate Redbeard and get him to confess."

Quinn picked up a stack of papers and dropped them back on the desk. "Just got a copy of the forensic reports so far."

Jinks caught Adam's eye and winked. They knew how much Quinn hated looking at computer screens and always wanted the printed version. Quinn asked, "Did Joe Brimm brief you yet?"

Adam nodded. "He's been working with ATF on the pipe bomb and arsons, particularly the type of materials used. As far as my house bombing, definitely a pipe bomb made of copper tubing and explosive powder. Maybe fireworks powder. They think the device was likely around six inches long and an inch in diameter. Typical size. Plugged ends and a green fuse."

"Is that related to the arsons?"

"With the incendiary device at Annika Grimes's store, yes. So it's looking like those two incidents are related. We may yet find details linking the other arsons."

"What about a copycat?"

"Wouldn't make much sense, given the details have been kept out of the papers."

Quinn dialed a number on his intercom and asked for Joe Brimm to join them in the office. The bespectacled Brimm was still wearing his white lab coat when he strolled into the room. "Hey, Quinn," he said.

Adam shook his head at that. Brimm was one of the few who could be that familiar with Quinn and not get his ear chewed off for it. Brimm asked, "What's up?"

"I was just talking to Dutton and Jinks here about your work into Adam's pipe bomb and the recent arsons."

"The new ones or the older ones?"

The chief blinked at him. "What?"

Adam explained, "We just found out last evening about two more antiques stores that burned earlier this year."

Brimm added helpfully, "It's in your report."

The chief grumbled, "Probably on the bottom. Haven't got that far yet."

Adam continued, "They were in farther parts of the state. At first, they were deemed accidental, so they didn't land on our radar until now."

"But they're no longer 'accidental,' I take it?"

"No, sir."

Adam gestured toward Brimm, who said, "We used gas chromatography-mass spectrometry to create a chromatogram of Jared Lake's arson. Several details matched up with the others. Kerosene was the accelerant with added fireworks powder. Designed to spread fast along the underside of a ceiling. Started on a wall adjacent to the most flammable wall and added in some tinder around. Multiple ignition points. A fire-spreading trailer from one outlet to another. Very professional."

"In your expert opinion, the attack on Adam's house and all the arsons *are* likely related?"

"I think the operative word is likely. Ironclad proof, not so much."

Quinn grunted. "Still, good work, Brimm."

As the forensic tech ducked out of the room, Adam said to Quinn, "Did you know Sergeant Moody has an explosives background from his military days?"

"I was aware of his Army stint. But no, I hadn't heard about that particular unit. How long have you known about this, Dutton?"

Adam cleared his throat. "I found out after the bombing on my house."

Quinn glared at him. "And didn't tell me until now?" Then, he sighed. "Hell. I understand you've been put in the middle, thanks to Moody, Lehmann, and their grudges."

"I had no proof—and still don't—Moody was behind the attack on me. And you're right. I was afraid it would look like sour grapes." Adam rubbed his eyes. "What do you want me to do about this, sir?"

"Keep your distance as much as possible, both of you. Be professional when required, and let me do some discreet inquiring myself."

"Inquiries, sir?"

"This matter has to be handled delicately due to potential political and financial repercussions. As a matter of fact, we shouldn't even be having this discussion. But I want to reiterate that I'd hate to lose two of the best detectives this department has ever had."

Jinks spoke up, "Thank you for that, sir."

"Moody may be a dirty cop. If so, one way or the other, I'll find that out." Chief Quinn's expression darkened. "But if it's true, he's a well-connected dirty cop. Making this a far more delicate problem than it would be, otherwise."

Quinn stabbed the stack of papers with a pencil, make a hole through the center. "Getting back to the arsons, what else you got?"

Adam replied, "We're having problems getting in touch with Belle Lake. I want to see whether Kozak tried to buy her brother's antiques store like Annika Grimes and Justin Garone. It would be too coincidental if all three had the same offers and refused right before their businesses burned to the ground. And we'll have to contact the owners of the two older arsons."

Quinn nodded. "No luck tracking down Redbeard?"

"The local PD around Stowe are on the lookout. We couldn't get the state police to send up one of their recon drones."

"They're pretty squirrelly about using those."

Jinks piped up, "Might not matter. A fugitive might see them and be able to hide in time, anyway."

The chief leaned forward over his desk and scanned the top of the paper stack. "Are you keeping the state BCI detectives apprised of your progress?"

Adam answered in the affirmative. "But if we don't get something to break soon, they may want to start poking their noses around. And you know how we love being busted down to 'assistant.'"

Jinks added, "Had some luck getting Jared Lake's bank records via subpoena. To dig into that sudden infusion of funds."

"What did you find out?"

"All cash, no checks or money transfers."

"How much cash?"

"Oh, just some little mad money. To the tune of a hundred thousand dollars."

Quinn whistled. "Mad money, indeed."

"The credit card companies came through, too. All his debts had been paid off recently."

"You don't say. Sounds like Jared Lake took some tantalizing secrets to his grave. But it just so happens we're in the business of uncovering secrets, so—"

"We're on it, sir." Jinks smiled.

Once the chief dismissed them, they headed back to Adam's office, where Jinks brought him up to date on her pharmacy robbery case. "We had a break, lucky for us, so that's one case looking like it's close to being solved."

"What happened?"

"The poor schlub wanted to get his hands on some opioids. But what he didn't realize was you have to go through the Seven Circles of Hell to get to them these days. What with all the high-tech security."

"Pharmacies are becoming more like bank vaults."

"You'll have to give a kidney and your first-born just to get some Tylenol."

Adam grinned. "Jacob?"

"*He* was a pill this morning, so handing him over sounds good right now. But ask me later when he's all sweet and innocent again."

Jinks leaned against the wall. "Felicia ran into Beverly Laborde the other day."

"Where?"

"Miralee's. Felicia liked her. Even invited her to our Christmas party. You know you're welcome, as always. Felicia's going to make her famous Pork Wellington with Prosciutto and Spinach-Mushroom Stuffing."

Adam looked at her askance. "Are you going to cook, too?" Jinks's lack of cooking skills were legendary in the department. No one ever asked her to make anything for the company picnics anymore.

"You're in luck. I'm in charge of the drinks. Pomegranate Cosmos with orange liqueur and extra vodka."

"Sounds good." Then Adam started salivating. "Is Felicia making those Cranberry Brie Bites again?"

"If it'll get you to come, it's on the menu. One day, you're going to have to unleash your amazing gourmet self again and host the Christmas dinner."

"You remember what happened last time I tried."

"We got a call right in the middle of it."

"Exactly. Cooking is best left to civilians, especially when there are kids involved. Don't want to ruin their holiday fun."

"Well then, you can bring the dessert."

He grinned, "I have a great recipe for Christmas Bombe. Spiced cake and chocolate-brandy glaze with sparklers on top."

She snorted at that. "Maybe *you're* the real arsonist."

24

Beverly waited with anticipation alongside Mr. X in her car outside their next target. She wanted to get their stories straight, but first, she had to know something, "What happened to your ex-wife of one month, the opera singer?"

"I was attracted to her voice. But then I found out I was attracted to her brother even more."

Beverly laughed. "Oh, the relationship-merry-go-round. Everybody seems so ready to get on until they've had a few spins. And then they're quite ready to get off."

"Have you not felt the nesting urge, Beverly?"

She looked down at her magenta nails. "I don't do relationships well."

"Not even with the dashing Detective Dutton?"

"Don't know where our relationship, or lack thereof, stands right now. Or what I really want."

"It's best not to push yourself into these things. They tend to play out as they are meant to."

Beverly nodded. "You think you can draw on your one-month stint as a husband to play one now?"

He tilted his head. "Come again?"

She ducked out of the car long enough to grab a few items from her kit in the trunk. After she slid into the driver's seat, she put on her curly red wig and popped in some green contact lenses. "If we're going to check out this guy, I think it would go better if I went as a wife with a husband in tow. Men tend to talk to other men more than they do single women."

"Do they really?"

"Not you, perhaps. But it's that way with car mechanics. And one study even found doctors listen more to women when they have a male partner with them."

"I offer apologies for my gender on your behalf."

"Nice to know there are exceptions." She smiled at him. "Thanks again for letting me tag along with Gorrie Sidman."

"That was a spot of fun for me, as well." He glanced out the window at the sign on the office in front of them. "Though I'm a bit puzzled why we're at an insurance business."

"Adam let it slip about the attorney, Douglas Marcell, that Gorrie Sidman mentioned. And now I want to find out more about him since he's in thick with the whole NAL crime syndicate. Maybe even Kozak and by extension, the arsons."

"I'm familiar with Marcell from my Forsythe days, and he with me. I would be recognized."

"That's why we're here instead. Marcell was in private practice when he repped Redbeard and the Forsythes. But he was once part of a firm, Lassetter & Lorens."

"I'm not following."

"Lassetter & Lorens used to represent both Forsythes. One of the other former members of that firm now works someplace else. And get this, as an insurance rep. Business insurance in case, say, a business burns down."

"And you're thinking this person had something to do with the arsons?"

"One way to find out. Besides, the guy sort of has a connection to Redbeard and Forsythe and Marcell, too, so it's a win-win. Even if he didn't have anything to do with the arsons himself."

"What's the man's name? I need to be certain I've not had any dealings with him."

"Oh, you haven't. His name is Mark Grightell, originally from Maine. He only joined Marcell's old firm, Lassetter & Lorens, three years ago. And then abruptly quit and set out his shingle as an insurance rep."

"Intriguing, I will hand it to you. Are you sure you want to do this, Beverly? You have mentioned on several occasions how Detective Dutton feels about you stepping on his cases."

Beverly stared down at the steering wheel. "I don't want to step on his case, but I want to protect Harlan and Agnes. And avenge Annika Grimes in my own way."

"All right, then. I shall join you in this charade." He looked bemused when she pulled out a charcoal-gray fedora and some large black-rimmed glasses for him to wear. "And we'll need to make an appointment since these people rarely do drop-ins."

"I might already have made one earlier this morning."

"Isn't that a little presumptuous of you? What if I hadn't been able to come along?"

"I'd not really thought that far ahead yet. But having you along is merely a happy stroke of luck."

She reached into the back seat and grabbed some other items she'd stowed there. "I brought along some insurance of my own in the form of this."

He studied it. "Cups and a thermos? What's in it, arsenic?"

"Something I had the resort whip up for me. A tasty hard cider, with emphasis on the hard. One hundred proof. In my research on Grightell, I found a photo in the *Herald-Gazette* where he was at a party drinking some hard cider. With ruddy cheeks. I suspect he might be a fan."

Mr. X grinned. "You are quite a clever girl. And devious. I'm so proud."

They walked into the office, where Beverly announced to the receptionist she had an appointment. The woman, who sported Christmas-ornament earrings and a reindeer brooch with a flashing red nose, ushered Beverly and Mr. X into a smallish space with standard office furniture. Nothing fancy, just functional. Maybe Mark Grightell, Esquire's business wasn't all that well established just yet?

Beverly reached out to shake Grightell's hand, noting how hairy it was. The hair must have transferred down from his head because the man had a chrome dome. She said, "I hope you don't mind if I brought along my husband."

"Ah, of course not, Mrs. Kornelson." Mark Grightell turned to Xenakis and shook his hand, too. "Mr. Kornelson."

Beverly dug right in. "As I mentioned over the phone, Mr. Grightell, we're setting up a new restaurant nearby and want preliminary information on business insurance. Especially after the recent fires in the area."

She placed the thermos on the desk. "I took the liberty of bringing along some refreshments. My famous cider. In honor of the season." Before he could refuse, she poured Grightell a full cup of the hard cider and gave herself and Mr. X a teensy amount.

Grightell seemed a little hesitant at first, but once he got a whiff, he said, "That smells quite good. And this place is a tad drafty."

Beverly said, "As I'm sure you can understand, we like to check out our partners before we settle into any sort of agreement. You worked for a law firm before going into insurance. Lassetter & Lorens?"

"Yes, that's correct."

"What made you want to switch from the legal field to the insurance field just like that?"

He squirmed a little in his seat and took a deep gulp of the cider. He struggled to put on a neutral expression as he stammered out, "I feel I can help more people this way. Less red tape and legalese."

Mr. X got into the spirit of things and said in a conspiratorial tone, "You got out just in time. I understand there's been quite a spot of trouble at Lassetter & Lorens lately. Or so the rumors go."

Grightell squirmed a little more. "I suppose so."

Mr. X continued, "I've had dealings with a man connected to them before, when a friend of mine was setting up an antiques store. Reggie Forsythe was the man's name. Quite a piece of work, that one."

Grightell took another big gulp of the hard cider, and the tension in his shoulders started to relax. Beverly hid a smile. Maybe the cider was already beginning to work.

He licked his lips. "To be honest, that's why I got out of that biz. I can't really speak about my former employer per se, but . . . I was no longer comfortable there. Lots of bad vibes, lots of strange goings-on. Lots of clients charged with crimes who got out on bail and then disappeared. Far more than average."

Beverly put her hand over her throat and feigned shock. "I think I read about the latest client in the papers. Some guy arrested for being an accessory to the murder of that man who had a sword run through him into a tree. How ghastly. I believe his name was Darnell something, like the movies. Warner Brothers. That's it, Darnell Warner."

She put on a show of appearing triumphant that she'd thought of the name. "Such an odd name, don't you think? It could be fake."

Grightell was obviously enjoying the cider now, and Beverly poured him some more. He seemed oblivious to the fact Beverly and Mr. X weren't having much at all. "Yes, I read that, too. His attorney was Douglas Marcell, used to work for Lassetter & Lorens the first year I was there. Speaking of pieces of work. Marcell scared me, to be honest. Very shady character."

Grightell belched. "This is like the third client of Marcell's who's up and disappeared while on bail Marcell arranged. I think all three of 'em were associated with a murder, which makes it even more remarkable he got 'em out. Some kind of magician or he bribed a corrupt judge or something."

Beverly shook her head. "I hope you don't know this Darnell Warner character first-hand. If he's out there, he's probably still dangerous."

"As a matter of fact, I did run into him. He's been a client of Marcell's for a while. Low-level stuff. Attempted robbery and burglary."

"Where does he live? I mean, surely the police can just go and find him there?"

"Think he's got a friend who lives in Brattleboro. I think it was Brattleboro. Heh, funny name for a town, isn't it?" He sounded it out slowly. "Bratt . . . ull . . . burro."

"Your friend's name wouldn't be Kojak, would it?" She mispronounced the name.

"Kojak? Oh, you mean Ivon Kozak." Despite his increasingly inebriated state, Grightell's face turned serious. "Not Kozak, no. Graves or something, I think."

Worried her cider-ploy might be working too well, and the man would be useless, Beverly hastily changed the subject back to Warner. "I do hope they catch this Warner fellow soon. I'll feel much safer when he's not out there on the streets. Can you imagine? Him being connected to a murder and out there free as you please?"

"Not just murder and robbery. I think he also likes to play with matches. If you get my drift."

Beverly clucked her tongue and patted Mr. X on the arm. "Oh my. I think we'll be locking our windows extra tightly tonight, won't we, dear?"

Mr. X replied, "You know how I love security, darling."

With Grightell nearly three sheets to the wind after Beverly refilled his cup again, she gave Mr. X a small nod, and they asked some questions about business insurance and then left.

Standing outside her car, Beverly said, "Yes, I do know how you love security. But, 'darling?' Wasn't that laying it on a bit thick?"

"You'd already used 'dear,' so I had to scrape the barrel. 'Sweetie' seems gauche for you, Beverly. You definitely look more like a darling that a sweetie."

He gave her a stern look. "I know what you're thinking Beverly Laborde, and I'm afraid I will not let you drive down to Brattleboro looking for Darnell Warner's friend. If I have to, I'll kidnap you and hide you behind some of that security."

"Redbeard was in a military explosives unit, and he also likes to play with matches. And he has ties leading right to Kozak. I hate waiting around for justice. It's downright glacial."

"Not to mention that sometimes justice also gets lost in the process."

"And there's that."

"Beverly, we nailed Reggie Forsythe, we can get Kozak if he's the person responsible. Remember, we have a lot of hearsay but no proof."

She tapped her foot. "You're starting to sound like Adam."

"In a good way, I hope."

"That remains to be seen."

He wagged his finger at her but said, "I forgot to mention I've heard via my antiques connections that Jared Lake recently sold a very valuable piece of Burmese sapphire jewelry to a dealer in Canada. An under-the-table deal. He must not have wanted it to be known to the taxman ... or someone else, perhaps."

"But why did he sell it now if he owned it all these years?"

"Why, indeed? Seems unlikely, don't you think?"

Beverly thought about that. "Especially since he'd had chronic financial problems."

"There was no provenance attached to the item, so they had no idea of its recent ownership other than Lake."

"How much did he get for it?"

"A hundred grand."

Beverly whistled. "That's a pretty big under-the-table deal."

"Quite."

"Kozak is an expert on that type of jewelry. Are you thinking what I'm thinking?"

Mr. X nodded. "If Jared Lake stole such an item from Kozak, and Kozak discovered it ... I can imagine there would be some animosity."

"The murder-by-arson type of animosity."

Beverly tossed her used cup into a nearby trashcan, and Xenakis followed suit. He opened his mouth to say something, but she anticipated his question. "I think I drank about four tablespoons. I'm okay to drive."

"We should probably hide the thermos in the trunk. Just in case you get pulled over."

"Yes, dear."

Mr. X held open the car door for her. "After you, darling."

25

Adam dropped his keys on the table next to his door while he kicked off his shoes and pulled off his tie. He examined the front window, admiring the work his contractor had done on it so far. Along with the new red door, Adam was pleased at the way the repairs were turning out. Could hardly tell someone had sent him a pipe bomb that nearly killed him and Beverly.

Too bad he wasn't as pleased with the way the murder and arson cases were coming along. He rubbed the muscles on the back of his neck, the source of a headache he hadn't been able to get rid of all day.

But maybe he shouldn't feel too bad since the PDs in Burlington and Montpelier hadn't solved the antiques store arsons in their jurisdictions yet, either. Maybe if they had, he wouldn't be dealing with it now. He'd tipped them off about Kozak and Redbeard in the hopes it would jumpstart their investigations.

After grabbing a bottle of lager from the fridge, Adam sat on the sofa next to his cellphone, thinking. Ivon Kozak didn't look the part for some sort of criminal mastermind. Zelda used to call such things a case of "short man syndrome."

But if Kozak was their man, he seemed to be having quite a bit of fun at their expense. He had to know that one arson target on a business he'd tried to buy but was rebuffed wouldn't look that suspicious. But three? At least three. Tomorrow he'd try to chat with Belle Lake again to see if Kozak had approached her brother, too.

What would make the man feel so confidant he'd get away with something like that? If it was him, naturally. Jenny-Lee Salant had mentioned large insurance polities on Justin Garone's and Jared Lake's businesses. Maybe it *was* just one big fraud ring. Beverly had been trying to get Adam to tag Ivon Kozak all along as their primo suspect, and maybe she was right—but fraud was the motive.

Adam swallowed some of the beer and relished the sour taste. What in the world was he going to do about Beverly Laborde? If she'd been to see Kozak—and with that fake name, he was sure she had—who knows what else she'd been up to? As if he didn't already have enough on his plate.

Guess he knew how much a promise from Beverly was worth. No, that was not entirely fair, was it? She'd promised only to *try* to avoid using her con-woman skills.

Deciding the beer and gentle stretching weren't doing much to help his sore neck and headache, he headed for the shower. Thank god Zelda had renovated the bathroom and installed that rainfall showerhead before she left him.

He lost track of time standing in the hot water, not wanting to think about anything or feel anything other than relief. But when he started to feel like a lobster, he reluctantly got out. Time to cool off with more of that unfinished beer. He walked out toward the kitchen while rubbing his wet hair with a towel and then became acutely aware he wasn't alone.

Zelda stood in the middle of his living room, staring as his naked body with a big smile on her face. "You're every bit as sexy as you were when we were married, Adam Dutton."

Adam hastily wrapped the towel around his waist, making her laugh. "We were married for ten years. It's nothing I haven't seen before."

He glared at her and perched on one of the kitchen bar stools, making sure the towel was still firmly in place. "Why are you here? And how did you get in?

"As to how, I still have a key. You may have changed the front door, but it still works on the back one."

Adam made a mental note to change the back-door locks tomorrow. "And the why?"

"I've been reading about the antiques store arsons. I wondered if Harlan is okay. I mean, he just got over being charged with murder. It would be horrible if he had to deal with a fire on top of everything else."

"Harlan is fine. And he has some new security tech to help keep him safe."

"I still have a soft spot for Harlan, despite the divorce. And Titus's antagonism and all." She added softly, "He's a good man."

"Yes, he is." Adam drank some more of the beer, wishing it was something stronger.

She pointed at it, "Aren't you going to offer me one, too?"

"You're driving, I assume."

"A soda, then."

He got up to get her an orange soda, which she accepted with a wink. "You still buy these? I'm touched. You must have remembered it's my favorite. Maybe you kept hoping I'd show up again someday?"

Adam rubbed his forehead. The headache seemed to be shifting toward his temples. But she had a point—why hadn't he got rid of those orange sodas? He didn't like the stuff. They must have been in there since the divorce.

Zelda moved closer to where he was standing. "You remember what I said at the courthouse the other day? When I gave you a key to my house? Titus is going to be out of town for eight days in two weeks. I want you to come see me, Adam."

She put the soda down and rubbed her hands up and down his chest. "Adam, I'm so lonely."

"Titus isn't keeping you warm at nights?"

"He's lousy in bed. I crave you, Adam. I need you. And this might be our last chance."

"What do you mean?"

"Titus is definitely throwing his hat into the ring, to officially announce his run for governor. If he wins, it'll change everything."

She looked up at him with a mischievous grin. "I think unwrapping you in your towel might be the best Christmas present I'll get this year. Did you do that just for me?"

He should have reached out a hand to stop her as she grabbed the towel, really he should. But his lower regions were already beginning to respond to that look on her face. She pressed her body against his and pulled his head down into a kiss. And god help him, he kissed her back.

Little alarms kept flashing through his brain. Mayor Lehmann! Illicit affair! Job killer! Alert! Alert! But the limbic part of his brain pushed them away as he succumbed to the feeling of Zelda in his arms again, just like old times. When she "unwrapped" him and tugged him toward the sofa, he knew he was in trouble. Part of him cared, part of him didn't.

She straddled him on the sofa and nibbled on his neck before kissing her way down his chest. Adam closed his eyes and gave in to the sensations with a sigh . . . until his cellphone broke the mood.

He grabbed for it and answered, "Dutton."

It was Jinks reporting on some calls she'd just finished making, nothing urgent. But he'd never been happier to hear from her in his life. He pretended to listen intently, and when he hung up, he told Zelda, "Something's come up. I have to take care of this."

She frowned. "Can't it wait?"

"You may recall that's one of the reasons you left me."

"I do remember. But *you* may recall that I always cashed in my rain checks for sex, so I'm not letting you off the hook. Adam, you are by far the most amazing lover I've ever had. I don't want to give that up."

"I doubt I'm all that." He edged out from under her and rescued the towel again. "I've got to get dressed and go. Duty calls."

Zelda pouted. "You were responding to me. You still have feelings for me, don't you?"

"Zelda, I can't talk about this now."

"Later, then."

He managed to get rid of her but was shaken up at how close he'd come to having an affair with a married woman. Even if she was his ex-wife. He recalled the chief's question to him only a few days ago, "Seen Zelda lately?"

Adam had to laugh and shake his head at that. Oh, yes, he'd seen her all right. Although she'd seen a lot more of him. He didn't know what was more disturbing—that he'd let himself get carried away in a moment of weakness or that it wasn't Zelda he'd been thinking about when he closed his eyes as she seduced him.

Wherever Beverly was tonight, he hoped she was safe. Although knowing her, she was probably taking lion-taming lessons using only a fork and spoon as weapons. Or maybe she was learning to ride one of Xenakis's yaks. She was trouble with a giant, flashing "T." Perhaps that was why she was making more frequent appearances in his dreams. Yeah, that must be it.

26

Thursday, December 17

Beverly sat down across from Adam and studied his face. He seemed a little off, but she couldn't quite put her finger on it. She'd asked to meet him here at the Crossroads Café in hopes she could declare a truce. She owed him that. And more.

She looked at the menu. "As I recall, you said the fist-sized bacon cheddar muffins and homemade chorizo hash are their specialties."

"None any better that I've found."

When the waitress came to take their orders, they ordered the same thing along with some coffee Adam asked to be "extra black." She raised an eyebrow. "Didn't sleep well?"

"Not much."

He didn't seem forthcoming with any further details, and she didn't want to pry. Well, actually, she did, but she bit her tongue. Instead, she told him, "I'm going to order food to go when we're ready to leave. For Annika Grimes."

"Have you talked to her lately? How's she doing?"

"Much better. Still upset about her business. But Harlan, Prospero, and other folks they corralled picked through the remains from the fire to rescue what they could." When Adam opened his mouth, she added quickly, "Harlan checked with your Chief Quinn first. He said it was okay."

Adam mumbled, "Could have asked me."

"He didn't want to put you in the middle again. Says he's been doing too much of that lately. This way, if anyone got in trouble over it, it would be your boss, not you."

Adam still looked upset, but after he'd settled down again a bit, he asked, "I gather this is a 'working' breakfast?"

Oh, how she wished it weren't. She'd like nothing better than to be just enjoying a nice meal with him. But she'd decided to tell him what she'd learned yesterday. "Mr. X found out Redbeard was in the Army along with Sgt. Moody in the same explosives unit." She left out the part about Gorrie's museum.

Adam whistled. "That may be how Redbeard and Moody are connected. And may point to both of them being behind the bombing on my house."

"And the arsons?"

"Maybe even the arsons. The report from the arson techs came in, and it appears the same sort of technique was involved in two of them, and Joe Brimm has found some links to the other three."

Beverly frowned. "Five? I thought there were only three?" She started to panic for a moment, thinking Harlan's shop had been targeted, and he and Adam hadn't wanted her to know.

"In addition to Justin Garone, Jared Lake, and Annika Grimes, there were two earlier fires this year in different parts of the state."

"All antiques stores? Where?"

"There was a place called What on Earth up in Burlington. And a Yesterday's Curios in Montpelier."

Beverly whipped out her cellphone and called up a bookmark she'd saved. As Adam watched with a curious expression, she turned the phone around to show him.

"Those five stores—look at their names. Yesterday's Curios. What on Earth. Vintage Vibes. True Gems. Y, W, V, T. It's like the arsonist is going in reverse alphabetical order." She pointed at the list. "Which would make Tossed Treasures close in line. Harlan's store."

Adam considered that idea for a moment. "What about Garone's shop, Main Street Antiques? It doesn't fit."

"Oh." She frowned. "Still, if I'm right, then . . . "

"We've got patrols around Harlan's shop. And there's all the new security he's added."

"I hope so." She waited as the waitress refilled their cups. When the woman had left, she continued, "Mr. X found out something else about Redbeard. He has a friend who lives in Brattleboro. Something you could check into, maybe?"

"Do you know this friend's name?"

"Graves, I think. It was kind of hazy."

Adam looked over his coffee mug at her. "Hazy?"

Beverly didn't want him to press too deeply, so she changed the subject to give him more of the Gorrie Sidman intel. "Moody had dealings with a bookie and loan shark, Leroy Schick."

"This also via Xenakis?"

Beverly nodded.

Adam wrinkled his nose. "Gotta wonder how your Mr. X is getting this information all of a sudden."

"You know how connected he is with all the former NAL gang. He knows a bit about everyone."

"Why do I think you aren't telling me the whole story? You weren't out on your own getting into trouble again?"

His accusation, although accurate, still stung. Why wouldn't he just let it go? Wearily, she laughed it away, saying, "I paid a visit to Mr. X, that's how I found out about it. We . . . *he* had done some more digging. He also found out Moody was deeply in debt to Forsythe and maybe even Kozak. Off-the-book debts."

Adam grunted. "Maybe I should just hand Mr. X my badge and retire. Someplace warmer. With a lot of fishing."

He was scowling now, and Beverly didn't know how much more she should reveal of her "investigating" with Mr. X. Not wanting to deepen his foul mood, she said, "I did a smidgeon of antiques investigation, myself. Found out that Ivon Kozak has a fondness for Burmese sapphire jewelry."

"What is that?"

"Burmese sapphires among the finest in the world, known for their royal blue color and superior luster. And a Burmese sapphire necklace came on the market recently. Guess who the seller was?"

"Who?"

"Jared Lake. To a dealer in Canada, but it was off the books. For one hundred grand."

"Funny, that. Lucas stole an item or two from Jared Lake's shop that he sold to make money." Adam tilted back in his chair. "So, Lucas, the assistant, steals from the owner, Jared Lake, who in turn steals from another owner, Ivon Kozak?"

"Seems like a logical leap."

"Before I met you, I had no idea the antiques business was so cut-throat and filled with intrigue."

"Every tree has some bad apples. Look at the police business. I mean, there's Moody, right?"

Adam grimaced. "Yeah. Crooked cops made us all look bad."

"But you do such great work. Most of you. Although I'm getting impatient with all the side investigations. I still firmly believe Ivon Kozak is behind all the arsons."

"Con woman's intuition?" He gave her a half-mocking smile.

"From my experience with my uncle, I'm sure this guy is cut from the same cloth. And used the same sort of underhanded tactics my uncle did."

Realizing she was getting too animated, she took a few deep breaths and added, "I won't rest easy until all of them are behind bars or gone on to their own forever judgment day."

"Including your friend Annika Grimes? If she's involved, that is."

"You can't seriously believe Annika Grimes had anything to do with this, can you?"

"We haven't ruled out anyone completely."

Damn, he really was in a foul mood. Was he angry with her? Or was it simply work-related? She got a little testy, herself. "You don't seem happy about the news of Redbeard and Moody. Won't it help solve the case of who's behind the pipe bomb and arsons?"

"It's more complicated than that."

Their food arrived, and he seemed to be as eager to have an excuse not to talk as she was. This certainly wasn't going the way she'd planned, not at all.

After several minutes of chewing in silence, he said, "Leads are always appreciated. I just don't want you to get involved and almost get yourself killed again. Especially when I'm still not one hundred percent sure I trust Xenakis's motives."

"And let yourself get killed instead? That's okay?"

"It's my job, Beverly. But it's not yours. Speaking of which, have you thought some more about getting work in the area? Agnes's shop or Harlan or another place, perhaps?"

"I'm not so sure you want me around getting in your way, as you say."

He looked at her with exasperation. "That's not what I said, and you know it. Stop trying to be so obtuse."

She smiled briefly at that. "Obtuse? That's not a word I'd expect you to say."

"Why, because I'm a hick cop who didn't go to Dartmouth?"

Beverly could tell he regretted saying it as soon as the words left his mouth. But the damage was done. She hadn't done anything to deserve being the target of his ire, not like this. She had no idea why he was in such a bad mood, but right then, it didn't matter. He didn't trust Mr. X? And it sounded like he didn't trust her, too?

They managed to finish the rest of their meal in complete silence, and Beverly hurriedly placed a to-go order for Annika and left as soon as she could. What in the world had gotten into him?

She'd put it down to stress—but she'd seen him under much worse, and he hadn't reacted that way. Whatever it was, she was going to be giving him a wide berth from now on. Until he apologized. Or until she was through with this whole NAL mess.

Who was she kidding? She missed him already.

27

Adam stomped into the station, but if anyone was taking note of his mood, they didn't say anything. He did notice Joe Brimm starting out into the hall until he took one look at Adam and walked right back into his lab.

Jinks, as always, wasn't shy about stating the obvious. "Aren't we Mr. Sunshine this morning?"

"Not now, Jinks."

She folded her arms across her chest and stared him down. Finally, he muttered, "I'm surprised you didn't see my tail tucked between my legs."

"Let me guess. Woman trouble."

Adam's eyes widened. "Is it that obvious?"

"I've been with you how long now? So who is it—Beverly or Zelda."

"Both."

"Any time you need me to put on my boxing gloves and take 'em down for you, just ask."

"Gee, thanks, Jinks." But that made him smile a little.

She said, "Got some news for you. I checked around on couriers. To see if I could track down who arranged for the package with the pipe bomb at your house."

"You had some luck, I take it?"

"Yeah, after your neighbor said she thought she saw the delivery van dropping off a package that day. With her teensy bit of description, think I've found a good prospect. A one-man company that specializes in odd but discreet deliveries."

"How discreet?"

"His motto is 'we specialize in fab, not gab,' according to his website."

He snorted. "That's terrible. But it does sound like a good target. Thanks, Jinks. Want to come with?"

"I'm waiting on some calls from the DFR and NAIC about some fraud claims. Might be related to our cases. But if you get in a bind—"

"I'll whistle for you."

Adam waved Jinks off to work on her fraud line of investigation and sat staring at his computer. He was still smarting from his less-than-satisfying breakfast with Beverly, something he felt pretty bad about. Maybe it was a reaction to Zelda and his almost giving into temptation? Some of it was genuine concern for Beverly's welfare since he knew what these NAL gang people are capable of. She'd already been in jeopardy far more than he'd like.

But he wasn't at all proud of himself for the way he handled it. Hell, maybe that's yet another reason Zelda left him. Not just because she wanted to be Mrs. Somebody Mayor's Wife. He hadn't always been the greatest communicator.

He sighed and tackled the computer keyboard with a little too much vengeance. The letters were already wearing off with all the pounding he'd given them. He started off with digging through some records but was interrupted by the "ding" from an email notification. It was from a source who'd known Darnell Warner, aka Redbeard, and was able to verify that the guy was indeed in the same unit as Sergeant Moody, explosives and all.

Adam stared at the email, then jumped up and stalked down the hall to find Moody. The sergeant looked up with a surprised expression when Adam found him in the break room, where fortunately, he was alone. "Did you know Darnell Warner? You were in the same Army unit together."

Moody jutted his chin out. "I was in the unit with a lot of guys. Think I might recall that name, but if was the same fellow, he left shortly after I transferred in."

"You were both in a unit that handled explosives, right?"

"You go where you're assigned. I mean, I didn't ask for it or anything."

Moody whirled around in his chair to face Adam. "I don't see it would have much to do with your arson case. I mean, Warner wasn't into antiques. No reason for him to be involved with arson. Besides, I don't think he's all that creative. Or that bright."

Ordinarily, Adam would have laughed in Moody's face at the intimation that Moody was a much smarter fellow who'd made something of himself, unlike Redbeard. But he wasn't in the mood for Moody's smug arrogance. "Have you been in touch with Warner recently?"

"Why would I? Like I said, I don't really know the guy." Moody narrowed his eyes at Adam. "Thought you would have caught him already. Maybe he's brighter than I thought if he's given you the slip this long."

Moody maintained his usual combative asshole persona, even as he was trying to deflect attention away from himself. Fine. Adam would play that game for now, but he didn't know how much longer he could take the sergeant's attitude.

Remembering how Chief Quinn had said to leave Moody to him, Adam made nice with Moody by offering him a couple of tickets to a rock concert that weekend a friend had given him. The last thing Adam wanted to do was spoil Quinn's plan, whatever it was.

Adam returned to his office long enough to grab his coat and the directions Jinks had printed out for him with the courier's street address. Her directions were always spot-on, and he found them easier to follow than a GPS. Diligent Deliveries wasn't exactly in the best part of town, situated next to the infamous Class-A Massage Parlor—what his fellow cops had dubbed the "touch my ass" parlor. Just what kind of business did the guy expect to get with that address?

The proprietor, Leon Nolen, looked like he fit the area. He gave off a '70s vibe with shoulder-length dark, wavy hair and a mustache. He even had his shirt unbuttoned half-way, exposing gold and silver chains.

Adam showed him his badge, and Nolen's hands immediately started twitching. "What seems to be the trouble, Detective?"

"A couple months ago, you delivered a package to this address." Adam pulled out a piece of paper with his own address printed on it.

Nolen frowned. "Maybe. I don't remember everywhere I go, man."

Adam pointed to the date he'd written on the paper. "It was on this date."

"Look, Detective. I'm an honest businessman. But I don't have a way of checking what people put inside their packages and whether *they're* honest. I have them sign a waiver, that's it. I don't X-ray or open the packages to make sure. Just like the post office."

"Do you keep logs?"

"You bet, but I don't wanna give up that information without a subpoena. Customers like to know their privacy is gold."

"I can return with one of those subpoenas. But if I find out you've tampered with the logs in the meantime, it won't go well for you. Something to keep in mind."

Nolen shrugged. "Whatever, man. You won't find

anything, so I'm not worried." His words might say so, but the way his hands were twitching even harder said otherwise. Afraid of Adam? Or someone else?

"Have you seen this man?" Adam showed Nolen a mugshot of Redbeard.

"Red hair and beard? Somebody like that would stand out, wouldn't they?"

"Did you see him or not?

"I don't have the greatest memory, you know?"

Adam looked around the space and spied a computer and laser printer for customers to print out copies of documents. "Mind if I use that?"

"Sure, man." More hand twitching.

Adam sat down and created a test document similar to the threatening notes, with a series of different fonts and colors. He also printed an envelope, using his own address. But it didn't seem to match the threatening notes he and the others had received.

Then he spied a computer and printer in a far corner off by themselves. He hopped up and headed for them as Nolen called out, "Those aren't for customers."

"I'll pay you for all the copies." Adam didn't wait for the man to head him off and sat down to make a similar note to the one he'd created at the first printer. He noted this printer was an inkjet, not a laser.

After he printed out his test, he waved it at Nolen. "The red ink is faded."

"That piece of crap is old. Can't get cartridges for it these days. I told ya, it's not for customers."

Adam paid Nolen for the copies and promised to return with a subpoena.

Nolen shrugged again, but his twitching hands were now like drums on the counter. "Sure, man, sure. Whatever floats your boat."

When Adam climbed back into his car and pulled away, he saw Nolen peering out the window after him with his hand glued to a cellphone. Somehow, Adam didn't think he was calling for a pizza delivery.

§ § §

It had been a couple days since Adam had tried to get in touch with Belle Lake over the phone, so he decided to stop by her house before heading back to the station. She was home, but to his surprise, she seemed hesitant to talk to him. Since she couldn't exactly refuse, she opened the door and showed him to a hard wooden chair. Her posture was as wooden as the chair, and her demeanor decidedly cooler than before.

"Mrs. Lake, I won't take much of your time. I'm curious— did your brother Jared ever get an offer from Ivon Kozak to buy out his business?"

"Ivon Kozak?" She sounded out the name slowly. "I'm not sure. I never knew those details about Jared's business."

Adam took a stab in the dark. "Has an insurance investigator by the name of Jenny-Lee Salant been talking to you? Perhaps about insurance fraud?"

Belle's face turned red. "Yes, I've talked to 'that person.' But I really don't want to discuss anything further without my lawyer present."

Adam was concerned about the attitude change, so he took another chance and pulled out one of the threatening notes he'd created at the delivery shop. "Have you received something like this?"

Her eyes were frozen in shock. She didn't answer right away, so he took that as a yes. "Several people have been getting them. Do you mind if I see yours?"

She hesitated. "Still think I should call my lawyer first."

"Letting me see the note won't get you into any trouble, I promise. In fact, a similar note was even sent to me."

After sitting there wringing her hands for a moment, she got up and disappeared into the back of the house. When she returned, she handed him an envelope and note. He held it by the corners and studied it. It looked like the same kind the others had received. Maybe Adam should rethink his earlier idea that the letters were only being sent to people he cared about as a veiled threat to him. On the other hand, it didn't mean the same person was behind all of them.

Hoping he'd made a little thaw in her ice, he asked again about Kozak. "Are you sure your brother never received a buyout offer?"

"I think I might have heard my brother mentioning something about such a sale offer. But no matter who offered to purchase his shop, he wouldn't have sold it, I don't think."

"Didn't you say he was having financial problems?"

"Yes, but he loved that place. Had too much history and emotional stakes tied into it."

Adam described the antique sapphire necklace Beverly had told him Jared sold recently and how much he'd got for it. Belle shook her head in surprise. "I helped him out from time to time when his staff was sick. Just to man the cash register. It's been months now, but I certainly don't recall anything expensive like that. He would surely have sold it long ago to pay for his debts."

The next topic was a little dicier, and Adam hoped she wouldn't shut him down. "Belle, the wife of a former employee of Jared's said that Jared may have taken some items from other businesses to sell as his own."

"Stolen, you mean?"

"That was the implication, yes."

She frowned. "He was knee-deep in debt. Folks do desperate things when that happens. To be honest, I guess I wouldn't be surprised."

"You didn't hear your brother mention any vendettas against him for this? Perhaps someone found out and threatened him?"

"No, nothing like that."

Adam had one other thing to ask, and it was an even trickier question. "This former employee also indicated Jared was a little too friendly when teenage girls who came into the store."

Belle sat up straighter and stayed silent for a few moments. When the moments stretched out to a full minute, Adam was afraid she'd show him the door.

But she finally said, "That would surprise me even less than the thefts. I witnessed something like that myself a few years ago. Put it down to middle-aged-man syndrome. But then, Jared was never good with strong women. The younger ones might have seemed less threatening."

"And again, no hints of jealous boyfriends or angry fathers?"

"Not at all. I'm sorry, Detective. Guess I really didn't know my brother as well as I should have." She looked down at her hands as she picked at her nails.

"I know this has all been quite hard on you, Belle. And thanks for being honest with me." He gave her a big smile and thanked her for her time, exacting a promise she'd let him know if she received any other strange notes or saw anything suspicious.

Before he left, though, he wanted to say one other thing. "Since we're on the topic of thefts, I feel obliged to tell you Lucas Barratt confessed to stealing an item from your late brother's store. He's offered to pay back the money he got for selling it."

She waved it off. "That's ancient history. Like everything else. I have to deal with the legal and insurance aspects of my brother's estate, and that's all I want to deal with. Besides, if my brother had been a better businessman, he could have paid his employees better. And then that poor man wouldn't have felt it necessary to resort to such an act in the first place."

Once back in his car, Adam placed Belle Lake's note on the passenger seat and stared at it. More fodder for Joe Brimm, and more headaches for Adam. Had Jared Lake received one, too, before he died? If so, all traces had likely burned up and vanished in the fire along with all the other aspects of Jared Lake's unfortunate life.

28

Beverly kept going over her breakfast meeting with Adam in her head. Had she said something wrong? Had he received some horrible news that set him off? Something he didn't want to tell her about?

She'd put on a happy face when she stopped by the give Annika the meal she'd bought at Crossroads Café, but Annika could tell she was upset. Beverly changed the subject and focused on the other woman, who was thankfully doing much better. She talked nonstop about how generous Harlan and others had been and how she was looking forward to re-opening her store in a few months or so after repairs were made.

After spending an hour with Annika, Beverly politely excused herself to pick up some pain meds from the drugstore. During her little outing with Mr. X at Gorrie Sidman's strange museum, she'd hit her knee on a wooden crate in the basement. She'd ignored the pain at first, but it hadn't improved as much as she'd hoped.

Just as she was heading into the store, she spied a familiar woman with short auburn hair who made her want to turn the other way. Zelda Lehmann. But it was too late—Zelda had also seen her.

She gave Beverly a haughty smile. "Beverly Laforde. As I live and breathe."

Did people really still say that? And still the wrong name, of course. Beverly gritted her teeth. "How are you, Zelda?"

"Oh, I'm doing quite well, thank you. I mean, it's such a lovely day with all this sunshine. And I enjoyed seeing Adam last night. With emphasis on the seeing part."

Beverly stared at her but didn't say anything. Where would she have seen Adam?

Zelda patted her perfectly coifed hair. "When I arrived at Adam's house to drop off something for Titus, I caught him right as he was coming out of the shower. Naked as the day he was born. You know how things go." Zelda laughed. "One thing led to another and let's just say it was a wonderful evening."

"I see." Beverly kept her face neutral and imitated Zelda's syrupy tone. "I'm sure Mayor Lehmann was happy to have your assistance playing delivery girl. And just how is your fine husband? Does he know about you 'seeing' Adam?"

Zelda tugged on her opal earring. "Titus is Titus. Busy as always." When a car drove up and parked right in front of them, Zelda waved and turned to leave.

Beverly called out after her, "It was so nice running into you, Zelda."

Sure it was. Beverly marched into the drugstore, grabbed her pills, and got out as soon as she could. But the whole time, she was seething. Oh, she knew Zelda was jealous of Beverly's relationship with Adam. And she knew all about Zelda's attempts at seducing Adam because he'd been forthright with her about it. At least, she'd thought so. Had he changed his mind about getting back together with his ex-wife?

Afraid she'd turn into a road-raging driver if she wasn't careful, she climbed into her car, took some deep breaths, and focused on her driving. What she needed was a friendly face, and one of the friendliest she knew was Agnes Flamm.

What she hadn't expected was for another friendly face to be there, surprised to find Harlan at Agnes's shop again. In fact, she was fairly sure he'd been there a lot lately. She gave him a big hug and asked, "Is the antiques store okay? No attempted arson?"

"Prospero and that Mr. X fellow have set me up with some amazing security. Maybe you were right about him, after all. I'll be fine, Beverly. Don't you fret now."

She looked around for Agnes and the other staff, and Harlan helpfully told her, "Sharon's on the café side working with customers. Blaine's in the stock room. Agnes had to run to the bank but should be back any minute."

Any minute was right, as the woman in question strolled into the store at the exact moment. She smiled when she saw Beverly, but her smile morphed into a small frown when she got a better look at her. "You look you've had some bad news. Spill."

"I'm not sure I want to talk about it."

"Sharing burdens makes them lighter."

Beverly sighed, and Harlan patted her on the shoulder. "She's right, you know. Maybe we can help."

"I had an unpleasant encounter with the mayor's wife."

"Ah." Harlan gave a half-smile. "I know Zelda well, of course. I have mixed feelings about her. I kind of liked her when she was married to Adam, though I never thought they were a good match. But after she left him for the mayor, I didn't think as kindly of her. And why is she giving our poor Beverly a hard time?"

Agnes gave Beverly a knowing look and said to Harlan. "We'll discuss it later."

Beverly was grateful Agnes had saved her embarrassment over her feelings—and Zelda's—about Adam. The whole thing was excruciating. This is why she didn't trust romantic attachments. They always turned out badly.

Harlan scratched his chin. "Sometimes I wish I could just deck Mayor Lehmann over his treachery. And the way he puts pressure on Adam and Chief Quinn. In my younger days . . . "

Agnes tapped her foot on the floor. "I don't understand why everyone can't see he's corrupt. Why did he get re-elected?"

Harlan replied, "He tells people what they want to hear, don't you know. Makes for a great politician but a lousy human being."

Beverly stayed a few minutes longer, but they were quite busy with several customers streaming through the store. Feeling like she was in the way, she returned to the Apple Valley Resort. But she didn't go to her room just yet. She was still unsettled and restless.

§ § §

Beverly was in luck because Gloria was working in the resort's café. Beverly also liked talking to Nyssa, but she felt more of a connection to Gloria, who already knew about Zelda and Adam. They sat down at a table since the café was empty at that time of day.

Gloria listened as Beverly vented, nodding in sympathy. "She probably made all of that up, Beverly. You can't believe a word she says. And do you really think she'd leave the mayor—who might be governor someday—and all that money and fame and glory to go back to a police detective? It's not her style."

"Suppose you're right." But there had been something in Zelda's swagger that wasn't there before. Did she and Adam really have sex? After everything he'd said about her?

Gloria frowned. "I've got a little venting to do, too."

"Really? What's the matter?"

"I'm furious with Ramsay about his lawsuit against Harlan. I mean, I understand it's as much about getting revenge on his estranged late father as anything."

"Must have been hard for him with their toxic relationship."

"Ramsay's father never seemed to love him and chose to part ways with him after Ramsay married a Vietnamese wife. Prejudice and all. So while I'm understanding to a point, at the same time, I'm angry." Gloria sighed. "I'm also falling for him more. That makes it harder."

"Harder seems to be the operative word these days."

Gloria looked past Beverly out toward the lobby and sat up straighter. Beverly turned around as a male voice said, "Thought you were going on break soon."

Ramsay Ryall walked toward them and stopped in his tracks when he recognized Beverly. He gave a little bow. "Miss Laborde."

Never one to back down from a fight, Beverly came right out and said, "What's all this about a lawsuit aimed at Harlan, Ramsay?"

"Just looking out after my interests. I only want what's fair, nothing more."

"But a lawsuit? That'll just mean money for lawyers. And it could drag out for years. Neither one of you can afford that."

Ramsay rubbed his hand over his face. "Look, I have to do this. I can't expect you to understand."

That face of his was on the haggard side, and he also walked with a slight limp. Beverly had seen first-hand how hard he worked at the resort, often putting in large amounts of overtime. It wasn't exactly a lucrative job. Extra money sure wouldn't hurt.

She hopped up and grabbed three cups, poured coffee from the urn in each, and handed them out. "My treat."

Ramsay sat down at the table after she added, "Not a bribe. You just looked like you needed it."

He nodded his thanks, added some sugar and cream, and gulped some of the liquid down. Beverly asked, "I've been meaning to talk to you, anyway. Not about Harlan, about Darnell Warner."

"That red-bearded guy? The thug who aided in the murder of my brother? What about him?"

"Have you seen him lately?"

"Why? You think he's stalking me?" Ramsay's eyes widened.

"No, not that. But there's been at least one sighting of him."

Ramsay slumped over the table. "To be honest, I've been looking over my shoulder ever since that guy went AWOL. When that dirty attorney bailed him out. The thing I don't understand is why a slimy lawyer who usually takes on sleazy *rich* clients would represent Warner."

"It's complicated, but Warner—I call him Redbeard—has ties to powerful people."

"Figures. It's funny you should ask if I'd seen him. That's why I asked about the whole stalking thing. Because I thought I noticed Warner following me the other day."

"Are sure it was him?

"Caught a glimpse of red hair. But then, I figured it was my imagination playing tricks. I make sure I carry my gun with me now."

Beverly gave a quick glance at her purse, where her own gun was stowed. "Where did you think you saw him?"

"Over in Mapleville."

The insurance rep, Mark Grightell, mentioned Redbeard had a friend in Brattleboro. Mapleville was even closer. Was Redbeard circling around to the scene of his crime again? Didn't make any sense and seemed far more likely the guy would be in Canada by now after smuggling himself over the border. Or on a boat to the Caribbean.

But Redbeard had been one of Forsythe's lackeys and stayed loyal to his crime boss. It was possible he'd switched loyalties to Ivon Kozak. Could Kozak possibly give him the protection he needed to stay at arm's length from the law in exchange for Redbeard's "talents?"

Forsythe's words in the nursing home haunted her, "Dutton will pay, and so will you." Maybe Forsythe had somehow managed to order Redbeard around during other periods of Forsythe's return to consciousness. And maybe it was he who was running the show and not Kozak. If true, then Adam was in very great danger.

29

Adam stood in front of the old grain elevator factory, studying the deserted building that had graffiti plastered across in neon letters. When he'd looked up the address, he discovered it had been abandoned for a while after a downturn in the grain industry.

It was hard to see all the details in the waning light of the day, but he spied two entrances, one in front and another on the side that was boarded up. It was an unlikely place for a meeting, but this is where his anonymous "informant" had said to come for information about Ivon Kozak.

Adam would have brought Jinks along, but she was delayed tying up pieces of her pharmacy robbery case. He patted the gun in his shoulder holster and peered inside the main entrance. It was even darker than the outside, and when he flipped the one light switch nearby, nothing happened. Figured. Why would anyone pay for electricity in an empty building?

And it was indeed empty, save for all the rotting wooden pallets, rusted metal bars, and leftover equipment lining the two-story structure. The layers of dust must be a foot thick, making it hard sometimes to tell where the floor was. He fought the urge to sneeze and slipped inside the main hall which was open to the second floor—basically a second-floor platform all the way around—with smaller offshoot rooms on the first floor.

There didn't seem to be anyone there, but Adam was sure he had the right place and the right time. He called out, "Anyone here? It's Detective Dutton."

The only reply was more silence and the steady rustling of the wind through the cracks in the walls and ceiling. He kept scanning the space in a methodical manner listening for even the slightest sound. That's why he was able to duck when a shot rang out, a bullet missing him by inches.

Adam skidded into a nearby room, although the cracked walls only gave him partial cover. He didn't return fire, not yet. No reason to give away his exact location.

He wiped his sweating palms on his slacks and tiptoed around a stack of metal containers to get a peek through a section of missing wallboards. But he accidentally kicked an empty aluminum can sending it flying, and the clattering sound echoed throughout the building.

Another shot flew through the opening in the wall, and Adam ducked again. He was at a disadvantage in more ways than one. His attacker had likely scouted the place out beforehand and was more familiar with the layout.

Adam edged through the room toward the end where he spied a small sliver of light pouring through. Another opening, he hoped. He slowed his breathing and listened again for any slightest hint of a noise, rewarded when he heard a scraping sound from the upper story.

With his gun in hand, he picked his way through the room and slipped out the doorway at the rear which brought him out into the larger room. Another bullet rang past him, and he ducked behind a stack of concrete slabs. Bullet-resistant, even if his location wasn't exactly a big secret any longer.

He'd be a sitting duck if he stayed there, so he headed for another room to his right. At the sound of a loud creaking, he looked up just in time to avoid being pummeled by a pulley swinging at him from an overhead chain that crashed into the wall, splintering it.

The bastard had launched a chainsaw blade at him. But Adam's dive out of the way of the pulley had cost him—it knocked his gun out of his hand, and it slid into an opening between the concrete slabs, burying it.

Adam rolled into the room and leaned against the wall. He had a reasonably good idea who his opponent was, and he needed to keep him talking. "That you, Warner?"

A loud bellow of laughter answered him. "You think you're so smart, Dutton. But you couldn't keep me nailed down, could you? I've eluded you and all of those state keystone-cops for weeks."

"Why don't you turn yourself in? The charges you're already facing pale in comparison to shooting an officer of the law."

"That's rich. You've already got enough to put me away for life, and you know it."

While Redbeard was talking, Adam found a hole in the wall of his present room to look out of. His gaze followed the other man's voice toward the top of the second floor, open to the main floor below.

Adam could just make out the other man's silhouette. He must have climbed up the ladder Adam spied, meaning he wouldn't have an easy way down. That might work in Adam's favor.

Redbeard hooted, "You're cornered, Dutton. You aren't going anywhere. But I must admit, you're a hard man to kill. Did you not like that little present I sent you?"

Adam said, "If you mean the pipe bomb, it was real thoughtful."

"Maybe things are getting a little too hot to handle. For you and your friends, wouldn't you say? You think you're smarter than someone like Ivon Kozak, but you're not. He's way ahead of you. And so am I."

The wind had picked up, and the howls coming through the cracks in the building were louder, almost sounding like a movie-ghost groaning. Adam needed to distract the man, and for that, he needed him talking. "I don't think you're so smart at all, Warner. One of the Forsythes is dead, and the other is as good as, right? You and your new pal Kozak will end up just like them."

"Wouldn't count on that."

"What makes you so sure?"

That started Redbeard off on a tirade about the police and how he'd had enough of rules and regulations while he was in the military. Taking the opportunity, Adam spied a tall board with a flat bottom and stood it on its end. He then took off his coat and draped it over the board, pushing it as quietly as he could toward the room's entrance and parking it there.

Time for a little of those hunting and tracking skills Adam's father had taught him when he was just a boy. Think SSS, his father had said—scan your surroundings, study your escape routes, and spot every movement.

At the end of the room Adam was currently in, he spied the outlines of a rope dangling from the ceiling. Another way up to the second floor, perhaps?

Knowing he didn't have a lot of time, Adam gingerly moved to the rope and tugged on it. Seemed safe. It was now or never since Redbeard's rant would wind down any second. Adam was also grateful for his boxing training with Frank Ethridge because it had built up his muscles enough to make the climb up the rope easier than he'd feared.

Somehow, he managed to swing himself over the edge onto the second-floor platform where he rolled behind some boxes that smelled of mold and old grease. Now, if he could just keep Redbeard talking long enough to make a run at him.

But the other man finally stopped his rant and said, "Isn't that right, Dutton?"

When Adam didn't answer, he heard Redbeard shifting his weight around on the second-floor platform, and another shot rang out. From the sound of the bullet's trajectory, Adam was certain the man had aimed for his "double" with the coat.

This hypothesis was proved correct with a loud clattering in the room where his dummy stood. The poor wooden schlub had taken a dive for Adam, and Adam was grateful. But that meant he had no time left for finessing his attack, so he stood up and charged around the boxes toward Redbeard's position.

The man's surprise made him freeze for an instant, but that was all Adam needed to pick up a small wooden pallet and heave it at Redbeard's gun hand. Redbeard started cursing as his gun fell out of his hand and skidded off the edge to the floor one story below. He squatted down to the floor, grabbed something, and then flung handfuls of dust in Adam's direction.

Adam immediately started coughing, and his eyes burned and watered, making it hard to see. He heard the crash of glass breaking, followed by the telltale odor of fire and smoke. First one crash and then another.

Redbeard laughed. "You'll never get out, Dutton. The entrances are all blocked now. Or will be soon."

Adam wiped his eyes with his sleeve and tried his best to clear his vision enough to see what was going on. Redbeard's Molotov cocktail was already spreading a roaring fire at the main entrance to the warehouse. And a second was now blocking Adam's path with tongues of fire lapping at the floorboards.

Redbeard wouldn't have done this without a way to escape. Must be behind the trail of fire ahead. Adam took off his belt, slung it over an exposed pipe above him, and kicked off the wall. He pulled up his feet and propelled himself over the flames until he could jump down in a clear spot ahead.

That's when he spied a glass-free window, and when he looked out, there was a ladder leading all the way to the ground. Damn the man. Adam wasn't about to let him get away a second time.

Adam scrambled down the ladder in record time, ignoring the splinters slicing through his palms, and raced around the front of the building. There, he saw Redbeard standing very still. With his hands in the air.

Adam walked over to the woman holding a gun on Redbeard. "Glad you could make it, Jinks."

"Can't let you have all the fun, Dutton." She nodded at the handcuffs lying on the hood of her car.

Adam grabbed them, twisted Redbeard's arms behind him, and slapped on the cuffs. "Feels good out here. Things were getting a little too toasty inside."

Jinks snorted. "Should have brought my marshmallows."

Redbeard glared at each one of them in turn, and Adam said, "You're really going to owe me this time, Warner. I lost my good winter coat and my best gun."

Redbeard mumbled something that would have made a sailor blush. Jinks said, "Aww, now you've gone and hurt my feelings. And I'm going to have to wash your mouth out with soap for all those curse words."

Adam grinned. "I don't think we have that much soap at the station, Jinks."

30

Friday, December 18

Beverly awoke to the sound of her cellphone ringing. She fumbled around on the nightstand and grabbed the phone as the adrenaline rush made her pulse race. Early morning calls were never good.

But Mr. X greeted her with, "Beverly, I thought you would like to know that Redbeard has been arrested."

"How? When?"

"Yesterday evening. As I understand it, when he tried to kill Detective Dutton by luring him to an abandoned warehouse."

Beverly's brain was now wide awake as she processed that information. But it was the latter part that had her pulse pegging the stratosphere. "Is Adam okay?"

"He is fine, love."

She breathed a huge sigh of relief and immediately wanted to head over to the mini-fridge to pour herself a glass of bubbly. "Thank god for that. And thank god Redbeard is behind bars. Again."

"I have the distinct feeling he won't be let out on bail this time."

Beverly slid out of bed and headed straight for the fridge. Screw the early hour. She was definitely going to have that champagne. "You're a doll for keeping me in the loop. I wouldn't expect Adam to call me about this."

Or would she? After what she'd been through at the hands of Forsythe and Redbeard, didn't Adam owe her that?

After she hung up with the gleeful Xenakis—well, she thought he was gleeful since his voice always had the same emotionless timbre—she pondered what to do next. Hallelujah for Redbeard being in jail, but the story wasn't over, not by a long shot.

There was Ivon Kozak. And Sergeant Moody. Especially after everything she and Mr. X had learned from Gorrie Sidman about Moody's explosives past and his being in debt to Forsythe and Kozak. Being Mayor Lehmann's cousin wasn't exactly a point in his favor, either. Did black-sheep genes run amok in that family?

Beverly tapped on her computer as she sipped on the champagne. Maybe she should start with Mike Moody. Mr. X had let it slip the other day where Moody lived, and Beverly looked up the address in the county tax records. The homeowner was listed as a Donella Seagraves. So the house belonged to her, not Moody? A sister, perhaps, or a cousin or a girlfriend.

It wouldn't hurt just to take a little peep at the house, would it? After throwing on a pair of skinny jeans, a yak-wool cable knit sweater—Mr. X would be so proud—and her favorite Chelsea boots, she made her way to her car and entered the address into the GPS.

As she drew nearer, she looked for places to park where she could observe the house and not be seen acting suspiciously. A holly bush poked out into the street between her target house and its neighbor, so she cut the engine and went into surveillance mode.

She didn't have to wait long and was surprised when Sergeant Mike Moody himself opened the front door of the house. He kissed an attractive red-haired woman who waved after him as he got into a car and headed off.

Beverly called Mr. X on her cellphone. "Do you know anything about a woman named Donella Seagraves?"

"The name sounds vaguely familiar. Let me check for a moment."

She waited as she heard rustling and tapping in the background, and then Mr. X returned. "Donella Seagraves is Redbeard's maternal-side cousin."

Beverly said, "Now isn't that convenient? I just saw Sergeant Mike Moody kissing her as he left Ms. Seagraves's house. Well, technically, the house is listed in her name, so I assume it's hers."

Mr. X said, "Beverly, I applaud your initiative on the one hand. But I urge caution. You wouldn't want to jeopardize any work Adam Dutton and his colleagues are doing."

"I'll be careful. Aren't I always?"

That elicited something that sounded like a bemused chuckle, but he didn't comment on the fact she hadn't exactly promised not to proceed with her plan. After she hung up, she hopped out of the car to rescue some items from her effects-kit in the trunk. Nothing too fancy, since women were more perceptive than men when it came to other women. She didn't want to seem too "fake." Her brown, curly wig and headband, along with fake square-frame eyeglasses, should suffice. And the clipboard, of course.

She knocked on the door and waited.

Donella Seagraves hesitated when she saw the clipboard, so Beverly hurried to say, "Good morning, my name is Barbara Beale. I represent the FEP, an organization that lobbies for firefighters, police officers, and other emergency responders.

We're raising money and awareness and helping to support state legislation to expand services and compensation."

The other woman's expression relaxed into a smile, and she showed Beverly to the front seating area, which was furnished with antiques. If you counted second-hand used furniture as "antiques." The sofa was threadbare, the coffee table was an old footlocker, and the bookshelves were boards propped on top of concrete blocks.

Donella said, "I'm all for helping out first responders. My boyfriend is a police officer, so you can imagine."

"I have a boyfriend who's also an officer," Beverly lied. "But he's in Alaska right now. He grew up in Vermont."

"Must be hard being that far away from him."

"You go where the jobs are. But he hopes to move back here soon." Beverly added, "He's a former enlisted man. He had some kind of dangerous job in the Army. It's classified, so he doesn't talk about it much."

Donella settled into the chair cushions and grabbed a bright purple one with fringe she picked at. "Mike used to be in the Army, too. He worked with explosives, so he knows all about dangerous jobs."

"I've met so many Army types who've returned from combat with PTSD and were wrecks." Beverly felt a little guilty about using that sympathy ploy since she *had* read about military vets committing suicide in way too large a number. She made a silent vow then and there to make a real contribution to a veterans' group after this charade was over.

Donella replied, "Fortunately, Mike managed to avoid combat. He wasn't in for long."

"You must be lucky your boyfriend didn't have all that baggage."

Donella lifted an arm to run through her hair, and Beverly spied bruises on her wrist. Bruises with finger-like tendrils, as if someone had grabbed her. Hard.

Beverly pasted on a smile. "He must be doing very well to buy you this home."

This time, Donella didn't hesitate and jut her jaw out defiantly. "It's my house. He moved in with me."

Beverly said soothingly, "I understand all too well how police officers aren't paid enough. Which is why our lobbying is so important."

"Yes, they're underpaid, but it's not that." Donella sighed. "To be honest, Mike isn't very good with money. He's also a clutterbug. Into video games and has all this paraphernalia lying around. Steampunk gear, consoles, controls of all kinds, goggles." Her cellphone chirped, and she excused herself to take the call.

Donella headed toward the kitchen and closed the swinging door behind her, but Beverly got snippets of the conversation after it appeared to get heated. She tiptoed to the door to eavesdrop.

Donella said, "Look, he'll get the cash. You just got to give him a little more time."

The other woman's voice dipped low again until she uttered a name that made Beverly's blood run cold ... Forsythe. When she heard Donella ending the conversation, Beverly hurried to her seat and pretended to be checking her notes as the woman returned. She looked up to see a mixed expression of fear and anger on Donella's face.

Beverly asked, "I do hope everything's all right. You look like you've had a spot of bad news."

"It's nothing. Just those credit card people. You know how they are." Her laugh rang hollow, and she didn't sit down, rubbing the arm with the bruises.

"It's probably not as bad as you think. And we should all count our blessings considering the horrible stories on the news every day. Like those arsons recently and that poor man they found dead inside one of the buildings. How tragic."

Donella only seemed to half-hear what Beverly had said. The woman was still visibly upset, and Beverly wasn't sure if it was the phone call or her questions, so opted to leave and apologized for getting Donella at a bad time.

Should she call Mr. X or not? She'd promised Adam she wouldn't do this sort of thing, and Mr. X had warned her against it. What to do? But the mention of Forsythe was too great.

She slid into her car and called Xenakis to tell her what she'd been up to.

He sighed. "Oh, Beverly. That is most distressing." He also sounded a little amused until she told him about the Forsythe reference, and he sobered up instantly. "You didn't get any more details from her end?"

"No, and I barely missed her catching me snooping."

"That is still quite interesting. It would certainly seem Sergeant Moody owes money to people he should not. Gorrie Sidman was correct."

"Maybe I needed to bring you along again. Although I suppose you're too recognizable, especially to Moody. Donella might have let Moody know your description, and that would have tipped him off."

Beverly paused for a moment and then sucked air through her teeth when a car drove up to Donella's house. "Speak of the devil," Beverly said. "Guess who just returned home? I got out in the nick of time."

"That was a short trip for him."

"Perhaps he forgot something." But this new development was making her nervous. Even though she had on a disguise, she didn't want Moody to see her, so she ducked down on the passenger seat as she wrapped up her phone call with Mr. X. "I'd better go before he sees me."

She peered over the dashboard and waited until Moody had disappeared inside the house. Then she cranked up the engine and turned around in the direction she'd originally come. She *really* hoped he hadn't seen her. And maybe Donella would be too upset to tell him about Beverly and her imaginary FEP.

She just hoped she hadn't unintentionally made things much more difficult for Adam. She hadn't, had she? Surely, not. Then why was her stomach churning?

Beverly's foot gunned the accelerator pedal as she hurried to the resort and her waiting computer. With a sigh, she resigned herself to creating yet another fake website. And with any luck, she could do it before Sergeant Moody or Donella tried to look it up.

31

Redbeard had immediately demanded his attorney. When he tried to call Douglass Marcell, Esquire, Adam was about as surprised by that choice as he was that rain was wet. Except Redbeard was unable to reach the slimy lawyer. So, they'd decided to let their prisoner stew on that overnight before tackling questioning this morning.

Adam and Jinks took him to the interrogation room, where he gave them the silent treatment as they stood looking down at him. Adam said, "Well now, seems to me you confessed to sending me that pipe bomb that redecorated the front of my house. And I'm guessing you arranged with Leon Nolen to drop it off that day via his shady delivery business."

Redbeard didn't look at Adam or Jinks and kept running his finger along the edge of the table. When Adam mentioned Nolen's name, Redbeard paused his motion for a second before continuing. That was "tell" number one.

Adam continued, "I understand you're friends with Mike Moody."

Redbeard shook his head. "Don't know anybody by that name." This time, the man's eye twitched. "Tell" number two.

"Oh, really? You were in the same Army unit together. You seem to have some selective amnesia."

Adam sat down across from him. "We already have you on accessory to murder and capital felony murder of Wallace Ryall. So, you're looking at maybe thirty years there. And we might be adding bombing and attempted murder to your charges. That's another six to ten years added on to that sentence."

The other man snorted and kept running his finger on the desk. Adam said, "If you cooperate, we might be able to plea it down to less than life. You might even get out on parole in thirty. Or less. We know you're working for other people. They're the ones we're gunning for."

"I'll take my chances." Redbeard raised his head to stare defiantly at Adam.

"Your buddy, Douglass Marcell, isn't here to save your sorry ass this time. And I haven't even started talking about the arsons recently and the murder of Jared Lake. You're in criminal waters so deep, you're drowning. And we're offering your only lifeline."

Just then, the door forcefully opened, and Redbeard leaned back with his arms folded across his chest when none other than Douglass Marcell, himself, stomped in. The man said, "You don't have to tell them anything, Warner."

Adam didn't bother looking at the attorney and kept staring at their suspect. "This doesn't change anything. I'm sure your attorney here realizes plea bargains are often the way to go."

With a quick glance at Marcell, Adam said, "And I'm sure the judge won't be as likely to grant bail this time after your little escape-artist trick. That'll give you a nice long time to sit and stew in a jail cell. And begin to realize what it'll be like to spend the rest of your life behind bars."

Marcell interrupted, "My client has a mental handicap and didn't know he was supposed to return for his hearing."

Adam laughed in reply. "I don't know if you've had time to get caught up on all the new charges against your client, counselor. But in addition to the accessory to murder charge, he now faces first-degree murder, possession of explosives with the intent to kill or injure, arson, and attempted murder of a police officer."

Redbeard whined, "You can't pin that bombing on me. And I wasn't going to kill you. Just have a friendly chat about turning myself in."

Marcell jumped in, "Darnell, keep your goddamn mouth shut."

Adam ignored Redbeard's lie. Redbeard knew full well the murder attempt on a police officer was what he might get nailed for most. Adam aimed his next words at Marcell. "It's possible he could plea bargain from a mandatory first-degree murder charge for Jared Lake to a second-degree charge. Life versus a long stay."

Marcell replied, "I want a private word with my client, detectives."

Jinks spoke up, "That's your right, of course. We'll let you two alone but be waiting outside." She and Adam knew Marcell would have been frisked prior to being hauled into the interview room. Still, it didn't hurt to let the man know not to pull any funny business.

Fifteen minutes later, they ushered Marcell to the front lobby while Sergeant Bill Naigle returned Redbeard to his cell. Jinks said to Adam, "Guess we should update the chief."

"Hooray that we can give him good news for a change."

Chief Quinn congratulated them on their capture of Redbeard, although Adam had to be honest with him, "The evidence isn't terribly strong for the explosives and arson charges yet. But he did try to shoot me at the warehouse. We've got him on that plus accessory for Wallace Ryall's murder. Skipping out on bail for that charge only served to buy him a few weeks' time."

Quinn asked, "You think he's behind the arsons and Lake's death, then?"

"Still not sure about that, although the Molotov cocktails he used at the warehouse can't be coincidental. We aim to pursue some more leads."

"Guess this is a good time to talk to you two about my inquiries into Sergeant Moody's background. Your sources were correct, Adam, about Moody and Darnell Warner being in the same Army explosives unit."

Adam cleared his throat. "I recently asked Moody about Warner. Moody said he didn't recall him per se. And that he must have left shortly after Moody arrived."

The chief growled, "They were in the same unit for at least a year. That's far more than 'shortly.' I also talked to Moody's former commanding officer about the fact Moody was discharged dishonorably for fighting and other code violations."

Jinks asked, "What type of code violations?"

"Sexual assault. Being AWOL. Had to pull a lot of rotten teeth to get that info. His record had been mysteriously buried."

Adam spoke up. "Buried, sir?"

"Very. And I found out it was at the urging of none other than the late Representative Arlen Strudwick."

That made Adam wince. "Probably doing the bidding of Reggie Forsythe and his buddy, Mayor Lehmann. I suppose Lehmann put added pressure on you to hire Moody, too."

"And how. The whole vetting process was rushed primarily at Lehmann's directive."

"Pulling heavy-duty strings?"

"Let's just say, I felt like a puppet." Quinn sighed. "FYI, I also spoke again with Moody's former chief at the Concord police department. The man just retired so he can speak a little more freely. Anyway, Moody was a troublemaker from day one. But he hid it well, always making sure he didn't leave behind any crumb trails to lead back to him."

Jinks rolled her eyes and poked Adam in the arm. "Figures."

Quinn took a sip of a drink that smelled a lot like coffee. Real coffee. "Funny thing . . . they had a couple of arson cases while Moody was on the force. Both times, Moody just happened to be passing by and was the first responder."

Adam replied, "How convenient."

"The ex-chief wondered about it but didn't have any evidence Moody set the fires. After that, he did try to keep Moody on a tight leash."

Jinks said, "He's a real charmer, our Moody. And he's been protected and shielded all along. So, how should we handle him going forward?"

"As I told Adam before, be polite and professional and try to stay out of his way. Leave the rest to me. The mayor's trigger finger is too ready to accuse our department of imaginary transgressions. Don't want to give him any fuel for the fire, pardon the pun."

Adam nodded. "I also learned Moody was in debt, maybe to Forsythe and Kozak, and that he's had dealings with a bookie, Leroy Schick. If he's that much in hock, he's also ripe for bribery, blackmail, and a host of other crimes."

Jinks added helpfully, "Including helping out with arson. If Kozak and Forsythe were part of all of that, he's definitely compromised."

Quinn said, "That's why I'm keeping him off major cases right now and assigning him to small-time stuff on the pretext he needs extra time to study. He's taking online classes to get a Bachelor's in Criminal Science and scheduled training with Vermont's CJTC."

When Jinks snorted again, Quinn raised an eyebrow. "If and when any of Moody's misdeeds become public, I don't want any major cases compromised by him being attached to them."

Adam and Jinks looked at each other. Adam knew what Jinks was thinking. They were both recalling previous cases where Moody had "helped" out. Having his name associated with those cases might raise enough alarm bells for the defense attorneys to call for new trials and dismissals. Another reason dirty cops were lower than pond scum.

"It should go without saying you two should be very careful what you say around Moody," Quinn looked at each of them in turn.

They agreed, but Adam had one other tidbit he wanted to pass along. "FYI, Jinks saw Moody snooping through my office."

The chief looked like he was about to have a stroke as his face grew red with veins on his neck popping out like fiery trees. "Might want to lock your offices when you're not around, then."

Adam and Jinks waited for him to dismiss them but he didn't right away. He grabbed a bottle of antacids and popped a few. Quinn added, "Mayor Lehmann is pushing through a proposal that reduces our budget by one quarter."

"On what justification, sir ?" Jinks looked like she was going to join Quinn in having a stroke.

"Says it's a necessary cost-cutting move. But I think it's to put pressure on me to push Moody into a detective slot. Our department bylaws do specify we should give preference to ex-military. However, they don't say anything about dishonorably discharged ex-military."

Chief Quinn popped a few more antacids and waved at his two detectives by way of dismissal. Adam and Jinks filed back to Jinks's office, where they sat down without saying anything.

Jinks finally broke the silence with a simple, "Fuck."

Adam grinned, despite the seriousness of the situation, taking note of some dessert thing on her desk. "What's up with that?"

"Didn't I tell you? My sister has decided to become a chef and is taking classes. She's in the dessert section right now. She's sending me all these goodies. You should try one."

Adam studied the heart-shaped pastry that had something pink and white on top. It looked . . . slightly repulsive. Maybe it was just his foul mood. "What is it?"

"A dragon fruit custard with meringue hazelnut tart. I like it."

"This from a woman who loves lutefisk. I'll let you have it all to yourself. Don't want to lose my girlish figure."

He left Jinks with her tart-thing and checked in with Joe Brimm. Time to see if he'd had time to compare the fake note he made from Leon Nolen's business printers in various fonts and colors to the other notes.

Brimm blinked at him. "Do I look like I never sleep, Dutton?"

"Now that you mention it."

"Maybe I just dreamed it, then. Under a microscope, the ink patterns on the threatening notes you gave me match the ones from the fake note you printed. Not the laser one, the inkjet."

"No microdots?"

"Nope, but it's off an old inkjet, so I didn't expect to find them. But, there's the same faded red ink and all. I'd bet large sums of money they were created on the same machine."

"Thanks, Joe. I owe you some of Jinks's lutefisk."

Brimm threw a small stuffed pink pig at him as Adam left. Well, then, they might have just found a possible link between the threatening notes to Beverly, Harlan, Jinks, and Annika Grimes and the bomb that was delivered to Adam's house. All running through the delivery business of sleazy Leon Nolen. That took Adam's mood up several notches.

He returned to his own office to start working on reports, by way of coffee in the breakroom, but Jinks was waiting for him. He said, "Miss me already?"

"I just put in the subpoena request."

Adam stared at her in confusion. "Subpoena request?"

"Brimm called me. Told me you'd be asking for a subpoena for Leon Nolen's delivery business records."

"But I didn't . . . " Adam must be getting too predictable if his colleagues were already two steps ahead of him.

Jinks grinned at him. "It's with Judge Mollin, so you can expect results faster than usual. In fact, I'll be happy to pick the subpoena up myself and hop on over to Nolen's little rat house to get a copy of those records. Haven't had any good brawls lately. Don't want to lose my touch."

Adam laughed. "Not a chance, Jinks."

"Oh, and I've also got feelers out to all the stores in the region that would possibly sell gunpowder or black powder. And the other bomb-making ingredients of the lovely pipe bomb that hit your house. Can't let the ATF guys have all the fun."

"As well as any unusual arson-related purchases?"

"Naturally."

Adam tightened the lid on his coffee. "Since you're cruising for a bruising, why don't we go see that bookie, Leroy Schick."

"The one that might have Moody by the short hairs?"

"That's the one."

"Lead on, McDuff."

"Isn't that 'lay on, McDuff?'"

Jinks folded her arms across her chest. "Since when did you turn into a Shakespeare geek?"

"Don't blame me. My father read the plays to me when I was a boy."

She unfolded her arms to poke him in the chest. "Lay on, then, McDutton. And prithee let us proceed to pick a quick trick with Mr. Schick."

When Adam groaned, she added, "Don't worry. I'll shape it into iambic pentameter later."

32

When they pulled up to the drab gray-and-black building that was located next to a pawn shop, Adam pointed at the sign. "It actually says 'Leroy Schick, Wealth Consultant,' on the sign. I thought Cray was making that up."

Schick's bald head broke out into little beads of sweat when Adam and Jinks walked in. He was wearing dark glasses—indoors—making Adam think the guy didn't want people to read his expressions. Fancy that.

The plaid-clad bookie looked at Jinks without registering any recognition, but he said to Adam, "I know you. You're a cop."

Adam flashed his badge. "Detective Adam Dutton. This here is my partner, Detective Jinks."

"Yeah, Cray's mentioned you. He says you're tough. But fair."

"Cray says you dealt with the late Jared Lake. He owed people money, and his sister told us he'd fallen on hard times. Might have had to declare bankruptcy soon. But lo and behold, he suddenly got an infusion of cash."

Schick rubbed his hands together. His knuckles were irritated and raw, maybe a touch of OCD repeated hand-washing. "I did some business with Jared Lake. Since the guy's dead and all, it won't hurt his reputation none, right?"

"What kind of business?"

"He needed a loan. He paid me back. So don't look at pinning his murder on me."

"Wouldn't dream of it."

Adam picked up a gold paperweight in the shape of a dollar sign from the counter. "Did he say where he got the money to pay off the loan?"

"Nah, I never ask. As long as it ain't counterfeit, I just count it and put in the bank."

"Such a good businessman you are."

Schick scowled at him. "Funny man."

"I heard you also did some business with a Mike Moody."

Schick licked his lips and looked from Adam to Jinks. "Moody? He's a cop, right? You're a cop, he's a cop. Why don't you talk to him?"

"Because we're talking to you," Jinks chimed in. "Just answer the man's question."

"I never discuss living clients. Much safer that way."

Jinks eyed Adam as she asked, "You're admitting Moody is a customer of yours?"

"I can neither confirm nor deny. That's what all those politicos say, right? And the legal beagles?"

Adam put the paperweight down and leaned on the counter. "Let's speak hypothetically, then. Let's say you had a customer *like* Mike Moody. A man who does some gambling on the side. What sort of gambling do you think he'd be interested in?"

"I don't know. Sounds like that sort of guy might like to bet on sports. Football, the ponies."

"Uh-huh. And how much money would this type of guy typically bet, I wonder?"

"Around a couple grand per pop. Speaking hypothetically, as you say."

"I see. And I can't imagine the odds would be too hopeful in his favor. Since they rarely are. I suppose such a customer might hemorrhage money pretty fast."

"Yeah, you might guess that. And it would be a good guess."

Adam stood up to his full height. "I don't suppose you would loan our hypothetical customer money for all that betting?"

"I like to play both ends. Would make sense if he knew no one ever gets by with welshing on me."

"And did Moody—sorry, our hypothetical customer—'welsh' on you?"

"Came close. Went down to the wire, but he came up with the money. Hypothetical money."

"Now, where do you think this customer might have got that money if he didn't have it in the first place?"

Schick shrugged. "Do I look like a mind reader?"

"Maybe you can read my mind. I'll give you a hint. Forsythe. Kozak."

"I'm just an honest businessman. I don't deal with those types." More hand rubbing. Those poor knuckles would be bleeding any second at that rate. "But I might have heard something about our customer getting some of that hypothetical money from those two."

"Well, Mr. Schick, if you 'imagine' anything else about this hypothetical customer, give me a call." Adam handed over his card. "And good luck with the wealth consulting."

Back in their car, Jinks said, "Gotta wonder just how deep in doo-doo debt Moody might be?"

"And which of our many players does he really owe the money to? I would love to find out how much Mayor Lehmann knows about this."

"He'd better know if he wants to run for governor and avoid any more scandals peeking out under his bonnet than he already has."

Jinks turned on the radio to a classic rock station. The song currently playing was, "Love is a battlefield."

Adam glared at it, and Jinks turned it off. "Still smarting about Zelda?"

"Part of me hopes Lehmann does become governor. Zelda won't have time for me anymore."

"Then I'll hold my nose and vote for him if he runs. And don't say I never did anything for you."

"Gee, thanks, Jinks. I'm truly touched."

"But you will owe me."

"More lutefisk?"

"After my sister's monk fruit tart things, I'm thinking something bigger. Like monk fruit wine or monk fruit-flavored caviar."

"Monk fruit caviar?" Adam's stomach turned a little queasy at the thought. But he was grateful to Jinks, as always, for trying to turn his mind away from Zelda and all the other grim issues in his life. She might have terrible taste in food, but she was a damned fine partner.

Beverly stepped back as she surveyed the evergreen wreaths and garlands dotted with white lights, red ribbons, and miniature glass ornaments—snowmen, pinecones, and nutcrackers. "*Better Homes and Gardens* couldn't have done any better."

Agnes beamed. "Sharon and Blaine and Harlan pitched in to help. You don't think we overdid it on the tchotchkes?"

"Quite tasteful, I'd say." Beverly glanced over at the music stage. "And that looks finished."

"Just in time for the holiday concerts I booked."

"Which ones? You didn't have a firm list the last time we spoke about it."

"For starters, Adam must have worked his magic with Blaine, because the boy agreed to perform some of his songs right before New Year's."

"That's wonderful! You and Adam have been so good for Blaine. He just needed somebody to care, for a change."

Agnes reached over to add a couple of glass ornaments to one wreath. "He reminds me of my Willem, in a way. A little rough around the edges but a good soul." She peered at Beverly. "Haven't heard much from Adam lately. I'm getting a little worried."

"Oh, he's fine." Beverly didn't really want to talk about Adam. The news about Redbeard's murder attempt would definitely worry Agnes, for one. And Beverly certainly wasn't going to mention her argument with Adam at the Crossroads Café.

She picked up a bag she'd set next to the door and handed it to the older woman. "This is why I stopped by. It's for you."

Agnes peered into the bag and pulled out the hand-painted keepsake box Beverly had bought from Kozak's store. "Oh, my. This is beautiful. Where in the world did you find this?"

"Just something I ran across. I thought of you immediately. Maybe it will bring some good luck."

Agnes put it next to the cash register and gave it a pat. "I'll find it a place of honor." She hugged Beverly. "Thank you, dear."

"You're most welcome. Wish I could stay longer, but I have some errands to run."

"Sure you can't stay a while?"

"Yes, but I'll be back soon. Wild horses couldn't stop me from enjoying Blaine's concert."

Agnes shook her head. "But that's over a week from now."

"Sooner, I promise."

Beverly reluctantly left the cheery shop and its inviting warmth and good company. She'd been thinking about what Sheila Kozak's handyman said—that if she wanted to find out about Kozak, she should talk to Lucas Barratt. If Adam asked, it was just a little get-acquainted chat, commiserating with a fellow antiquer, right? She looked up Barratt's number and called him to see if he was available.

When she got out of her car at the address Barratt gave her, she saw she wasn't the only new arrival. She thought to herself, *Speak of the devil.* Adam was also just getting out of his car.

When he spied her, he growled, "What are you doing here?"

Beverly crossed her fingers behind her back. "I felt sorry for him. Losing his boss and his business and all."

When Adam stared at her for several moments without saying anything, she added, "And Mr. X might have told me a handyman who works for the Kozaks said to talk to Lucas Barratt if we want to find out more about Ivon Kozak." It was getting too convenient to blame it all on Mr. X, and she was going to owe the man one enormous apology.

Adam frowned. "I have police work to do, Beverly. The *official* kind."

"I already called ahead to make an appointment."

"On what pretext?"

"On being an antiques consultant to the police department."

Adam rubbed his forehead and sighed. "Not that again."

"Shall we go in?" She gave him her best Zen-esque smile and knocked on the door.

They found both Lucas and Jeanne Barratt at home, and to Beverly's surprise, the couple didn't seem at all upset by their visit. Jeanne said, "I came home early from work to talk to Lucas in person. I just found out I'm pregnant again. We're over the moon."

Beverly glanced at Adam. She knew what he was probably thinking, and she shared that thought. Neither of them was happy to worm in on the Barratts' good news with questions about a decidedly less pleasant topic of conversation.

Lucas invited Beverly and Adam to sit down while he and his wife held hands on the sofa. Lucas said softly, "We were both a little afraid at first. Because of the loss of our first child." He looked briefly at Adam. "And there's my green card status. And the arson case since we might be suspects."

Adam cleared his throat. "First of all, congratulations and best wishes to both of you. Can't think of a better Christmas present than that."

Lucas's eyes lit up. "That's exactly what I told Jeanne."

"Mr. Barratt, I had some questions I wanted to ask you about the arsons, but I could come back at another time."

The other man shook his head. "No, it's okay. Then I'd just be wondering and worrying."

Adam hesitated, then continued. "A source," he didn't look at Beverly, "told me you know more about Ivon Kozak than you let on. Can you fill me in on that? When I met you the first time, you said you didn't know him. And that you hadn't heard Jared Lake mention anything about him."

Lucas looked regretfully at his now-pregnant wife, and she squeezed his hand. "Guess I should come clean. When I was at my darkest, I was terrified I'd be deported and lose my family since I was in deep debt. That's when I accepted money from Ivon Kozak to spy on Jared Lake."

"Spy on him? In what way?"

"Mostly his profits and debts, bankruptcy status, all the financials. Kozak said it was something everyone did, corporate espionage."

"How did this scheme work?"

"I went to Kozak's house to turn over my findings a couple of times, although I tried to hide my visits. Kozak also paid me to run some errands for him. Secret errands. He made me sign one of those NDA things."

"A non-disclosure agreement?"

"Yeah."

"What type of errands?"

"I had to hand over some papers to this guy. Never learned his name. Quite an imposing man, red hair, red beard."

"What was in those papers?"

"The envelopes were double-sealed, so I don't know. But I dropped them off at prearranged meeting points behind buildings, in dark alleys, and such. The more I did it, the more sorry I was for having gotten involved with Kozak."

Barratt closed his eyes for a moment. "At first, it was just about the money. But as time went on, I began to see what kind of man Kozak was. All charming on the outside, but he can put up this curtain of such a cold, dark stare. It's like looking into the eyes of the devil himself."

Barratt turned to his wife. "I know it wasn't smart, and then there's that whole antiques theft thing, too. The couple of items I stole from Jared's shop." Barratt directed his words at Adam, "I told Jeanne about that."

Jeanne reached around his shoulders to give him a hug, and his eyes teared up. "But I did it for you, for us, for our future."

Jeanne spoke up, "Lucas is a good man, Detective Dutton, Miss Laborde. He's hard-working, he's a loving husband. Please don't hold any of this against him. You don't know what it was like for us."

Lucas Barratt's expression morphed from anguish to fear. "My work for Kozak didn't have anything to do with the fire and Jared's death, did it?"

"I understand your motivations. If your courier duties had something to do with the arsons indirectly, and you didn't know anything about it, you likely won't be held accountable for that."

Barratt looked slightly less tense than before, and Adam leaned forward. "I must caution you and Jeanne, though. Don't have anything else to do with Ivon Kozak. Stay as far away as possible. With any luck, you won't have any further dark clouds hanging over you from your spying."

Beverly noticed Jeanne had grown quiet and seemed to be struggling with something on her mind. Beverly said to her, "Are you feeling all right, Jeanne?"

Jeanne nodded. "But I want you to know, Detective Dutton. I've overheard Mayor Lehmann talking about his plans to 'get' you, one way or another. In fact, I've been quite uncomfortable with the mayor's attitude and behavior lately. Especially toward the police department. I mean, I've only had positive dealings with you."

Beverly asked, "Can you leave your position?"

"We can't afford it. I need the health insurance for me and the baby. And the money, of course. Just until Lucas finds another job."

Beverly frowned at that. Mindful of the fact she'd already played "career counselor" by helping Sharon get the job at Agnes's shop and Nyssa the waitress position at the resort, she figured she might as well do it for Lucas, too. "I might be able to help with that. I'll get back to you."

Beverly ignored Adam's questioning look and pulled the little octopus-ashtray from her purse. "By the way, did your store sell anything like this?"

Lucas studied it for a moment. "Yes, I recall when we got that one in. We had several items like that. Steampunk is popular these days with the younger set. All those fantasy video games, you know." Then he frowned. "Where did you find that?"

"It was at the arson site. Well, not in the building per se, but several feet away."

"Really?" Lucas frowned. "I guess that's why it wasn't burned or even singed." He pointed out the dent in the side. "Looks like it's been dropped, though."

Beverly returned the item to her purse. "Thanks, I was just curious."

After Adam and Beverly excused themselves from the couple and headed outside, Adam said, "Okay, I'll bite. How exactly are you going to get Lucas Barratt a job?"

"I don't know yet. But I'll think of something."

Adam huffed. "Good luck. You're going to need it. And also, what's up with that ugly octopus thing? Why does it matter?"

"I'm not sure. It just seemed odd."

"Whatever. I'm not particularly interested in anything that doesn't relate to our case."

"You're Mr. Positive today."

He growled again. "Because of Moody. And Lehmann. And having to deal with attorneys like Marcell when trying to get information out of people like Redbeard."

She tried to ignore her sudden guilty conscience when he mentioned Moody. She was already having second thoughts about her unofficial sleuthing attempted via the man's girlfriend. "I heard about Redbeard's arrest. From Mr. X."

"Of course."

"It's not like *you* called me." She folded her arms across her chest.

He looked up at the dark sky where the clouds blotted out the stars and didn't reply for a minute, then surprised her. "You want to get an early dinner—or maybe it's a late lunch—from the Sugar Train restaurant?"

"I've been wanting to go there ever since Harlan recommended it. When I was still new in town." She knew it was his way of making a peace offering, and she didn't want to be the one to disturb the peace. It was also as close as they'd come to that "real dinner date" she knew Adam had been angling for.

"Okay, then. Guess you'll have to follow me."

"Or you can follow me." She managed a slight smile.

He held out his arm and gestured toward their cars. "After you, Miss Beverly Laborde."

34

Adam sat across from Beverly, unsure of what to say. Since they'd parted on less-than-happy terms at their last encounter, he didn't know how to break the ice. Maybe the make-up dinner at the Sugar Train restaurant would help.

Beverly studied the menu. "Harlan said they make a mouthwatering maple pecan-glazed trout. And that this time of year, they have these 'killer' pumpkin biscuits."

Adam put down his menu. "Harlan doesn't often steer anybody wrong. Sold."

"I hear you've been encouraging Blaine to step out of his shell. You're quite the musical impresario."

"He's got quite a bit of talent. Sure hope he can stay out of trouble long enough to take advantage of it."

"Is it true you also offered to take him fishing?" Beverly bit into one of the pumpkin biscuits that had just arrived. "Oh good lord, these definitely are killer. They'll kill my diet and figure, but it'll be worth it."

Adam felt a little stirring where he probably shouldn't. There was absolutely nothing wrong with her figure. He replied, "I felt sorry for the kid since his alcoholic father has practically disowned him."

"I wonder if the alcoholism started after the mother died in the accident? I almost feel a little sorry for Blaine's father. But I hate him a little bit at the same time. How could he cut himself off from the one good thing left in his life?"

Adam studied Beverly's face. "Like your grandfather did to your grandmother and your Mom?"

"In a way. Though I think my grandfather's demons were worse than just alcohol, as with Blaine's dad."

"But a demon is a demon is a demon, if it destroys you in the end."

She took a sip of hot tea. "Speaking of demons, one down . . . Redbeard. And only a couple more to go. Kozak and Moody."

Adam half-expected her to blurt out their social-security numbers, bank accounts, and favorite colors. Her ingenuity and bulldog pursuit were both exasperating and admirable. He alternated between the two emotions most of the time when he was around her.

She finished the biscuit and licked her fingers. "Mr. X found out Sergeant Moody's girlfriend is Redbeard's cousin. The girlfriend owns the house and said Moody wasn't good with money."

"Mr. X told you all that?" He uttered a humorless laugh. "Are you sure it's Mr. X who is finding out all of these things? Not a certain con woman playing at being an unregistered private eye?"

"I don't want to fight with you, Adam."

"We're not fighting. Just discussing. Friends discuss things, right?"

"Is that what we are? Friends?"

He was relieved when the waitress brought another basket of biscuits. How did he answer that loaded question? Friends? Adversaries? Partners? Antagonists? Would-be lovers?

She picked at a biscuit. "I ran into Zelda the other day."

"Oh?" That couldn't be good, and he steeled himself for what was coming.

"She pretty much said the two of you had sex."

Adam hated to see the hurt expression on her face. Hurt, betrayal, suspicion. He opened his mouth to reply, "I wasn't—"

"I thought you had higher ethics and morals. I mean, it's really none of my business and all. But maybe I was naive, and you aren't quite the man I thought you were—"

"We didn't have sex, Beverly. She's lying. She still had a back-door key I didn't know about and came over unannounced. Caught me getting out of the shower, and then *she* came on to *me*."

Beverly's face turned pink. "Naked? Out of the shower?"

"It was . . . awkward. And to be honest, I wasn't sure how to feel about it."

"You weren't tempted? Even a teensy bit? She's your ex, and she did offer to have an affair with you."

"Part of it felt natural since we were married for ten years. And yet . . . I don't know. It didn't feel right."

When their entrees arrived, he almost wolfed it down in a few gulps but forced himself to take his time. Anything to keep from talking about his feelings toward Zelda or Beverly or whatever passed for his love life. For her part, Beverly seemed just as eager to use the excuse of eating to avoid having to talk any further, except for comments on the food and the restaurant's enormous ten-foot Christmas tree.

When the waitress asked about dessert, Beverly said, "Why don't we have some at the resort, Adam? You can follow me again to make sure I don't do any of that unregistered private eye stuff. Besides, they have some 'killer' chocolate mousse there. I'll need the drive back for all of this lovely dinner to settle before I can even think about dessert."

Adam followed her as she'd asked, keeping an eye out for deer crossing the winding road that led to the Apple Valley Resort. When they headed inside, Beverly stopped at the café long enough to grab some mousse.

Gloria Gelling was on duty in the café and waved at him. "Long time, no see Adam Dutton."

Beverly told her, "Just bringing Adam by for a nightcap."

Adam didn't miss the little wink Gloria gave Beverly when she said, "We're about to close for the evening. Maybe you should take it to your room instead?"

Beverly replied, "If you don't mind making it to go."

Adam took the desserts and coffees from her as she swiped her key card to get into her room. He whistled as he looked around the place. "So this is what two hundred fifty a night gets you. Impressive."

He took in the king-sized four-poster bed, elegant sitting area with two turquoise and gray damask chairs, and the Jacuzzi tub next to the fireplace. And where was that strong cinnamon smell coming from?

She opened the mini-fridge to show him its contents, "Complete with stocked bar."

They sat a table in the sitting area, enjoying the mousse and coffee. She told him, "I'm glad you didn't give up on inviting me to dinner. The Sugar Train tonight was amazing. Thanks for that."

"A growing girl's gotta eat."

She smiled at that. "There goes my figure again."

This time, he couldn't stop himself and blurted out, "Your figure is perfect."

Her eyes widened, but she didn't say anything. After they'd finished the mousse, she finally said, "I'm sorry about our argument."

"Which one?"

She smiled again. "All of them, I guess."

"It's my fault. I've been in a foul mood lately."

"With good reason. I don't blame you for that."

He chuckled. "Blame games are best left to investigations."

She startled him when she said with a grin, "It's nice to get all this out in the open, finally. But isn't this when the make-up sex usually happens?"

Maybe she was joking, but right then, he couldn't tell for sure. He'd got mixed signals from her since day one. And when she'd been a suspect in a murder, he hadn't had any time to consider a relationship. Well, mostly.

The way his body was responding to her "joke" was no laughing matter, and he squirmed in his seat. She reached over for her coffee and accidentally knocked his empty mousse plate onto the floor. They both jumped up, colliding in the process.

He could tell from the look on her face she'd felt that "response" of his quite clearly. He started to back away, but she grabbed his shirt and pulled him closer. He'd never wanted to kiss anyone more than he wanted to kiss her right then. His fears at initiating unwanted overtures melted away when she put her hands behind his neck and pressed her lips onto his.

Hot damn, that woman could kiss. He wrapped his arms behind her back, enjoying the softness of those lips and the tantalizing closeness of her breasts. She moved her hands from his neck down to his ass and rubbed them along his backside.

She broke the kiss to nibble on his ear and say, "The Jacuzzi is big enough for two."

"I didn't bring a swimsuit," he squeaked out.

"Don't need one."

Their lips locked together again as they did a slow-motion dance toward the hot tub. She reached her hands up under his shirt as if to pull it over his head. And just then, his cellphone rang.

"I should have turned that off," he grumbled. *Talk about mood killers.*

She sighed. "Maybe you should check it? It might be important."

He looked at the caller. "Jinks," he told her.

Jinks sounded a little nonplussed when he growled at her on the phone. She said, "Caught you in the middle of something, lover boy?"

"You have no idea, Jinks. What's up?"

She filled him in on some tidbits that had come in concerning Redbeard's attorney, Marcell, and Redbeard's alibis. Finally, she said, "Most of this can wait until tomorrow. You carry on doing whatever it was you were . . . doing."

Adam hung up and shook his head. When Jinks had interrupted his almost-sex with Zelda, he'd been grateful. This time, he wasn't so sure.

Beverly asked, "Something you have to do right now?"

"It's not urgent. But I probably should get back home and do a little checking into it." That was partly a lie, and he could tell she knew it. But she was also looking at him a bit sheepishly, too.

She walked over and grabbed their coffee cups. After making some fresh java in the room coffee maker, she refilled his cup and handed it over. "For the road, then. Better than all the booze in the mini-fridge. Wouldn't do to have a detective getting pulled over for DUI."

"Lehmann doesn't need much of an excuse to have my badge, that's for sure."

If he'd wanted to kill the mood completely, that had done it. Not sure whether he was making the right call to leave or not, he was rewarded when she stood up on tiptoe, kissed him on the cheek, and then whispered in his ear, "You should know I always call in rain checks."

That was what Zelda had said to him, too, wasn't it? Although this time, it wasn't filling him with dread like when his ex had said it.

With his hot, fresh coffee in hand, he headed toward his house. Although as warm as he was feeling right then, the coffee wasn't really needed.

35

Monday, December 21

Beverly hadn't seen Adam in two days and hoped he wasn't avoiding her. Surely he was just busy, right? She picked at the last bit of the room service breakfast, not really hungry. When her cellphone rang, and she saw it was Adam, she got a smile on her face. Maybe she wasn't on his shit list.

But her smile quickly faded as he asked with evident agitation in his voice, "Did you pull one of your con jobs and talk to Sgt. Moody's girlfriend, Donella Seagraves?"

Beverly's face grew hot. "Why would you ask that?"

"Moody has a formal complaint against the department with the mayor's office. Something about harassing him via his girlfriend. Said a woman showed up at his house saying she was with an agency that supported cops, but he couldn't find anything about it other than a website."

Beverly said, "Adam, I—"

"We're having to be ultra careful in how we handle Moody. Chief Quinn is in the middle and trying his best to hold everything together before the mayor lowers the boom. And this little con job of yours just made things a whole lot worse."

"Worse?" Beverly stammered out. "How much worse?"

"The mayor is making noises now that he's going to fire Chief Quinn. The only thing holding him back is he knows how well-liked Quinn is in the area. And if Lehmann is gunning for governor, he doesn't want to be seen firing a chief who has a great track record on crime and no reports of wrongdoing."

Beverly stared at a little painting on the wall of a bucolic Vermont scene with woods and a stream running through, wishing she were there right now. She wasn't sure how she was going to make this up to Adam. Or if there was even a way to repair the damage. Mr. X had been right to warn her.

Finally, she asked, "You know where the cabin is? The one you showed me the picture of, that you wanted to buy when you married Zelda?"

"Of course, I know where it is."

"I have some news about that. I'll pick you up in front of the station in fifteen minutes." Before he could say anything else, she hung up.

When she arrived at the police station, she half-expected not to see him standing outside. But there he was, with a frown as wide as the White River after a flooding rain. His expression was just as stormy.

He slammed the door after climbing in and gave her one of his piercing stares. "What's this all about?"

"You'll see."

He stayed silent for a moment and then said, "You shouldn't go around behind my back like that, Beverly."

"I just wanted to help dig up some dirt on Moody since he's trying to make your life miserable. And since he's tied to that unethical bastard, Mayor Lehmann. Justice moves too slowly for me. I'm not used to that, I'm used to being in control."

"And taking that justice into your own hands? There are laws against that."

"I never hurt anyone. Maybe I got a little revenge on evil people who hurt other people. But even then, it was just antiques."

"Any other cop might have arrested you by now for impersonating an officer of the law."

"And when exactly did I do that? I never pretended to be a cop, just a consultant to cops."

Adam rubbed his eyes. "Beverly—"

"You know things aren't always black and white. Even when it comes to the law. You've bent it a few times, yourself."

He didn't answer, instead gazing out the window at the newly snow-dusted pines as they headed farther out of town. She hated to see him avoiding even looking at her and didn't want to dwell on how much it hurt. But she deserved it.

She said, "I guess I can tell you now, then. Remember when I asked Lucas Barratt about that octopus-ashtray thing? He said it was a Steampunk item and they sell a lot of those, mostly to gamers. Well, Moody's girlfriend told me that she was tired of his clutter, particularly his gaming and Steampunk collection."

"Could be a coincidence."

"Yes, but why was this octopus outside the arson site? Why not inside with all the other items? And it wasn't even singed. As Lucas pointed out, it also looks like it was dropped, causing the dent. What if someone took it while setting the fire and dropped it in their haste to leave the crime scene?"

Adam was silent for a moment. "Speculation and hearsay don't convince juries."

She sighed and decided to give it a rest. For now. After another mile of silence, she asked, "How's the arson case going? Have you made progress in the past two days since I saw you?"

She sensed his posture stiffening at the mention of their last meeting, although he didn't address it. He sighed. "Redbeard's still not talking."

"You told him it would be in his best interests to cooperate, I hope. Cops still do that, right?"

"Oh, we told him. Especially after we got a subpoena for a package delivery from Leon Nolen's records. He was the one who delivered the pipe bomb to my house. And the signature of the man who signed the order, although it was a fake name, matches Redbeard's."

"You told him all this?"

"You bet. Plus, we have a positive lead on a store where someone matching Redbeard's description bought some gunpowder and other materials for a pipe bomb. We just don't know where he's been hiding it."

"You think that mob attorney, Douglas Marcell, will get him off?"

"Not out of jail time. Might plea it down. But there's too much evidence."

"Hope you're right."

"Redbeard should be more afraid of what might happen to him if by some miracle he got out on bail again. This time, his shady connections might see he disappears permanently. And I'm not talking an all-expense-paid trip to Bermuda."

"By connections, you mean Kozak? Or someone else?"

"I know you've had your money on Kozak from the start. I never liked the organized insurance fraud angle, either, and the evidence is weak. I don't think poor Jared Lake committed suicide by arson, and we haven't found any link yet between his sister and the arson."

"Okay, then. Have you found that Kozak has ties to Mayor Lehmann? Like Lehmann did with my uncle?"

"The more I learn about the guy, the more I think that unlike Forsythe, Kozak is more of a loner and a true psychopath. No feelings for anyone, totally driven by his own whims and slights. Cold and calculating."

"Then I feel sorry for his wife."

"His wife?" Adam stared at her. "How do you know about his wife?"

Beverly wasn't about to tell him she went to interview that woman, too. "If he's married, that is. Must be hard living with someone like that."

They pulled into a gravel driveway tinged with snow, and Beverly said, "You remember when you told me you'd driven by this cabin and were disappointed it was no longer for sale?"

"Sure, I remember. Hell, I doubt I could afford it on my salary right now. But I do wonder who bought it."

Beverly laughed nervously. "You're looking at her."

Adam turned to her with his mouth hanging open. "You? How?"

"I put a down payment on it, although the contract may not go through. My finances aren't exactly normal."

"What do you mean, 'not normal?'"

"I use some offshore banks and—"

"And I probably don't want to know or shouldn't anything about that."

"It's all legit."

"Yeah, but . . . "

Had she made the wrong call by buying the house? He seemed almost angry with her. She chewed on her lip, wondering what to say to him. "You keep asking me about when I'm going to settle down, remember?"

He nodded.

"And you did ask me if I'd considered buying something around here, right?"

He nodded again. As she watched him, waiting for a reply, any reply, the tension in his shoulders relaxed. He stared out at the house and said, "Looks about the same as it did when I first saw it."

"The previous owner kept it in good shape. It might need a little work. And since you're handy with power tools, well . . ."

The beginning of a small smile crept onto his face. "Cheap labor?"

"I would be forever in your debt. You'd be welcome any time. And I do mean any time."

"Hmm," he said, his smile growing wider. "It is a peaceful place around here. Isolated, too."

"Very."

After a few moments of more companionable silence as they looked at the cabin, he said, "I should get back to the station. Much as I hate to head into the lion's den once again."

They reluctantly returned to the car, and she started the engine. "I'm sorry Redbeard isn't being cooperative. Have you talked to Mark Grightell yet?"

"How did you learn about Grightell since I only learned of him yesterday?"

"Mr. X told me about him." There she went again, but Beverly didn't want to set off Adam again with the full story, especially since he was in a good mood for a change. "He was formerly with the same law firm that represented my evil uncle. Although I think he left that firm. Anyway, he apparently knows Kozak."

"Yeah, he did leave to become an insurance agent. As a matter of fact, he's on my list to interview. Why don't I do that right now?"

Beverly's heart sank as she tried to think of a way to escape the mess she'd just dumped herself into. Adam was suspicious, she knew that. And how angry would he get if they went to

Grightell, and the man recognized her from when she and Mr. X chatted with him? Unless she'd got the man too drunk to remember.

"You don't really need me for that. I'll drop you off at the station and let you have at him."

"I've never known you to pass up the opportunity to go with me on any interview or otherwise finagle yourself into a case. Why stop now?"

Oh, Adam was definitely suspicious. "I have a massage appointment at the resort in an hour."

"You can easily reschedule, right?"

What could she say to that?

§ § §

Beverly asked Adam for directions to Grightell's office as if she didn't know the way already. When they arrived at the familiar building and headed in, Beverly crossed her fingers behind her back again. She didn't have a disguise this time, so there was that. And maybe the hard cider would offer her some cover.

Grightell did look at her strangely and say, "Do I know you?"

"I don't think so."

"You just remind me of a woman who came in with her husband a few days ago. Except she had curly red hair and green eyes. And her husband was one of the palest people I've ever met. Scary pale."

"Well, I'm not married, you see."

The man scratched his head and shrugged.

Adam gave her a sharp look but plunged right in, grilling Grightell about his former employers, Lassetter & Lorens.

Grightell didn't have much to say until Adam asked, "We have reason to believe you're acquaintances with Ivon Kozak. Is that correct?"

Grightell fidgeted in his seat and tapped a pencil eraser on his desk. A few beads of sweat formed on his forehead despite the fact the office was on the cool side.

Adam pressed him on it, adding, "There's a possibility Kozak is involved with some serious crimes."

"I don't know anything about that."

"Are you sure, sir? I want you to think long and hard about your answers."

Grightell went from tapping the pencil eraser to chewing on it. Finally, he said, "I knew of Kozak through Lassetter & Lorens. I was assigned to one of Kozak's accounts. And the paperwork and discovery in that case was what ultimately made me leave the law firm."

He swallowed hard, and Adam prodded him, "Go on."

"After I'd left, Kozak came to my insurance firm on the pretext of wanting to buy some insurance. But I could tell he didn't really want insurance, at least not the tangible kind. He was buying himself personal insurance by letting me know I was on his radar. And he'd be keeping an eye on me."

"What was in those accounts that scared you so much?"

"Kozak's been ruthlessly trying to take over his competitors, one by one, to create one large antiques conglomerate. For some reason, he wants to be some sort of antiques kingpin. Doesn't want any competition. So, he was using every loophole he could to do just that."

"What about the Forsythes and their businesses? Lassetter & Lorens also did work for them."

"I knew about their shady practices, too. And I honestly feared what might happen with the Forsythes ultimately clashed with Kozak. I didn't want to be the one in the middle. I have a wife and kids, you know, and after what happened to Representative Strudwick . . . ”

“You knew about that at the time?”

“Only what I read in the papers.”

“There was a lot that was left out of the papers.”

Grightell swallowed hard again. “I knew what Reggie Forsythe had done. Essentially buying Representative Strudwick’s cooperation to push through an update to the state code that caused several antiques shops to go under. When Strudwick died, and they said it was murder, and then Reginald Forsythe, Senior, died, and they said *that* was murder, well . . . I saw what can happen to middlemen like me.”

“And those were the only dealings you’ve had with Kozak? Nothing more recently?”

“No, thank god. I’d be thrilled if I never see or hear from him again.”

“Well, sir, thanks for your time. And please contact the department if Kozak makes any return visits.” Adam handed over his card.

Right before Adam and Beverly left, Grightell said to Beverly, “Sorry about the confusion. Your voice sounds so familiar. But I’ve been under some stress lately.”

Outside the office, Adam confronted her. “Are you sure he wasn’t right? That you weren’t there before?”

Beverly reminded him, “I’m not married, remember?”

She dropped him off at the station, relieved to see he didn’t press her on it, and that they were back on better terms. She was still apologetic about Moody’s girlfriend, and Adam was still a little miffed.

But as he hopped out, he said, “I’ll see about keeping Moody and the mayor off our backs about that whole girlfriend thing. Chief Quinn didn’t seem too worried.” And then he added with a slight smile, “Oh, and you might want to tell your 'husband' he needs a better disguise next time. Tall, albino Nordic types are a little rare around here."

36

Adam and Jinks had a long confab at the station. She'd been busy delving deeper into the arson insurance-fraud angle, since her "fraud chops" were still fresh after tackling her local internet-fraud case. What she'd uncovered was most interesting. And so they found themselves driving to another interview, with Adam taking the wheel this time.

When Jinks observed his distracted mood, she asked, "Sure you wouldn't rather I drive?"

"It's therapy. I can take out my frustrations on the potholes."

"Let me guess. Does this have something to do with Hurricane Beverly?"

Adam sighed. "I want to trust her. But she hides a lot from me. And by so doing, may have plunged the department into hot water."

"Unintentionally, though, right?"

"Here I am having to do everything by the book, and she waltzes off and tries to do her unofficial private eye thing. And now the shit is hitting that leaf blower."

"Sometimes 'by the book' turns out to be a horror story."

"It's what the courts want, so I have no choice."

Jinks muttered, "Um-hmm," and then changed the subject. "You still haven't given Felicia and me a definite yay or nay on the Christmas party."

"Sorry about that, Jinks. It's hard for me to make plans this time of year. I hate it when tough cases stretch out over the holidays. You know the drill."

"The kids have got so used to me being gone on those special days, I don't think they even miss me."

"Of course they do. Felicia, too. Guess I don't have to worry about that with no family baggage." He hastened to add, "Not that your family is baggage, Jinks."

She grinned. "Depends on the time of day."

They headed toward their destination, which was the second time they'd made this particular trek. In Jinks's phone calls around the area to check on bomb and arson equipment purchases, she'd not only tied someone looking like Redbeard to the purchases but also had found a shop where a woman bought some items of interest to the investigation. A woman who matched the description of Jenny-Lee Salant.

As they arrived, the woman in question was heading out the door to her car, prompting Jinks to say, "Damn. We'll have to come back another time."

But Adam shook his head. "Not so fast. Think we'll do some judicious tailing." Adam's police instincts were pegging high on the radar with the way Salant was looking over her shoulder and clutching her briefcase to her chest.

They tailed her without her seeming to spy them, and she pulled into the parking lot of the same putting green facility where they'd first chatted with Joe Garone. Jinks said, "Kind of an odd place to conduct business, wouldn't you say?"

When they headed into the building, they were just in time to see Jenny-Lee putting an envelope on a chair and walking away. Moments later, Justin Garone grabbed it and put it into a duffel bag he was carrying.

Jinks said, "Should I go after Salant?"

"No, we'll start with Garone."

Justin Garone saw them coming and grabbed his clubs and bag, saying "If you want another interview, this is a bad time. I've got a meeting I have to go to."

Adam looked around the facility where a half a dozen golfers were on the various greens. "Either we have a nice discussion here in front of everybody, or we go to the station where there are fewer people around to spread nasty rumors."

Garone's face blanched at that, and he agreed to follow them to the station in his car. They put him in an interview room where Jinks started in on him right away. "What's in the envelope we saw Jenny-Lee place on that chair?"

"Paperwork. Just paperwork."

"And this paperwork isn't something she could just mail to you? Or you could go to her office to pick up?"

He squirmed in his chair and picked at his nails until he finally stammered out, "It saved me time. She was just being nice."

"If this is just ordinary paperwork, then you won't mind opening up that envelope and showing us what's inside, right?"

Garone swallowed. "I think I need an attorney."

"Why? You haven't been charged with anything. Unless you have a guilty conscience of, say, conspiring with an insurance rep to commit insurance fraud."

Not accustomed to being on the hot seat, Garone's façade crumbled quickly. He started blubbering and pleading for mercy. "I'm not a good crook. Just a desperate one."

Adam said, "About what?"

"I needed to sell my business. But Kozak's offer was the only one, and it was too low-ball. Far below what I knew the business was worth. So I decided the only way to get my money was to commit insurance fraud. When I met a kindred spirit, it all fell into place."

"Jenny-Lee Salant?"

"I bumped into her at a party. We hit it off, got to drinking, and I might have blurted out my problem. So, she schemed that I would start the fire. She'd make sure it got 'investigated' in a way that pushed suspicion away from us. Then I would give her half the insurance money. I'm ashamed to admit we were even happy when the other fires occurred. That is, except for the whole death of Jared Lake part. It was just dumb luck the other arsons covered for ours."

Adam pressed him, "You're saying you and Salant had no part in the other antiques store arsons?"

"I know *I* didn't. You'd have to ask Jenny-Lee about the others."

Jinks was jotting things down on her notepad and gave Adam a "you bet we will" look.

Adam asked Garone, "Kozak wasn't in on this fraud scheme of yours?"

"No, he didn't have anything to do with it. Funny, though. When I bumped into Kozak later, the man said something odd."

"Odd? In what way?"

"He said, 'saved me the trouble, didn't you, old man?'"

"What do you think he meant by that?"

"I wasn't sure at the time. But it was almost like he knew what I'd done. And that, well . . . "

"If you hadn't burned it down first, he would have later?"

"Sort of struck me that way."

After telling Garone he should contact that attorney of his now, they left him in the interview room for a moment. Jinks leaned against a wall. "Guess it's time to go round up our femme fatale, Miss Salant. But it just solves one of the five arson cases. Though you'll notice since Redbeard was put away again, there haven't been any more."

"If Kozak is behind those, then he would wait and see what happens with Redbeard. If he's smart, he'll just switch to a different enforcement method. Or find another willing arsonist."

"You really think Kozak is behind the other four arsons, then?"

Adam half-shrugged. "Even though I could always be wrong—again—I think he's our guy. But it's going to be hard to prove if we can't get Redbeard to sing. Kozak was very careful to let him do all his dirty work. And I'm guessing threaten him enough he wouldn't betray Kozak in return."

"But why? What could Kozak possibly have over Redbeard that would make him clam up totally?"

"Good question." Adam rubbed his chin and frowned.

"You've got that look again."

"What look?"

"Your 'what the hell' look."

Adam looked at himself in the reflective computer monitor. "I don't see any 'look.'"

"Trust me, it's there."

"I was just thinking. If Garone's Main Street Antiques is taken off the list of the other arsons, then something Beverly said makes sense."

"As in?"

"The other four arsons go in reverse order, alphabetically. Yesterday's Curios, which was in Montpelier, and What on Earth, in Burlington. Then, Jared Lake's Vintage Vibes store, and finally Annika Barnes's True Gems."

Jinks frowned. "Tossed Treasures seems like it might be up next. Or close to it."

"Yeah, Beverly and I were both worried about that. But Harlan doesn't fit the pattern in one way. Kozak never approached him about selling the store."

"Swell. We're still back to a serial arsonist, regardless of the motive. And Moody might be in the middle. The untouchable. I hate it."

"Maybe we should talk to Redbeard's cousin."

"You mean, Sergeant Moody's girlfriend?"

"Yep."

"How are we going to do that with Chief Quinn wanting us to stay as far from Moody as possible? And with Moody already having a bee up his ass about someone—aka Beverly—harassing said girlfriend?"

Adam replied, "Leave that to me. I think I may have an idea."

37

Beverly propped her feet on the footstool and gulped down some of the yak hot chocolate so fast that she burned her tongue. Good. Served her right.

Mr. X had been watching her carefully as she sat there stewing in her anger and self-loathing. Finally, he asked, "You have hardly said one word since you arrived. Are you in a spot of trouble?"

"I'm not, Adam is. Because of me. You were right, I shouldn't have done my little disguise with Moody's girlfriend. Moody got suspicious and called Chief Quinn, and now Adam and Quinn are in hot water with Moody and the mayor, who have accused them of harassment and underhanded tactics to force Moody out of the force, and Adam is furious with me." She knew she was rambling, but she couldn't seem to stop.

"I am not an 'I-told-you-so' type. I regret I didn't do more to dissuade you, but what's done is done."

"Maybe for good, if this means the mayor succeeds in finally getting Adam fired."

"That would not be politically expedient. And if Moody gets caught in the police dragnet, then another reason for Adam's removal vanishes. The mayor would no longer want to push his black-sheep cousin on the department, yes?"

"If. Always those pesky little ifs."

She stared at her mug. Even it seemed to be mocking her for drinking too fast. Her burned tongue was starting to throb.

"And what if Kozak doesn't get caught? What if he gets away with the arsons and Jared Lake's murder?"

"Don't forget the attempted murder of yourself and Annika Grimes."

"I *try* to forget that. But I've been having fiery nightmares every night since. Sometimes I'm burning, sometimes Adam is burning, sometimes you're burning, sometime's it's Grammie. Or my parents."

Months ago, after she'd first met Mr. X, he'd found out via his research that her parents had died in a car crash—a fiery car crash. That was probably why he was looking at her with such sympathy as he said, "Perhaps you should see a therapist. It might help exorcise those demons of yours."

She dropped her feet on the floor. "Have you ever seen a therapist?"

"Once."

Her eyes widened in shock. "You? Really? And why just once?"

"He told me my life was too boring, and I needed a more exciting job."

That made Beverly laugh. "Oh, brother. If he only knew where you'd been and what you'd done."

"I almost told him, to see how he would react."

"Wish you had." Beverly listened to the gamelan music he had playing softly in the background. He'd told her that this particular piece was supposed to ward off evil spirits. Appropriate—for her, anyway.

She sighed. "I know I'm impatient. But Kozak has plenty of time to flee the country if it comes to that. Then there never will be justice."

"Life is not a TV show, Beverly. Most of our existence isn't black or white but gray, and justice can be grayer still. But I might be able to help with that a little. Maybe we just need to flush our quarry out like hunters use dogs to flush out pheasants."

"You think that would work?"

"Done in the right way. If we can make Kozak act rashly and thus create an easier path for Detective Dutton and Jinks to nab the man."

She smiled. Mr. X knew she hated inaction more than anything else, maybe because they were cut from the same cloth—he'd been quite the man of action in his day, hadn't he? "What do you have in mind?"

"First, we need to check the list of antiques stores in the state."

Beverly had done that once with Adam, but Mr. X had a more complete and up-to-date directory. They split up the list, each calling antiques stores—and in some cases, former antiques stores owners—in the local region, to see if they'd been approached by Ivon Kozak to sell their shops. After almost an hour of calls, they discovered only two others who'd discussed selling with Kozak. In both cases, they agreed to sell. And their stores didn't burn down.

Mr. X was the one to contact a business called Treasured Remembrances, which was the only other remaining store alphabetically between Annika's True Gems and Harlan's Tossed Treasures. The owner said she was contacted by someone representing Kozak just the other day, but she wasn't interested in selling. Her store hadn't burned down yet, but Beverly feared it would be next, and Xenakis agreed.

They decided that was their "in." It would involve Beverly playing another role, but she was quite comfortable with that. Mr. X only agreed to it if he were allowed to be close by, just in case. Beverly relented but made him promise to stay out of sight so Kozak wouldn't get spooked.

Adam would be angry with her, yet again, if and when he found out. But she was a woman on a mission for a righteous cause, and she'd have to patch things up with him later. She had the momentary thought of just *how* she might patch things up—something involving a Jacuzzi and some champagne—but she didn't have time for a fantasy life right now.

Beverly got up to pace across the hand-woven wool kilim rug that covered the length of Mr. X's living room. A Metsovo Epirus style rug, if she wasn't mistaken. "What if Plan A doesn't work out?"

"Then, we come up with a Plan B."

Beverly stopped pacing to rub her temples. "Okay, but trying to think like a gangster makes my head hurt."

"Fortunately, I don't have that same problem. But then, I'm closer to being a gangster than you are."

She smiled. "Guess neither one of is exactly what you'd call an angel or a saint."

"My great aunt was a deeply religious woman. She liked to say that sometimes God uses sinners to do his bidding."

"Do you agree?"

"I do not share her world view in general. But there is much sin among the saints and some saintliness among the sinners."

"That whole everything is gray thing again?"

"I was thinking more of a rainbow."

He lifted an eyebrow at her, and she collapsed onto the couch, laughing. When she finally caught her breath, she said, "Let's hope our colorful Plan A works. I don't think I could take any more of your bad puns."

38

The first part of Adam's plan worked like a charm. Adam enlisted the help of his friend Cray to contact Moody's girlfriend, Donella Seagraves, under the guise of Cray's private eye shingle. Cray told her he needed information he was willing to pay good money for. But he didn't want to come to her, he wanted it to be in neutral territory because he knew her boyfriend was a cop and didn't want him to get suspicious.

Cray picked a tattoo parlor by the name of Sync Ink. When he told Adam of the site, Adam said, "This is the best place you could come up with?"

"Did some work for the owner. He owes me big time. Has this private room he lets me use from time to time."

"And Donella was okay with this place?"

"She doesn't have a choice if she wants her money. And if she and Moody are as hard up as you say they are, she'd show up naked in the middle of the Boston Bruins' TD Garden arena, if it meant cold hard cash."

They agreed that Cray would wear a wire, with Adam and Jinks listening in outside in the car. Adam joked, "Hey, you'll be warm. We'll be freezing our asses off."

At the appointed time, Adam and Jinks watched from afar as Donella Seagraves drove up and slipped into the building. That is, they suspected it was Seagraves from the description they'd got from Joe Brimm, the ever-helpful forensics tech who also happened to have known Donella from a bowling league.

As they listened in, they could hear the deep voice of the owner, Troy Gaetano, as he ushered the woman to the room where Cray was waiting. The private eye waited for her to be seated, judging by the creaking chair. Cray said, "I told you on the phone I needed information. Just some simple information. And I'm willing to pay pretty well for it."

A woman's girlish soprano voice replied, "What about?"

"Your cousin, Darnell Warner. Some folks hereabouts call him 'Redbeard.'"

There was silence for a moment until Adam heard the sound of a paper being slapped onto a table. Cray continued, "Here are a couple shiny new Benjamin Franklins for starters. Let's call it the first installment. The more you tell me, the more I hand over."

Donella's voice was all smiles. "Ask away."

"Tell me about this Redbeard fellow."

"We're not that close, but . . . he did call me from jail."

"When was this?"

"Yesterday. That's what I thought you wanted to talk to me about. I mean, I hadn't spoken to him in months, and all of a sudden, I get this call. Figured you were working for him."

"Nope. Just rooting around for some truth-berries. So what did he want to talk about?"

"It was really odd. He wanted me to tell my boyfriend, that's Mike Moody, something for him. Mike's a police sergeant with Ironwood Junction PD."

"Like what?"

Donella spoke slowly as if trying to recall the exact wording. "He said, 'tell K that I'm clean. No dirt. You should use the same soap.'"

"You're right. Definitely odd phrasing. Do you know what it meant?"

"Sounded like nonsense to me."

"Did you tell Moody?"

"Well, yes. I mean, he asked me to, after all. I didn't see any reason not to."

"How did Moody react?"

"He seemed a little nervous, kind of spooked. But he said not to worry about it, he'd take care of it."

Adam strained to hear what was happening, but he guessed Cray had just slapped another hundred-dollar-bill down on the table. "Has Moody ever mentioned Ivon Kozak?"

"I overheard him talking about Kozak with Darnell. They didn't know I was listening in. And I didn't tell Mike, either. He gets a little . . . testy about such things."

"Why were they talking about Kozak?"

"Some deal they were making. Then they lowered their voices, but I heard a few words. 'Black powder' and 'trailers.'"

Cray replied, "Those types of things are used in arsons. Did you know that?"

For the first time, Donella's voice sounded nervous. "No, I didn't. Not at the time. I looked it up, though. I guess I thought maybe it was just police business or something. Look, Mike is in debt, and he's maxed out my credit cards. I'd kick him out of my house except he's a cop, and he's threatened to turn me in on a trumped-up charge."

Donella cleared her throat. "And then there's that Kozak guy. I think he might have come by the house once. That is, I think it was the same guy. Even Mike was afraid of him. So there's no way I was going to get involved in any of that."

Cray slapped down another hundred and said, "If Moody were to store something he didn't want anyone to see, where would he do it . . . at your house?"

"It's not that big. And the garage is filled with gardening tools and other stuff of mine. But . . . " Her voice trailed off, and there was silence for a few moments.

Cray prompted her, "But?"

"There's this old storage unit place. It's for sale now, but I overheard Mike talking about it on the phone. Maybe it was with that Kozak guy again, I'm not sure. Mike wears his police uniform like he's a security guard so no one seeing him there would be suspicious."

Cray slapped down another two bills, which by Adam's math was about five hundred dollars. The tone of her voice seemed grateful, but she added, "You're not going to let Mike know I said any of this, are you?"

"Moody and I are on opposite sides of the fence these days. You're safe. You can trust me on that."

After Donella had exited the building and drove off, Adam and Jinks made their way into the back room. It was pretty small with just two chairs and a small table between. Not much bigger than Cray's own micro-sized office. Adam refrained from making a crack about that, tempting though it was.

Cray asked, "Did you hear everything?"

"We did. Sounds like with that message to Moody through Donella, he was telling Moody to alert Kozak that he wasn't talking. And that Moody should do the same if he wanted to stay out of trouble. And stay alive."

Jinks spoke up, "I'd give my first-born to catch that crooked cop at his own game."

Adam squinted at her. "You don't have a first-born since you were never pregnant. Felicia was."

She grinned. "Semantics. But still, we gotta nail Moody somehow."

That prompted Adam to say, "I've got another idea about that one."

She beat him to it and said, "Bet I've got an even better one."

Adam looked over at Cray. "This could be fun."

Cray wrapped one of his bear paws around each of their shoulders. "I like fun. Fun's my middle name. Count me in."

39

Tuesday, December 22

It had taken some sweet-talking on Beverly's part, but she somehow managed to get the owner of the Treasured Remembrances store, Rachael Pyke, to agree to Beverly and Mr. X's scheme. The two agreed it was too risky to let Rachael know all the details about Kozak and the arsons and simply told her this was a way to protect her store from the recent fires.

Beverly was pleased to see from meeting Rachael that the woman was youngish and had a voice not too far off Beverly's. Perfect. With Beverly's acting experience from Dartmouth, she was confident she could impersonate Rachael without any problems. She just had to add a thicker dark wig that was a little longer than her own and some horn-rimmed glasses.

The next step was setting up a meeting with Ivon Kozak, at a place of his choosing to set him at ease. He selected Capp's Tap House, which made Beverly a little nervous when she scoped out the bar in advance. It had mostly private booths. And that meant she couldn't be certain they'd find a way to get Mr. X involved as he'd insisted.

He calmed her nerves by saying, "I'll take care of it."

"How?"

"Money talks, love."

After he'd bribed the waiter, Beverly was seated at a table on the left side of the bar in the middle, and Mr. X sat at a table in the back where he could keep an eye on the proceedings. Before he took his spying-perch, however, he wired Beverly's table with a hidden recording device.

Beverly was tremendously grateful for his foresight when Kozak arrived. The first thing he did was demand that Beverly-as-Rachel put her purse, coat, and cellphone in a locker in the hatcheck room.

Beverly thought to herself, *So's that why he chose this place.* She asked aloud, "Then how am I going to pay?"

"I'll buy your drink to toast our agreement since you've apparently changed your mind. I assume that's what this meeting is all about?"

After they'd ordered Beverly a Tom Collins and Kozak a White Russian, Beverly studied her opponent. How to describe him? The best she could think of was a slimy weasel in a worsted vest, but that wasn't being fair to weasels.

The drinks arrived, and Beverly told him, "I'm afraid the toast may be premature. I've been thinking about your offer to buy my shop, and I only came today because I want to hear more details about the offer. Seemed a bit low to me."

Kozak almost spit out some of his White Russian as he frowned. His appearance had changed from a benign—if unctuous—slimy weasel to snarling wolverine in seconds. It gave her a chill. She hadn't experienced anything quite like it with the various crooks she'd dealt with in the past. Not even her uncle.

"It's a very fair offer, Miss Pyke. I'm sure you won't get anything better."

"I'm not convinced about that. You see, I contacted the sister of Jared Lake, the deceased owner of Vintage Vibes. And also the current owner of True Gems, Annika Grimes. Funny thing—after Lake and Grimes turned down your 'generous' offer, their businesses burned to the ground only a few days later. I can't help but wonder if that isn't a coincidence."

Kozak's face was dark and threatening, which he had a way of channeling only at her. Anyone else in the room looking at them right then might see him as merely being polite, if a bit "focused."

He sipped some more of his drink and took his time answering. "You should be quite careful about making such false accusations."

"But are they so false? What are the chances something like that would happen on its own? I mean, there have been rumors about you that are going around in the antiques world in this state. Ugly rumors."

"Miss Pyke, I must firmly reiterate that my offer is the very best you are going to receive. And you should really keep your mouth shut regarding things you have no business digging into."

"Why is that?"

"You might not like the consequences."

"Are you threatening me, Mr. Kozak?"

"I don't threaten, Miss Pyke. But I do believe you're a little too smart for your own good."

"Like Jared Lake, perhaps?"

Kozak downed the rest of his drink in two gulps and rose stiffly as he prepared to leave. He said, "I'll give you a few days to think about it. But only a few days. After that . . . "

Beverly had a good idea of what would happen "after that." And she and Mr. X had to make something happen very soon or else the real Rachael Pyke and her business would be in great jeopardy in a couple of days' time. Maybe Mr. X could rig up some extra security from his vast collection of devices and tools. But would it be enough?

Before Kozak left, she had to get in one more dig at the man and said to his retreating back, "Reggie Forsythe."

He stopped in his tracks for a moment and turned around slowly to face her. "What about him?"

"He thought he was a Big Cheese, too, but look at where he is now. In a nursing home in a coma. Well, he *was* in a coma, that is."

Kozak blinked at her. "Was?"

"I hear he's awakened and is doing much better."

Every muscle in Kozak's body seemed to tense into a missile of sinew and gristle, and he looked as if he was ready to rocket through the ceiling right then and there. He gritted his teeth and slapped some money done on the table for the drinks. "Three days, Miss Pyke."

After he was gone, Mr. X slid into his seat and rescued the recording device. Beverly put her head in her hands. "What if we've doomed Rachel Pyke's store?"

"Not to worry. I've thought of that."

"What are you going to do?"

"Not do, did."

"Still not following."

"Kozak is going to be at a meeting today in . . . " Mr. X looked at his watch. "A little over half an hour. And I've arranged for the real Miss Pyke to attend the meeting and introduce herself in person."

"What?" Beverly's jaw dropped open. "But he'll know I was a fake."

"Precisely."

"Oh, I see. Yes, I suppose that might work." Beverly was a little more skeptical of the outcome than he was, but she hoped his instincts regarding Kozak were correct. Having worked alongside both Forsythes for years, Mr. X knew his way around evil pretty well.

He tossed the little recording device into a pocket. "We didn't get him to admit to anything directly. But it's very suggestive."

"Isn't recording someone without their permission—"

"Against the law and inadmissible in court?"

"Something like that."

"Oh, this isn't for your detective friends, Beverly. This is insurance for us. And if Detective Dutton should need additional convincing, this may do the trick."

Beverly signaled the waiter to order another Tom Collins, and Mr. X said to "Make it two."

"One of us should be the designated driver."

He replied, "Then let's have some food. We can stay awhile and scheme. I've heard scheming burns calories and reduces blood alcohol content at the same time."

She smiled and tipped her glass. "You always know how to say the nicest things to a girl." After grabbing a menu from the end of the table, she added, "Did you see his face when I told him about Forsythe?"

"I did. Most rewarding. Although I feared for a moment, he might hit you."

"As the bearer of bad tidings?"

Xenakis nodded. "But he's such a physically mousy little man, I doubt he would have had the strength to do it. And he didn't have Redbeard or any other of his minions along to do it for him."

Beverly closed the menu, realizing she wasn't all that hungry. "Adam called Kozak a true psychopath. No feelings for anyone, overly sensitive about whims and slights. A very cold and calculating man."

Mr. X agreed, "A fair assessment."

"What do you think he'll do? Now that he knows his rival, Reggie Forsythe, might not be out of the picture?"

"Bide his time, perhaps. Even if Forsythe lives, several of the man's former criminal associates are now in prison. Kozak may feel Forsythe's glory days are behind him, either way."

"I guess. But it was still fun to see that smug expression wiped off his face." She took a few sips of the cocktail. "As you say, we've flushed out the pheasant. We'll just have to wait and see where he lands."

40

Adam had conspired with Joe Brimm to be in the lobby of the police station as the two men innocently chatted about the weather and the UVM hockey team. While they were standing there near the front desk, Cray walked into the station and handed over a note to the receptionist. "This is for Sgt. Mike Moody. It's rather urgent. Could you see he gets it?"

Cray turned on his heel and left, and Arline Newton, the PD senior receptionist, called Moody on the intercom. Minutes later, Moody showed up at the desk while Adam continued to "chat" with Brimm as he flipped through a file folder.

When Moody picked up the envelope, Arline explained, "The fellow who brought this said it was urgent."

Moody opened it, and his face darkened. He said to Arline, "I've got to leave for a while. If anybody needs me, I've got my cell." Then he practically flew out the door.

Adam waved to Joe Brimm and Arline with a big smile. "I've got to head out too. Early lunch. Anybody need anything?"

She blew him a kiss and said no. Adam gave Brimm a knowing look and headed out the exit, still trying to look nonchalant.

Adam didn't have to tail Moody because he knew exactly where the guy was headed. Moody's target—and therefore Adam's—was in a section of the county Adam didn't get to that often. But when he got closer to the shuttered storage units, he recalled seeing them a few years before. Back when they were newer and filled with the various so-called treasures of the customers. Most of the units weren't even locked anymore, their open doors yawning into the afternoon air.

It was rare Adam could take his time getting to a stakeout, and he relished not having to speed. But his pulse was still elevated, all the same. This bit of theater could go in several different ways, depending on how it all shook out.

He spied Moody's maroon pickup truck parked outside the gated facility with the entrance open. Moody must have a key— or an unlawful way of picking the front lock. Adam bided his time while Moody scurried around the corner toward the rear storage units.

As Adam followed the man and peeked around the wall, he saw Moody fumbling with the lock on one particular unit. It was the only unit Adam saw that was locked. Why just the one? In an abandoned storage facility, no less?

Moody finally managed the lock and flung open the door. He looked inside it with a frown. After he'd disappeared inside, Adams spied Jinks heading out from around the other side of the building where she'd been hiding.

Jinks used the sign language she'd taught Adam to tell him it was time to make their move on Moody. They stood outside the unit and peered inside. Adam saw several things in one quick glance—for one, there were more funky items like that little Steampunk octopus-ashtray of Beverly's. But even more interesting, Moody was pawing through a box and pulled out some materials that looked for all the world like pipe bomb and arson ingredients—wires, tubing, fuses, timers, and a canister filled with black powder.

Adam called out, "Want to tell us what you were going to do with those, Mike?"

Moody whipped around, his eyes wide as he stood frozen in place. He didn't say anything at first. Then he threw the box down and pushed past Adam, almost knocking him over in the process. As he scrambled in the direction of his truck, Adam and Jinks took off in hot pursuit. But they skidded to a halt when they saw a car blocking the exit to the gate.

Chief Quinn stood in front of the car, watching the proceedings. He said to Moody, "Going somewhere, Sergeant?"

As Adam and Jinks rushed up to handcuff Moody, he started yelling at them. "This is harassment, pure and simple. Planting evidence to try to trap me. My cousin, the mayor, will hear about this."

Quinn replied, "Yes, yes he will. You can be certain on that count."

Adam and Jinks hustled Moody into Adam's car as Joe Brimm, Sergeant Bill Naigle, Sergeant Gray, and a videographer carrying video gear climbed out of the chief's sedan.

Adam pointed toward Moody's unit in the back of the lot. "It's open and ready for you. You can't miss it. Just look for the one with all the black powder and accelerants."

Quinn watched them scurry in the direction Adam had pointed and said to him, "I'd like to supervise the whole procedure. Make sure everything is done to the letter, so Mayor Lehmann can't say it was a set-up. Dutton, you and Jinks take Moody to the station. The crew and I will arrive later."

Moody didn't say anything at first on the long ride back, but Adam saw the man via the rear-view mirror glaring at them. Adam said, "Did you know you dropped a little Steampunk octopus-ashtray item? When you were scurrying away from the arson you helped start at Jared Lake's antiques shop?"

Moody's jaw dropped. "What? I didn't . . . " and then he snapped his jaw shut with an audible click. He kept up his refusal to speak when they arrived at the station, saying only that he wanted his attorney. When Jinks asked which one, Moody replied, "Douglas Marcell."

Adam tsked. "It's probably not the best idea to be on good terms with the same lawyer who represents such criminals as Forsythe and Darnell Warner. And Ivon Kozak."

Moody's head snapped up at the mention of Kozak's name. He turned red but didn't say anything about Kozak. He just kept whining that he was being framed because they were trying to keep him from becoming a detective, adding, "You'll live to regret this."

Jinks just smiled at him. "Somebody will, that's for sure. Don't think it's going to be us, though."

They left him steaming in one of the jail cells and returned to Adam's office. Jinks plonked down into a chair. "Can't help but worry Mayor Lehmann and Marcell will somehow be able to beat this. And say it really was trumped-up charges."

"That's why Chief Quinn had Gayle Henley with Joe Brimm and the crew. She's the best videographer in the area. Has worked with most of the police departments at some point."

Recognition dawned on Jinks's face. "I thought I'd seen her before. Quinn decided to add her at the last minute?"

"Yeah. Good thing she was available. She'll document everything and make sure it's all on tape."

"And once they only find Moody's fingerprints are on the materials . . ."

Adam grinned. "Coupled with the photocopied threatening letters tied to the sleazebag Leon Nolen's delivery company, and we should have plenty enough to convince the internal affairs investigators, the FBI, the ATF, and any jury."

Jinks tilted back in the chair, almost making it tip over. "But now we've got two canaries that are mute and don't want to sing. How do we nab Kozak, then?"

"Once he knows two of his main cohorts are behind bars, he might start to get desperate. And desperate crooks get careless."

"What's next, then, McDutton?"

"All I know for sure is Redbeard and Moody better like mystery-meat surprise. Because that's what they're going to be enjoying for their Christmas dinner wearing their cute little matching orange outfits."

41

At any other time, Beverly would have relished the chance to just sit and chat with Mr. X away from his usual haunts and hers. To learn more about him. His origins, for one. And how such an educated, polished, cultured man ended up working with an antiques crime syndicate that he later disowned.

Fortunately, the food was good at Capp's Tap House, and the drinks weren't half-bad, either. She was just starting to relax from the effects of the Tom Collins when Mr. X got a call on his cellphone. Beverly couldn't quite tell the entire conversation from his end, but it was enough to know what the call was about.

When he hung up, she said, "Rachel Pyke? The real one?"

"It was. I asked her to report back after her meeting where Kozak was in attendance. To her credit, she followed my instructions to the letter. She went up to him and introduced herself."

"What did he say to that?"

"He said basically, *'you're* the owner of Treasured Remembrances?'"

"How did she respond?"

"She told him yes, and why was he asking? He replied that he met someone recently who pretended to be her."

"Uh-oh."

"But that's exactly what I'd hoped. She told him it was probably just a prank, and he shouldn't worry about it. And then, she told him she had changed her mind and was open to negotiations about the store but had to check with her attorney and insurance reps first."

Beverly leaned back in the booth with a smile. "And thus, her store is likely not to become arson-bait any time soon."

"Exactly."

She took one last sip of her drink. "And here I was worried. I should know you better than that."

When Mr. X's cellphone rang again, he apologized and almost tossed the phone on the seat next to him. But when he saw the caller, he added, "I think I'd better take this one."

He listened intently for a few minutes, with only a few murmurs of agreement in reply. When he finished, he said to Beverly, "I have a little bird who keeps me posted on all things related to the police in this area. It seems Detective Dutton and his cohorts have arrested Sergeant Mike Moody."

Beverly almost jumped out of her seat. "For real? They must have got something airtight on him. Otherwise, they would have waited until they could be certain they didn't upset Mayor Lehmann."

"I'm told they found him in possession of materials related to bomb-making and arson. Even Chief Quinn was in on the collar."

"The chief was there, too? Oh, that would have been fun to see." Beverly took a deep breath and exhaled loudly. "I feel like an elephant—make that a mastodon—was just lifted off me."

"It does seem to be a positive development. Leaving only one remaining actor in this drama."

"Kozak."

"Yes. I must say, Beverly, you are really quite the actress. I've enjoyed watching you use your talents in person."

"I don't know, I think I might have a rival in that department. Although I have a long way to go to match both your experience and expertise."

He gave a little head bow and then studied her "disguise," such as it was. "Are you up for another opportunity to win an Academy Award?"

She perked up. "I'm listening."

"I think I'd like to pay a little visit to the bookie, Leroy Schick."

"The one who loaned money to Moody?"

"And also to Jared Lake, it seems. I think I have a role for him, too, in this drama of ours."

"What do you need me to do?"

"What's one of your favorite personas? I don't want him to know your real name."

She thought a moment. "Kornelson will do."

"Excellent. Shall we start the performance?"

§ § §

When they pulled up in front of Schick's office, Beverly pointed at the sign. "Wealth consultant?"

"A little joke on his part. I don't really see the humor in it, myself."

Beverly bit back a smile. She hadn't seen Mr. X utter a good belly laugh since she'd known him. In fact, she wasn't even sure he knew how.

They walked into the office, and when Schick took one look at Mr. X, he stood up straight and gulped several times in a row. "Xenakis. You don't usually come slumming in these parts."

"It became necessary."

Schick's eyes widened, and he stammered, "I don't have any business with you. I'm an honest businessman. I don't want no trouble."

"Is there some sort of trouble I should know about?"

"No, none, nothing. Really. All's good, yep good."

"That is most reassuring. Because I have a little job for you."

Schick stared at him. "A job? From you? For me?"

Mr. X motioned with his hand toward Beverly. "My companion, Miss Kornelsen, has a beef with Ivon Kozak. I believe you've heard of him?"

"Kozak, sure? I don't got no business with him, neither."

"Naturally. Since you're an honest businessman. This is what we need you to do. You will give Ivon Kozak a call—"

"No, no, no. Not calling him. No way."

Mr. X stared at Schick for several moments without blinking. Finally, Schick said, "What would I be calling him about?"

"It's very simple. You'll just be relaying a message. You are to tell him Sergeant Mike Moody is singing in jail and that Kozak should watch his back."

"Is that it?"

"That is all."

Schick stood there in a quiver of indecision. He wrung his hands together and stared at Beverly and then Mr. X. Beverly was interested to see that Schick appeared more afraid of Xenakis than Kozak.

Schick gave a little sigh of capitulation. "Okay, I'll do it. If that's all."

"That is all, as I stated."

When they didn't leave the office, Schick said, "You mean call him right now?"

Mr. X nodded.

The other man picked up the phone and put it on speakerphone as he dialed. When a nasal voice answered, Schick repeated what Mr. X had told him to say. Afterward, he angrily punched the "off" button as he shook his head. "Hope I don't regret this."

"I want to congratulate you on making the 'right call.' And I have it on good authority that it's quite likely you won't be on the hook for the pipe bomb that detonated at a police detective's house recently."

Beverly held back her surprise that Mr. X knew this since she hadn't heard anything about it from Adam. When they finally left Schick's office, Beverly called him on it. "Where in the world did you learn that? And what does it mean?"

"Schick handled loans to Moody. Moody teamed up with Redbeard to buy the bombing gear and sent the pipe bomb through a less-than-reputable courier to Detective Dutton's home. Dutton knows about this. That is to say, most of it. The rest he will learn soon enough."

"Yes, but how did you find all that out?"

"I might have a mole in the police department. But I don't want to compromise my source. It would be better for you if you don't know who. And also for the source."

She shook her head. "How do you know all of these people? And Leroy Schick even seemed afraid of you."

Mr. X slid into the passenger seat of Beverly's rental car and closed the door. She took the hint and climbed in, herself, shutting the door behind her.

He said, "During my days in the employ of the Forsythes, I made quite a large network of connections, many of them highbrow and an equal number of them lowbrow."

After a short pause, he added, "As I have touched on before briefly, some of my interactions weren't always polite nor legal. It's also better for you that you remain ignorant of those."

"You're asking a con woman who's done some not-quite-legal things to understand what you had to do as part of your job? I think I understand more than you realize."

"Yes, I do suppose you would. And one day, perhaps I can be more forthcoming. For now, we all have our little secrets."

Beverly understood that one, too. She had a lot of secrets she hadn't told Mr. X. Or even Adam. Especially Adam. Her almost-sex with the handsome detective seemed like a lovely dream that had come and gone. Maybe it just wasn't in the cards that she and Adam ever have any sort of romantic relationship. They weren't exactly polar opposites, but they were on opposite sides of the ethical equator.

She sighed and told herself to focus on her task. Eyes on the prize, Beverly Laborde. Time to end the Forsythe and Kozak and NAL saga once and for all. If it didn't kill her first.

42

Beverly dropped Mr. X off at his castle and started the half-hour trip back to town. She was just on the outskirts of Ironwood Junction when she got a call from Mr. X. She joked, "Can't get enough of me?"

His voice didn't join in her joking tone. In fact, he sounded dead serious. "I have it on good authority via my police department source that Reggie Forsythe is awake again. Apparently, this time it wasn't just for a few moments."

Beverly's previous good mood started slipping away fast. "Awake as in coherent?"

"So I'm told. I don't know what this means going forward since I'm not a doctor. But I just thought you'd like to know."

She hung up and pulled over into a parking lot next to Devine's Drugstore while she digested that bit of news. She'd been certain she hadn't dreamed her encounter with her uncle in the nursing home, but this proved it. What was it he'd said again? Adam was going to pay for taking Forsythe down, and so was she?

She had no reason to doubt Mr. X or his source, but she couldn't just go back to the resort and not do anything—not knowing whether or not her murderous uncle had truly returned to the land of the living. His network of goons and thugs might have shrunk thanks to the efforts of Adam and

Beverly, but that didn't mean Forsythe was completely bereft of associates he could use to do his bidding. Like hurting Adam.

She turned the car around and headed toward the nursing home. She had to see what shape he was in for herself. Had to face this man head-on and let him know she wasn't afraid of him. And maybe convince herself in the process.

This time, she didn't bother to put on the lab coat and fake ID and kept on the long wig and horn-rimmed glasses from her earlier disguise with Ivon Kozak at the bar and later Leroy Schick, the "wealth consultant." She slipped into the building and walked confidently down the hallway as if she was accustomed to being there visiting family. The nurses at the nearest station to her uncle's room were watching TV again, making Beverly breathe a sigh of relief.

Her heart was racing as she tiptoed toward Forsythe's room. Maybe this was a bad idea. But what harm could it do to peek in on the man and make sure he wasn't a threat?

She entered the room and closed the door softly behind her. But as careful as she'd been, the slight click of the door shutting was enough to get the attention of the man lying in the bed. He opened his eyes and stared at her.

Try as she might, she couldn't look away from those eyes. They had a hypnotic quality to them that had drawn her in since she first met him, but they weren't the warm, soft eyes of Beverly's grandmother—Forsythe's own mother. They seemed almost devoid of life and light, piercing into her very soul as if to draw it out and consume it.

Beverly took a deep breath and steadied her nerves. This was silly. The man was hooked up to all kinds of machines. What could he possibly do to her now?

Forsythe continued to stare at her and then smiled coldly. His voice was raspy, but she could hear him well enough. "It appears my niece can't stay away. From me or my personal business. You thought I was dead. Or as good as, didn't you? Or you hoped for such an end. But as you can see, I'm not going anywhere."

"I think your doctors might have something to say about that." Beverly finally found her tongue.

"They will do as I tell them. And I will tell them to discharge me so that I can return home. Fortunately, I still have a home my ex-wife hasn't wrested away from me yet. No thanks to you, dear Beverly."

"Don't you mean they'll discharge you to a jail cell? Or have you forgotten you murdered your own father?"

"My attorney will see that I retain my freedom until any court case. Giving me plenty of time to disappear if I choose."

"By attorney, you mean Douglas Marcell?"

He bared his teeth into a half-laugh, half-sneer. "There you go again, poking your nose into my business."

"Your business became my business the moment I found out you were responsible for shutting down my grandmother's antiques business."

"It was my pleasure."

She glared at him. "Your father might have poisoned you against my grandmother, but she grieved losing you every day of her life. When your father took you away after the divorce and cut you off from Grammie, a little piece of her soul died. At the end, when she was dying in a nursing home like this one, she pulled out a locket she'd worn with photos of you and my late mother. With her last breath, she cried over losing both you. Do you know that?"

He shook his head. "She was heartless and cruel, she initiated the divorce. She left us."

"That's what your father told you. But it's not true. It was never true."

"What do you want from me, Beverly? To grovel? To cry? To tell you I'm sorry she's dead? The strong people in this world have no personal ties to anyone. Those personal ties only make you vulnerable. Make you a target, give your enemies ammunition to get to you."

Beverly moved to the foot of his bed to get a better look at him. Those eyes might still be piercing, but his body was frailer and more withered than he realized. She almost felt pity for him. Almost. Whatever heart—literally and figuratively—the man once had was slipping away. The shell of the man only held a shell of a soul.

Beverly started to reply to him when she felt the presence of someone else in the room. Whoever it was had entered silently without the telltale click of the door as with her own arrival.

She whipped around to see Ivon Kozak watching the two of them. It was apparent he'd been listening in for some time when he said to her, "So you're Reggie Forsythe's niece. Well, well. I don't know what stunt you were trying to pull this morning, but I see you inherited your uncle's flair for the dramatic. And his cunning. Brava."

Forsythe raised up in his bed a few inches. "Kozak? What are you doing here?"

Beverly jumped in, "Kozak's been busy taking over your antiques empire while you've been in a coma. Tried to buy out the other businesses. And when they didn't cooperate, he burned them to the ground."

Her uncle's face gained a bit of color for the first time. "You thought you could swoop in and take advantage of my situation, did you? As you can see, I'm back. And I'll make sure you're squashed beneath my heel. Like everyone else who's tried to cross me."

Kozak said calmly. "That will be hard to do from prison."

"You actually think I'm going to end up there? You don't know me at all, do you? Why don't you ask Beverly here? I'm sure she can tell you all about my Teflon shield."

Beverly moved toward the wall as if heading for a chair. She needed to distract them both so she could get out of there fast and call Adam. "Tell me, Kozak, did you kill Jared Lake because he defied you? Or was it because he stole that Burmese sapphire necklace of yours?"

Kozak clapped his hands. "I underestimated you, Miss Laborde. I had no idea you were so resourceful. I merely considered you a minor nuisance when I had Mike Moody send you that threatening note. My mistake."

"You and my uncle are peas in a pod. Equally evil and morally bankrupt."

"That I will take as a compliment. But perhaps I shouldn't since Reggie here is half-vegetable now. I'm the one who'll be left standing. King of the hill, god of the antiques world. I'll show all those people who doubted I'd ever amount to anything."

Forsythe started laughing. And he kept laughing as he pointed at Kozak. He only stopped long enough to take a breath and cough before starting up the laughing again. Kozak's face grew redder as Forsythe mocked him further, "You'll never be king of anything. You're too weak, too cowardly. Always have everyone else do your dirty work for you."

Before Beverly could react, Kozak strode to the side of Forsythe's bed in two quick steps and grabbed a pillow to put over the other man's face. Then he pulled a gun with a silencer out of a pocket inside his coat and shot Forsythe through it. Beverly watched in disbelief as blood soaked through the pillow, and Forsythe's body grew limp.

Kozak said to her, "I did a better job with the gun than Forsythe did, now, didn't I?"

She turned to flee out the door, but Kozak grabbed her hand and pulled her further into the room. His efforts made both of them off balance, and Beverly swung backward toward the wall as Kozak grabbed onto the bed railing to keep from falling.

Try as she might, she couldn't stop herself from toppling onto the floor, and he stumbled over to grab her again, saying, "You're coming with me. I may need a hostage to get me out of here."

But he never got the chance. Adam and Jinks swooped into the room in a full-run and shoved Kozak against the wall. Adam then threw Kozak down onto the chair while Jinks stepped out to call the nurses for help with Forsythe.

Keeping a close eye on Kozak, Adam offered a hand to Beverly to help her up. "You okay?" he asked.

"Fine. I might have picked up a new bruise or two."

"What were you doing here?"

"I heard Forsythe was awake, so I came to check it out. You?"

"The same. We got a call from the facility's staff."

Kozak had crumpled into an even smaller man than he was before, although he managed a glare in their direction. "You haven't heard the last of me. I'll beat this. And you."

Beverly looked over at the flat-lining heart monitor attached to her uncle. "Funny. That's exactly what Reggie Forsythe said to me once."

43

Thursday, December 24

Agnes Flamm giggled as Harlan opened a bottle of champagne and kissed her lightly on the cheek. While Beverly watched, Harlan poured champagne for himself and Agnes and got some on his shirt, making the woman dab at it with a handkerchief. Maybe having Agnes and Harlan get closer wasn't a bad thing at all. Beverly wasn't sure why she'd had those conflicted feelings in the first place.

Then again . . . as she watched the handsome man with the lovely mocha eyes approach her, she knew where the source of those feelings lay. She was just a whirlwind of conflicted emotions these days.

Adam looked around the wine shop. "Nice party."

"Haven't been to a Christmas Eve party . . . well Christmas Eve anything, in quite a long time. It *is* kind of nice." Thinking that sounded a little pathetic, she hastily added, "Everyone seems to be having a good time."

"Speaking of good times," Adam had been watching Agnes and Harlan, too, and pointed them out.

Beverly grinned. "They've both earned it, as hard as they work. Owning your own business is stressful."

Adam nodded. "You say Harlan and Ramsay Ryall came to an agreement over that estate-coin money?"

"When Harlan offered Ramsay half of the proceeds from the sale of the coin and the other items from Ramsay's father's estate, I guess Ramsay realized it was a better deal than paying out the money to attorneys."

"No doubt."

Beverly added, "Did you hear that Ramsay is going to use the money to start up his snowmobile business again? The promising one Wallace wrecked when the brothers were estranged?"

"No, but that's a good idea." Adam said, "And speak of the devil," as Ramsay and Gloria from Apple Valley Resort entered the store and gave them a wave before heading into the café.

Sharon Bogren was overseeing the café side of things, and the guests seemed to be enjoying the hard cider and spiced eggnog to go along with the music. Blaine Morland was on the stage, playing the guitar and singing some holiday songs as well as several of his own compositions.

Lucas and Jeanne Barratt stood in one corner chatting with Jared Lake's sister, Belle. Adam nodded toward their little group. "Awfully generous of Belle to hire Lucas as a chef in a restaurant she's going to open with the insurance money."

"She just didn't think she could salvage the antiques store. And I don't think her heart was in it anymore. Too painful with all those lost memories."

Beverly poked a stray strand of hair behind her ear. "Never did hear how Belle found out about Lucas's plight in the first place." She had a pretty good idea how, and her suspicions confirmed when Adam replied, "I might have made a call telling her about Lucas and his desire to open his own restaurant because he likes to cook."

"It might not be his own restaurant, but you have to start somewhere. He can get valuable experience. Maybe one day strike out on his own."

"Hope so. A little Christmas magic."

One person who wasn't present at the party was Mayor Lehmann, not that Agnes would have invited him—or he'd have come if she had. Beverly was hoping to never have to see the man again, but if he won the governor's race, he'd be all over the news.

She shuddered, making Adam ask, "Are you cold?"

"No, just unwanted thoughts trying to sabotage the party."

"What kind of thoughts?"

"Mayor Lehmann."

"Ah. Well, one thing's for sure. He couldn't cut ties with his cousin, Mike Moody, fast enough. I've never seen anyone pivot in such a fashion, practically 'disowning' him."

Beverly grimaced. "I heard about his public statement."

"What a piece of work that was. He actually said he personally turned in his cousin and would make certain his 'estranged' cousin was prosecuted to the full extent of the law."

"Has Moody said anything yet?"

"Still defiant and still silent. I think he knows Lehmann could make his life miserable in or out of prison and hopes if he keeps quiet, he'll get out faster." Adam added, "Thanks for handing over the octopus-ashtray, by the way. Finding a tiny trace left of Moody's fingerprints as we did will help our case."

"Did you ever nab Jenny-Lee Salant for the arson and insurance fraud?"

"My colleagues in Windsor County have her locked up, nice and tight."

The thought of Salant and her perfectly coiffed hair in an orange jumpsuit cheered Beverly up even more. By then, the party was in full swing as the shop filled with music, laughter, and conversation. It was getting so loud that Beverly could barely hear herself think. She suddenly felt overheated and said to Adam, "Think I might need a little fresh air."

He guided her toward the side door that led out onto a screened-in porch, but she carefully sidestepped the mistletoe hanging over the door. Once outside, she breathed in the cool air and watched the light snowflakes fall.

Adam kept studying her until she finally said, "I'm fine. Really. I just . . . it was a little too loud and hot in there."

He joined her in watching the snowflakes. "Reggie Forsythe's ex-wife is taking over his estate, as you might imagine. She bought a plot next to his father's at the cemetery for him."

Beverly sighed. "I don't think I'll be asking you to join me at that tombstone. In fact, I'd like to forget about everything Forsythe-related for a long, long time."

"Can't blame you. But you must be sleeping better at night now."

"Why?"

"Because you did it. You helped take down the NAL mob that have been terrorizing antiques shop owners for the past several years, your grandmother included."

Beverly ran her finger along a wooden slat in the screen and wiped away the tiny snow pile. "I don't know what to do with myself now. I mean, it's not like I'm going to go work in a cubicle and be happy."

"You have a new house. That's a start."

She smiled. "My first baby steps toward a more normal life. Though I'm not sure I'll ever be able to do 'normal.'"

Adam laughed. "Thank god for that. I like the ab-normal Beverly just fine, thank you very much."

"You do? You aren't angry with me anymore?"

"Ah, Beverly. I was never truly angry with you. Worried. Annoyed, maybe. But never angry, not with you."

"That's a relief." And for the first time in years, she felt her body truly giving in to something that felt almost peaceful. It was a new feeling, and she most definitely liked it.

Adam pointed toward the door. "Saw you skirting around the mistletoe. Afraid you might succumb to its powers?"

She grinned. "It has powers? And here I was thinking it was just a parasitic plant."

Adam pulled something out of his pocket and reached up to hold it over her head. It was a tiny sprig of mistletoe. "Let's find out how powerful it is, shall we?"

And they proceeded to do just that.